FAVOURITE STORIES
FROM AROUND THE WORLD

FAVOURITE STORIES FROM AROUND THE WORLD

Retold by
Jane Ives and Jean-Luc Billeadeux

Illustrated by
Luděk Maňásek, Vladimír Machaj,
Karel Teissig and Vladimír Tesař

CATHAY BOOKS

First published 1982 by
Cathay Books Limited
59 Grosvenor Street
London W1
Reprinted 1983, 1984

Text © by Octopus Books Ltd. 1982
Illustrations © by Artia Prague 1982
Graphic design by Aleš Krejča

ISBN 0 86178 179 1
Printed in Czechoslovakia by TSNP, Martin
1/18/05/51-03

Contents

PROMETHEUS

Long, long ago, when the world was young and the earth was green and peaceful, the gods lived in splendour on Mount Olympus. This high mountain with its tip wreathed in clouds looked down over the hills and valleys of Greece. This was a beautiful land created by the gods for their pleasure. The rivers were forever clear, the flowers never faded, the air was filled with the song of birds and the bright flashing wings of butterflies. Even at night while the stars shone down through the velvet darkness, the soaring song of the nightingale and the soft flutter of moths' wings filled the sparkling sky as if in praise of the beauty around them.

The gods looked down through the clouds and saw how lovely the world was. Only the animals of the earth, the fishes of the blue oceans and rivers and the birds of the clear heavens lived there — for as yet no men had been created.

The greatest of all the gods on Mount Olympus was Zeus. He, and his wife Hera, who was the most beautiful of all the goddesses, ruled firmly over the other gods. But the earth had not always been so peaceful. Many years before, when the world was born, there had been a terrible war between the Titans, a huge, warlike race of gods. Father had fought son, brother had fought brother. Finally Zeus, the grandson of the mightiest Titan god Uranus and son of the powerful god Chronos, conquered and forced peace upon all of them. That was why Zeus now ruled so firmly, helped by his brothers Poseidon and Hades. Never again would Zeus allow war to break out between the gods. With Poseidon as the King of the Oceans and Hades as the King of the Underworld they watched over the world. Nothing escaped their notice, no matter how small. Now, once again, trouble was coming to Zeus' peaceful land.

Prometheus, another grandson of the mighty Uranus, loved the earth. He was tired of living on Mount Olympus and wanted to live amongst the valleys and hills of Greece. With his brother Epimetheus they wandered through the countryside. Prometheus noticed that there were always most fish and animals where ever water flowed freely and where the soil was rich and dark.

'Water and soil give life,' he told his brother Epimetheus, 'we could create life from these two things.'

Epimetheus thought that this was a wonderful idea and set to work modelling men out of clay by mixing soil and water together.

Prometheus, who knew more than the other gods about the ways of the animals and creatures of the earth, helped him and soon Epimetheus had made a whole race of men and women. They lay on the ground before the two brothers but they did not move.

'We cannot breathe life into them,' cried Prometheus. 'We are only half-gods. I shall go to Mount Olympus and ask Pallas Athene, the wisest of all the goddesses, to help us.'

Now Pallas Athene, who was indeed the wisest of all the goddesses, often became bored on the cloudy heights of Mount Olympus. She too thought that Prometheus' idea of creating a race of men from clay was a splendid idea. Besides, she was curious to see how these strange little creatures would turn out. She came down from the tall mountain with Prometheus and breathed life into the clay figures that he and his brother had made.

The clay figures stirred, then stretched and stood up, stumbling at first because they had not yet become used to their legs and arms. They looked round them in wonder, for they knew no more than new-born babies, even though they were fully the height of grown men and women.

Prometheus realized that he would have to teach them how to survive, for although Pallas Athene had breathed life into them, she had not made them clever — that was the task for Prometheus.

For many seasons Prometheus lived with the men and women he had created. He taught them how to make houses from the stones of the hillside and the wood from the trees. He showed them how to plant grain and harvest it, how to fish in the streams and the sea. He showed them how to read and write, and how to foretell the weather from the clouds and the sun. He taught them about music and painting, and how to create beautiful and useful things from the tin, gold and silver they found in the caves of the hillsides.

And all the time Prometheus was busy with his teaching Zeus and Hera looked down at what he was doing and became angrier and angrier.

'Prometheus is teaching his men to be too clever,' boomed Zeus. 'These men of his will soon be almost too powerful for us. If they can do all these things, what is there to stop them from climbing Mount Olympus?'

'That is very true, dear,' replied Hera, 'and what is worse is that although Prometheus has taught them to be so clever, he has never taught them to be afraid of us. No, indeed, his men have made no temples or altars to worship us, they offer no sacrifices, no, not even the smallest gold ring or two . . .' sighed Hera, who rather liked the

8

look of some of the beautiful things that Prometheus' men had made.

'I shall teach them to respect us,' roared Zeus, and he stretched his arms wide and clenched his fists.

Immediately the sky darkened, purple and grey thunderclouds rolled in from across the sea. Strong winds whipped the sea into spray at first and then into enormous waves. The waves rose like mountains, dashing against the shores, while the wind roared and

howled across the valleys. Great bolts of lightning sped across the sky, splitting trees and breaking rocks. Then the rain started. It became heavier and heavier until the green valleys of the land were hidden by it and the drops fell like veils across the face of the land. Every single fire that Prometheus had built for his people was put out, every tiny cinder, every lighted torch, every spark of fire.

When the storm was over the land was very still and terribly dark.

'That will teach them,' roared Zeus, who could see that there was not a single spark of fire burning anywhere. 'Let us see how clever they will be without fire.'

Zeus had known all along that the one thing that Prometheus could not teach his people was how to make fire.

All through that dark night the people huddled in what shelter they could find and when the morning came they began to rebuild their houses. At first they did not miss the fire too much, but by that evening, when they could not bake bread or cook their food or even build a fire to keep themselves warm they began to understand what a dreadful thing had happened to them and how important fire was to them.

They went to Prometheus and begged him to help them. Prometheus loved the people that he had made and he was determined to help them. He knew that there was one place in the whole world where he could find fire, but he also knew how dangerous it would be for him to try to go there. He had seen how angry Zeus could be, and how powerful the greatest of all the gods was. Even so he decided that he could not leave his people without fire, so, late that night, taking a hollow branch with him, he began to climb Mount Olympus.

He climbed quickly, knowing that he must hurry before Zeus realized what he was trying to do. He reached the palace of the gods and crept into the sacred chamber where the eternal fire burned. Stealthily he stole several of the flaming embers and placed them in the hollow branch and just as stealthily he crept back down the mountain.

Using the embers he had stolen he brought fire back to his people, but as he looked up through the darkness towards the top of the mountain he knew that Zeus would punish him the next day.

The morning came and Zeus looked down on the land. To his amazement and fury he saw little columns of smoke rising from the houses in the villages and towns. He saw twinkling flames in the blacksmith's forges and the silver and goldsmith's workshops. He realized that somehow Prometheus had outwitted him. He raged through the palace, shaking his fists at the land below.

'Prometheus shall pay for this,' he vowed, and he sent for his powerful brother Hephaestus, the god of the forge and the fire.

'Prometheus has stolen your fire, capture him at once,' he shouted at Hephaestus. 'Bind him with chains to the topmost peak of Mount Caucasus so that he may never escape.'

Hephaestus did as Zeus demanded, although his heart was heavy and he felt that such a cruel punishment was too harsh.

Zeus still had not finished with Prometheus, the half-god who had dared to defy him. Every day for thirty years Zeus sent a gigantic eagle to attack him.

This eagle had a steel beak and claws and every morning tore at the poor chained Prometheus until it reached his liver, and every night Zeus caused Prometheus to be healed, ready for the savage eagle to attack him the next morning.

Although Prometheus was in great pain he would not give up, for he believed that what he had done was right and he was prepared to stand any pain if it would allow his people to keep their fire.

At last Zeus relented. He had come to admire the bravery that Prometheus showed. Zeus commanded one of his mightiest sons, Hercules, to release Prometheus by slaying the monstrous eagle. With a sweep of his great sword, Hercules slew the eagle and severed the chains that bound Prometheus to Mount Caucasus, but as he did he also sheared off a small piece of the mountain. The chains that Hephaestus had made to bind Prometheus were so strong that even the strength of Hercules could not part all of them from Prometheus. So for evermore this brave half-god carried with him a part of the mountain that had been his prison for so long — a reminder of his noble sacrifice in bringing fire back to the world of man.

DAEDALUS AND ICARUS

The ancient city of Athens has always been the mightiest city in Greece. Even today its temples and palaces, squares and meeting places are still impressive. Imagine how Athens must have looked when it was young, when the great Acropolis was first built.

This huge temple to Pallas Athene, the patron goddess of the Athenians, stands on the hill of the Acropolis, overlooking the paved streets and smaller temples of the city. Inside the Acropolis once stood a proud and awesome statue of the goddess. This statue was said to be so lifelike that when the people of Athens prayed to her she bowed her head to receive their prayers. Who built such a statue? Who could have made such a strange and wonderful thing?

This is the story of the man who was believed to have built not only this statue but many of the beautiful temples and palaces of Ancient Greece; the man who built the fabulous maze which surrounded the dreaded Minotaur of Crete. The man whose name meant 'cunningly wrought'. This is the story of Daedalus and his son Icarus.

Even when Daedalus was a young man he began to make wonderful sculptures. Most statues at that time were stiff and straight, their eyes were blank and they looked blindly out at the people who came to see them. The statues that Daedalus made looked as if they might step down and walk among the men and women of Greece. Some of these statues showed men throwing the discus — a popular sport in Greece; some of them showed the athletes and sportsmen who took part in the great Olympic Games that were held every four years. The statues that Daedalus made of the statesmen and leaders of that time showed them as if they were real men, not stiff and unnatural stone models. Their eyes seemed real, their robes looked as if they might move in the cooling breezes that blew through Athens.

Even more than this, the temples, palaces and houses that Daedalus designed were more comfortable than the houses built by any other architect. Their mosaic floors, pillared halls and painted walls proclaimed the genius of Daedalus. Whenever a new temple was built or a great palace was created for the rulers of Athens it was Daedalus who was asked to design it.

No wonder then that Daedalus became the greatest artist in all Greece. Students came from all parts of the ancient world to learn from him, songs were written praising him and his name was known all over Greece.

Daedalus became proud and haughty, and when one of his students, the son of his sister, began to show great promise as an artist, Daedalus began to watch him carefully.

Daedalus' nephew Talus learned fast, and soon there was very little that Daedalus could teach him. Talus knew how to carve the fine marble from the mountains round Athens, how to take a rough block of this milky stone and turn it into a fine likeness of a man. He carved little sculptures of animals; cats and dogs which seemed so real that they might jump down and scamper away. Then he turned his hand to making pottery. He invented a wheel on which beautiful vases could be made: vases which were smooth and shapely, unlike the crude pottery that had been made before. He even made small models of shrines to the gods. Talus became well thought of and some of the rich merchants of Athens began to ask him to design their cool marble villas.

Daedalus watched this and grew more and more jealous. He did not feel pleased that Talus had learned his skills only from him. He didn't listen when people told him how proud he must be of his nephew and how well he had taught him. Daedalus began to forget that he himself could still make fine sculptures, that he was still the greatest artist in Greece. He only looked at what Talus had made. He would not allow Talus to build any of the great temples of Athens and never asked for his help.

He tried to ignore Talus, but wherever he went people spoke so well of his nephew that Daedalus could never forget him. At last he became determined to destroy him.

One evening Daedalus sent a message to Talus asking him to come to a high cliff beside the sea near Athens. He pretended that he wished to ask for Talus' advice about a temple that was to be built there. Talus received the message, and, glad that his uncle, who had seemed so strange and silent recently, wanted to see him, hurried off to the meeting place.

Daedalus was waiting for him, pacing around the cleared space which was littered with blocks of marble ready to be carved into statues of the gods. Below him he could hear the thunder of the waves on the sharp rocks at the base of the cliffs. He looked around. This was a desolate place, a mile or so from the city and far away from curious eyes.

'Yes,' thought Daedalus. 'This place is ideal for my plan. No one can see me and the sea is deep and full of deadly currents.'

He looked down at the crashing waves and for a moment almost changed his mind. 'Talus is so young . . . my sister's only son . . . just a few years older than my own son Icarus . . .' he thought to himself, but then he hardened his heart again.

'There must be only one great sculptor and architect in Greece, and it must be me,' he said to himself. 'The gods will surely forgive me for what I do, I have built many temples to them, surely they will forgive me . . .'

The voice of his nephew broke into his thoughts.

'Uncle, this is indeed a wild and magnificent place for a temple, see how the mountains surround us and the sea stretches before us.'

Talus walked towards Daedalus and stood by him. Daedalus put his arm round the young man's shoulders and turned towards the cliff edge.

'See how far the sea stretches into the distance,' he said, urging Talus towards the crumbling stone that marked the edge of the sheer and fatal drop into the sea.

It was done swiftly; a scuffling of feet, a muffled cry and Talus fell into the darkness towards the hissing waves.

Daedalus turned away from the cliff, sickened at what he had done. Fearfully he looked up into the darkening sky, afraid that the gods had seen him. Pulling his robe round his face he crept back to Athens.

The gods had indeed seen what Daedalus had done and Pallas Athene was determined that Talus should not die. As he plunged downwards she turned him into a bird before he could reach the sea. She had saved him from death and for evermore Talus would swoop and cry round her temple on the Acropolis — one of the white seabirds that forever give thanks to the wisest of goddesses.

Daedalus hardly dared to go out among the men and women of Athens. He was sure that his face must show the dreadful thing that he had done. The days passed and at first Talus was not missed, but then people began to wonder.

'Where is Talus, the nephew of Daedalus?' they asked.

'Why does Daedalus look so pale and frightened?' they murmured in the streets.

'Daedalus was jealous of his nephew, anyone could see that,' they whispered in the alleyways.

'Perhaps Daedalus has . . .' they muttered in the squares of Athens.

Still the body of Talus was not found. Weeks passed and Daedalus began to feel bolder. He began to go out and about again, but wherever he went people stared after him.

'There goes Daedalus,' they hissed. 'His nephew Talus is missing, such a strange thing . . .'

'See how pale Daedalus looks, as if he had a guilty secret,' they said, and their voices followed Daedalus around.

Even the white birds that circled the temple of Pallas Athene seemed to be crying out — Talus . . . Talus . . . Talus . . .

Daedalus was frightened. No one dared to openly accuse him, for the body of Talus was still missing. But now, instead of being the proudest artist in Greece, Daedalus was the man who everybody thought was a murderer, and he knew that they were right. He had to get away, away from the whispering voices and the accusing stares.

He packed his belongings and persuaded one of the Athenian fishermen to take him and his son Icarus far, far away from Athens. And so they sailed far across the stormy waters of the Mediterranean Sea until they came to the island of Crete.

Minos, the King of Crete, was a strange man. He had heard of Daedalus, of the marvellous palaces and temples that Daedalus had built, and he had also heard that Daedalus was thought to have killed Talus. Minos did not care, for he had need of this man. Only Daedalus could help to hide the dreadful secret that this King kept in his heart.

Parsifae, the Queen of Crete, had a son, but this was no ordinary child. He was born with the body of a human but the head and shoulders of a bull. As the child of Minos and Parsifae became stronger he grew into a monster whose terrible rages· could not be controlled. Minos knew that Daedalus was the only man who could build a palace large enough and strong enough to hide his monster son, a palace so complicated and strange that no one could enter it. Even if they did, they would never be able to find their way out again.

'If you build a palace for the Minotaur, you may stay here and I will protect you from the Athenians,' Minos told Daedalus. 'You and your son will have the finest house and everything you could ever want. I will pay you handsomely and you will be safe.'

Daedalus agreed. He wanted Icarus, his son, to grow up without being taunted and bullied for having a murderer for a father.

For five years Daedalus worked at building the most fantastic palace the world had ever seen. Made from the pinkish stone of the island it had hundreds of rooms, countless courtyards and galleries and thousands of pillars. Some of the walls were painted with bright pictures. Carvings surrounded the doorways and windows, the floors

16

were paved with mosaics and patterned slabs of marble, but strangest of all were the passageways. These twisted and turned like a nest of serpents, doubling back on themselves. Some of them led nowhere, some made a complete circle and returned to the outside of the palace.

One of these passageways, so secret that only Daedalus and Minos knew where it was, led to a room at the centre of the palace. Here, far away from the outer walls, the Minotaur, the terrible son of Minos and Parsifae, was to live. The half-human, half-bull monster whose roars and screams would never be heard by the outside world.

When the palace was finished and the Minotaur safely hidden inside, Daedalus was tired. The island of Crete, although beautiful, was not as lovely as Greece. Daedalus was homesick. His son was nearly a grown man and Daedalus wanted to return to Athens.

'Surely the Athenians will have forgotten about Talus by now,' he thought.

He went to Minos and told the King that he wished to leave and take Icarus with him. Minos persuaded Daedalus to stay a little longer; he had no intention of letting this brilliant artist go.

'It is the feast day of my wife, Parsifae,' he told Daedalus. 'Make me a present for her, something that will astonish and amaze her.'

Daedalus set to work again. He made the most magnificent wooden model of a cow, so lifelike that no one believed it was carved.

When it was finished he went to Minos again.

'Now may I leave?' he asked.

But Minos still would not let him go, and Daedalus realized that he must devise a way to escape from Crete, a way that would take both himself and his son far across the Mediterranean to his beloved Greece. Daedalus knew that Minos had hundreds of fast and well armed ships.

'The sea is too dangerous,' he thought. 'The only way to escape is through the air: I must make wings for Icarus and myself and like birds we will fly to freedom.'

Daedalus secretly began to collect birds' feathers. From the wings of the tiniest thrush to the great pinions of the eagle, Daedalus hoarded the feathers until at last he had enough. He built a light framework of the hollow stems of reeds and attached the feathers to this with wax. When one pair of wings was finished he made another pair for his son Icarus.

At dead of night he and Icarus crept to the top of the highest cliff in Crete. They strapped the wings to their arms and launched themselves into the darkness.

The wings worked well and they flew on and on over the sea towards Athens. As dawn broke, Daedalus and his son could see the cliffs and islands of the Greek coast ahead of them in the distance. They looked down and saw the sea below them, wrinkled and blue. They looked up and saw the clouds and the sun above them and curious birds circling around them, wondering what these two strange winged creatures were.

Icarus loved flying.

'Look at me,' he called to his father. 'I can fly higher than you.'

'Come down, come down!' called Daedalus. 'The feathers are only glued to your wings with wax and the sun is too hot. Fly lower where the sea breeze can cool you. If the wax melts you will fall.'

But Icarus would not listen and flew up and up towards the sun, and the wax began to melt. Soon the feathers began to fall and spiral down towards the sea. At last so many feathers had fallen that the wings could no longer hold Icarus up and he fell, like a thunderbolt, down and down towards the blue Mediterranean.

Daedalus looked down at the sea. There was no sign of his son and he saw ahead of him the very cliff where he had murdered Talus.

He realized then that the gods had punished him for the death of Talus by taking the life of Icarus. He had no heart now to return to Greece. Instead he flew on towards Sicily. There he spent the rest of his life. Although he made many statues there he was never happy again. None of the statues he carved ever smiled, and their eyes always looked towards the cliffs of Athens and the sea which claimed the life of his son Icarus.

DEUCALION AND PYRRHA

Perhaps you have read about the story of the great flood in the Bible, but maybe you didn't know that the ancient Greeks had a story about a flood, too. Here it is, the story of the four ages of man, the great flood and of Deucalion and his wife Pyrrha, the couple who survived.

Before the great god Zeus ruled the heavens, Chronos, his father, who was one of the oldest gods of all, was king of the world and the sky. He created a race of men to live on the earth. They were tall and fair and lived a perfectly happy life. They wanted for nothing, the earth gave them all their food, the seas were warm and calm and full of fish. The forests and meadows abounded with fruit and flowers and there was no sickness anywhere. Nobody ever grew old and even death itself was no more than a delicious sleep. When the Age of Gold came to an end it was followed by the Age of Silver. The people of the Age of Silver stayed young for a century, only becoming adult after the hundred years of youth had passed. Unfortunately when they were adult, they changed suddenly and became cruel and unreasonable. They jeered at the gods who had given them life and would not care for the lands that had supported them for so long. Zeus became angry and turned them all into demons and banished them to the Underworld.

After the Age of Silver came the Age of Iron. The men of this age were created by Prometheus and at first behaved well, but as the years passed they became worse than any who had come before them. War was their favourite sport and they thought no more of killing than they did of eating and drinking.

Battles raged all over the earth, nation fought nation and even families fought amongst themselves.

Hermes, the winged messenger of the gods, was kept very busy flying between Mount Olympus and the earth, reporting what was happening. He told Zeus that the world was in a piteous state and that was why the king of the gods was constantly being asked to give judgement between the warring sides. At last Zeus could stand it no more and he decided that he would come down to earth himself to find out what was happening.

He disguised himself as a man and descended from the Palace of the Immortals to a little town called Lycaon. This town was governed by the king of the Arcadians and even for such a fierce and

warlike region was thought to be the worst of all the Arcadian towns. There Zeus hoped to see for himself just how the men of earth behaved. He discovered that Hermes had been telling the truth, and that not only were the Arcadians cruel and savage, but they also held no belief in the gods. Zeus decided it was time that they were taught a lesson. He caused a great thunderstorm to show the men of Arcadia that he was no ordinary man. He expected them to fall at his feet in fear and trembling, but to Zeus' fury, the king of the Arcadians pretended not to believe that Zeus was really amongst them.

'How am I to know that you are really an immortal as you say you are?' he demanded. 'It is an easy thing to say that you are a god; I should think that you go all over Arcadia pretending to be Zeus, just so that you can feast and drink at other people's expense.'

Zeus held his tongue and waited. He believed that even such a barbaric king would abide by the rules of hospitality and offer a stranger a meal and shelter.

'I will feed you,' said the king sarcastically, 'and it will be a meal fit for a god.' The king commanded that the oldest of his watchdogs should be killed, skinned and cooked and when this was done he served it up to Zeus.

This was too much for the proud father of the gods. He drew himself up to his full height and stretched out his hand; from his fingers flames burst forth and the entire palace of the king was burnt to the ground. Then Zeus turned on the king, who was weeping and wailing and grovelling on the ground. Once again the mighty Zeus stretched out his hand. The king's body stretched and lengthened, his skin changed into a furry pelt, his hands and feet turned into paws and in a trice the king was changed into a wolf. Then Zeus turned his might on the land that harboured such villains. He conjured up a terrible storm. The heavens grew dark and the winds rose. Poseidon, brother of Zeus and god of the sea, sent waves and tides sweeping inland. There they met the boiling waters of the rivers and swept away the trees and grass. As the waters rose men and women struggled to higher land, but the faster they climbed the faster the waters followed. Many days and nights passed and still the water rose steadily until no land could be seen anywhere. Only one place was spared and that was Mount Parnassus. This beautiful mountain rose above the plains of Arcadia, and there, huddling from the rain and the wind-blown spray, were a man and a woman, the only survivors of the human race.

Zeus loved these two, for the man was the son of Prometheus, one of his half-god sons. Deucalion and Pyrrha had never been like the violent Arcadians, but had lived quietly and industriously, looking after their flocks and tending their vineyards. Zeus had warned them of the coming flood and they had built a boat that rose with the waters until it had come to rest on Mount Parnassus. Deucalion and Pyrrha stayed on the mountain until the floods had receded and then they walked sorrowfully down to the drowned plains. Nothing stirred, no animals, no birds, no trees blew in the wind.

'What are we to do, my husband?' sobbed Pyrrha. 'There is nothing to eat and nowhere to shelter.'

They wandered on until they came to the ruined temple of Themis, the mother of Prometheus. There they knelt down and prayed to the goddess.

'Great mother of the earth,' they prayed. 'We cannot live so lonely a life; there are no men and no women but us.'

A strange light began to flicker over the tumbled stones of the temple and a mist gathered round the altar. From the mist came a silvery voice.

'I will help you,' the voice said, 'but you must do exactly as I say. Take the bones of your grandmother and throw them on the ground. Hide your faces while you do this.'

'Great goddess,' replied Pyrrha, 'you cannot mean this. How can I scatter the bones of my grandmother? The gods teach us that we must respect and care for the bones of our parents.'

Then Deucalion spoke, 'Pyrrha, do not be afraid, the gods would never ask us to do anything that was wicked. Is not Themis herself our grandmother and is she not the mother of the earth? Her bones are the stones on which we stand, that is what she means.'

So Deucalion and Pyrrha did as the goddess had told them and scattered stones behind them, hiding their faces as they did so. The stones thrown by Deucalion were changed into men and the stones thrown by his wife Pyrrha turned into women, and the earth was peopled by the men and women made from the bones of the mother goddess — Themis. These people of the earth were strong and honest and worked hard to repair the damage done by the great flood.

Zeus also created another race of men. They were noble and fair, but alas, in time they too perished, just like the three races of man who had gone before them. These men were the heroes of the Greek legends; they were half-gods and when they died they went to a heavenly island — the Island of Happiness where everything was peaceful and no sadness clouded the lives of those who dwelt there.

The people of stone lived on. They were only mortals and so it was their destiny to work and labour to survive, and so it is today for us.

TANTALUS

Zeus, the greatest of all the Greek gods, had many children. Some of them were born to his wife Hera and lived on Mount Olympus, but others were born to women of the earth and were only half-gods. One of these half-god sons was called Tantalus, and ever since he had been a baby he had been a favourite with his father. Like all the earthling sons of Zeus, Tantalus grew up to be tall and handsome and Zeus gave him everything he could ever wish for; lands and riches beyond belief. Tantalus became King of Phrygia, ruler of one of the wealthiest states of ancient Greece.

From time to time Zeus would invite his favourite earthling son to dine with him and the other gods in the marble hall of their palace on Mount Olympus. There Tantalus would eat delicious food and drink the Ambrosian wine that only the gods were allowed to drink. To be sure, Zeus spoiled Tantalus dreadfully, but then, even the gods are sometimes allowed their weaknesses.

Tantalus began to believe that he was as important as the gods themselves. He secretly laughed at Zeus and mocked the other gods, even going so far as to steal a flagon of the sacred Ambrosian wine and bring it back to earth. There he and his friends became very drunk and in their drunkenness sneered and laughed at the Olympians.

Zeus knew how ungrateful Tantalus was, but turned a blind eye to his son's stupidity.

'He is still young,' he told Hera, who was furious that a mere mortal dared to mock the gods. 'He will grow up and become wiser.'

But Tantalus did not grow any wiser. He became more and more haughty, refusing to make offerings to the gods or even to worship them. He began to forbid the people of Phrygia to build temples to Zeus saying:

'Zeus is not so mighty. I know Mount Olympus well and have met all the gods, they are just like us — a little larger perhaps, but they quarrel just like us and make mistakes just like us. Why should you worship them, why not worship me — I am just as mighty.'

Still Zeus did nothing about his wayward son; and then Tantalus went too far.

'The gods are supposed to know everything,' he said to the Phrygians one day, 'but I will prove to you that I can trick them.'

Tantalus then did the most terrible thing. He went to the nursery of his son Pelops and killed him. Then he ordered his cook to prepare a dish fit for the gods, and he gave the cook the body of Pelops to use for the meat for the dish. In fear and trembling the cook obeyed, for he knew that Tantalus would kill him if he disobeyed. When the dish was prepared, Tantalus took it to Mount Olympus and presented it to the gods. Zeus was away hunting at that time, but was expected back that night.

'I bring you a present,' Tantalus said to the gods, 'in thanks for all your hospitality to me. It is a dish prepared especially for you, but please save it until Zeus returns and then you may all dine together.' He placed the dish on the marble table and went back down the mountain, smiling to himself.

Now it was true that the gods knew everything that ever happened and they were horrorstruck at the dreadful thing that Tantalus had done. They also knew that he was trying to trick them. They left the dish on the table to wait until Zeus returned when he would decide what to do with his evil son.

Zeus, who in his wisdom knew immediately what had occurred, came back from the hunt early. His anger was terrifying. He hurled thunderbolts about the heavens and split the sky again and again with lightning.

'Tantalus will be punished,' he raged at the other gods, 'you may be sure of that, but first we must bring Pelops back to life.' He called for Clotho, who was one of the Muses and could restore life. She took up the dish and placed its contents in a large bronze cauldron.

'I suppose that no one has eaten of this?' she asked.

'Oh!' said the goddess Demeter in surprise, 'were we not supposed to eat it? I only nibbled a little, but I was so hungry.'

Demeter had just lost her only daughter Persephone to Pluto, the god of the Underworld, and had been quite distracted with grief. Normally she would have known at once what the dish contained, but in her misery had not noticed.

'Well, I shall do what I can,' said Clotho and took the cauldron away with her to a secret place where she chanted incantations and spells over it until Pelops was re-formed and came back to life. Where Demeter had nibbled away at his shoulder Clotho made a new shoulder from ivory, which Pelops in later life showed proudly to anyone who was interested, for, as he would say: 'It is not every mortal who has been nibbled away by a goddess!'

The punishment that Zeus devised for the evil Tantalus was indeed terrible. The wicked king was banished to hell, to the darkest regions of the Underworld. There he was to stay for eternity, standing in a pool of water which reached to his knees. Tormented by thirst, whenever he bent down to drink the water drained away and yet, when he stood up, the water rose again to his knees. Worse even than his thirst was his hunger, and there, dangling in front of him was the branch of a tree, laden with juicy peaches, apples, pears, grapes and olives, all growing from the same branch. The branch seemed just within his grasp and yet, whenever he stretched his hands towards it, it would draw away as if it were alive, until the fruit was a mere fraction beyond his trembling fingertips, so near but never near enough. Above his head was suspended a huge boulder, just on the brink of falling, threatening the terrified king: no matter how many years Tantalus might be there the threat of this heavy rock always hung over him, threatening to fall and crush him. So Tantalus was punished for his crimes — an eternity of yearning, an eternity of hunger and thirst and fear, but what was even worse — an eternity of unfulfilled hope, an eternity of striving and never gaining any peace.

THE TROJAN WARS

This is the story of Paris, the son of the King of Troy, and Helen, the woman he loved so much that he fought a war for her; a war that lasted for many years and finally led to the downfall of one the greatest cities of the ancient world.

King Peleus of Pythia had fallen in love with the goddess Thetis and she had agreed to marry him. Because Thetis was an immortal, all the gods were invited to the wedding feast, all, that is, except one. The uninvited goddess was Eris, the most unpopular of all the goddesses. No one ever invited Eris to any celebrations because she always caused trouble, for Eris was the goddess of discord. In the middle of the feasting and dancing Eris stormed into King Peleus' banqueting hall. She was furious that she had not been asked. She strode up to the top of the table where Zeus, Hera, Pallas Athene and Aphrodite were sitting. Without speaking Eris threw a golden apple onto the table and pointed at Zeus.

'Here is my wedding present to the bride and groom,' she said with a cruel smile, 'and to the guests, both immortal and human.' She then vanished with a clap of thunder.

'How unlike Eris to give anyone a gift,' murmured Hera. 'I wonder what she is up to?'

Zeus picked up the apple and turned it over in his hand. The apple was made of pure gold, and all the guests caught their breath in wonder. They had never seen such a beautiful thing.

'Yes,' said Zeus, 'it is unlike Eris to do anything that does not cause strife and war, and this gift is no exception, see . . .'

He handed the apple to Hera, who read out the words carved round it: 'To be awarded to the fairest of all.'

Immediately there was a hubbub, all the guests craned forward to look at the apple, and above their excited chatter the voices of Hera, Pallas Athene and Aphrodite rose the loudest.

'Well there is no question who should be awarded this apple,' said Hera. 'After all I have always been said to be the most beautiful of all the goddesses.'

'Fashions change, Hera,' retorted Pallas Athene, 'a few years ago golden hair and blue eyes were considered lovely, but you have grown a great deal fatter lately and now people think that tall, dark-haired and slender women are loveliest. I claim the apple.'

'Neither of you deserve it,' chimed in Aphrodite. 'Athene, you are too tall and Hera, you are too old. I am the youngest and fairest of us all. I claim the apple.'

Hera turned to her husband. 'Great Zeus, dearest husband, only you in your wisdom can decide — which of us is the fairest?'

This put Zeus in a quandary. He knew that Hera would give him no peace if he did not choose her and that Athene and Aphrodite would claim that he had only chosen Hera because she was his wife.

'I will not choose,' said Zeus. 'Surely there must be a mortal who can decide for me.'

At this Priam, King of Troy, stood up. 'My son Paris is the handsomest lad in Greece, he is just the person to choose,' he said. 'He is waiting outside.'

Paris was brought into the banqueting chamber. He was a tall, golden-haired young man, with the brightest blue eyes that Aphrodite had ever seen.

'Paris,' said Zeus handing the golden apple to him, 'look well at these three lovely goddesses and tell me which one you think is the fairest.'

First Hera stepped forward.

'If you award the apple to me I will make you the most powerful king the world has ever seen,' she told Paris. 'I am the queen of the immortals and can make your greatest wish come true.'

'I am the wisest of the immortals,' said Athene. 'I can give you wisdom and knowledge greater than any man has ever known. Give the apple to me.'

Then Aphrodite came and stood beside Paris. She placed her little hand on his arm and looked up into his bright blue eyes.

'I am the goddess of love,' she said, 'and if you choose me I promise that the most beautiful woman in the world shall fall in love with you.'

Paris looked at the three goddesses. They were all so lovely, but it was Aphrodite, with her smiling red lips and dancing green eyes, that seemed the most beautiful to him. Falling on one knee he presented the apple to her. Pallas Athene and Hera were furious.

'You will regret this, Paris,' raged Athene. 'Aphrodite may bring you success in love, but you will never have any success in war, Hera and I shall make sure of that!'

'Pooh,' said Aphrodite, 'with the woman you love by your side, what does that matter. Love will triumph over all. You have made the right decision, Paris.'

And she threw the golden apple up and down in the air and caught it in her little rosy hands.

'Where shall I find the woman I am to love?' asked Paris.

'She lives in Sparta,' Aphrodite told him, 'and you will know her the moment you see her. You remember that your father's sister Hesione was stolen away by Hercules many years ago? Why not ask your father to give you a fleet of ships so that you can sail to Greece and bring your aunt back. Greece is only a day's sailing from Sparta and so you may kill two birds with one stone by bringing back Hesione and finding the woman who is destined for you.'

So Paris sailed away across the blue Aegean Sea, down the coast of Greece towards the walled city of Sparta and the woman he was to love.

When he reached Sparta he sent messages to the king to announce his arrival. Menelaus was delighted to welcome him and even sent a troop of horsemen to ride with him from the coast to the city gates. There Menelaus and his wife Helen waited to receive their royal guest.

The moment that Paris set eyes on Helen he knew that this was the woman that Aphrodite had promised to him. It did not matter to Paris that Helen was already married to the King of Sparta. It did not matter to Paris that Menelaus, that very same king, was welcoming him into Sparta. All he could think about was the beauty of Helen's eyes and the way her hair curled softly around her shoulders. His days and nights became full of dreams about the lovely Queen of Sparta.

Helen and Menelaus had a daughter called Hermione and Paris would watch Helen playing with the little girl. He could see that Helen loved her daughter and her husband and although she made Paris welcome she showed no special sign that she was falling in love with him.

Paris prayed to Aphrodite and asked the goddess to honour her promise that he should be loved by the most beautiful woman in the world.

'Be patient, Paris,' the goddess told him. 'In a few weeks Menelaus must go away on a long journey and will be away for a month or more. Then I will make Helen fall in love with you, when it is safe to steal away with her.'

So Paris had to wait patiently. At last, Menelaus left Sparta; he kissed his wife and daughter goodbye and shook hands with Paris.

'Take good care of our guest,' he told Helen, 'treat him royally and see that he lacks nothing.'

Helen kissed her husband and promised to look after Paris.

As soon as Menelaus had left, Aphrodite cast an enchantment on

Helen. The Queen of Sparta suddenly saw the young man in a new light. She fell in love with him and forgot all about her daughter Hermione and her husband Menelaus.

When Paris begged her to flee to Troy with him she agreed and taking no more than she could carry she sailed away in Paris' ship, leaving her kingdom, her crown, her child and her riches behind. She was never to be known as the Queen of Sparta again, just as Helen of Troy, the woman who caused the Trojan Wars because of her beauty.

When Menelaus returned the whole of Sparta was agog with the news. Menelaus was terribly angry. He loved Helen with all his heart and now she had been stolen away from him by a man who he had welcomed and trusted as a guest. He sent soldiers out throughout Greece carrying messages to all the greatest kings and heroes of the land, telling them of the treachery of Paris and asking them for their help and support.

So a huge army gathered. Led by Menelaus and his brother Agamemnon, they prepared to sail for the ancient city of Troy, but before they left Menelaus went to consult the Oracle at Delphi.

People often consulted this miraculous oracle whenever they needed advice or were about to embark on a risky undertaking. Menelaus and Agamemnon made offerings to the gods. Then they asked the oracle what chances of success they had against the Trojans.

The oracle replied, 'Only with the help of Achilles will the Trojans be overthrown.'

This mysterious message pleased Agamemnon and Menelaus very much, for Achilles, one of the great heroes of Greece, had decided to march with them.

'The oracle is never wrong,' said Menelaus. 'We shall conquer and I shall regain my lovely wife. The treacherous Paris will be punished for his wickedness, as will the Trojans who harbour him.'

The great army set off, led by the King of Sparta. They marched to the seashore where they were met by Achilles and Patroclus, both worthy soldiers famed throughout the ancient world. Diomedes and Nestor also joined them, as did Odysseus, the widely travelled and greatly feared King of Ithaca. And so one of the largest armies ever gathered together in Ancient Greece set off across the sea for the city of Troy.

At that time, Troy was the strongest city of the ancient world. Surrounded by towering walls and battlements it guarded the plains and foothills of the peaceful land around it. King Priam was immensely wealthy and the Trojans lived in splendid houses. The Trojan army numbered thousands of men, but they were rarely called on to fight because King Priam preferred peace to war. The Trojans were not pleased that Paris had brought this disaster on them, and they muttered amongst themselves. Paris was hated throughout the city and even though the beauty of Helen was admired, many men thought that even her loveliness was not a good enough reason for war.

The Greek army camped on the plain in front of the walls of Troy. Their tents and campfires were spread across the grass as far as the eye could see, and at the edge of the sea some miles away the masts of the fleet of ships which had brought the soldiers from Greece nodded and swayed as the waves rocked the ships up and down.

For nine long years the siege of Troy continued and in all that time the Greeks could not take the city and the Trojans stood on the battlements and looked down at the army before them. The Greeks raided the cities of the Trojan Plain and it was in one of these raids, on the City of Chryse, that two slaves were taken. They both were beautiful young women; one of them was Chryseis, the daughter of the High Priest of Apollo, and the other was Briseis. These slaves were so beautiful that Agamemnon took Chryseis and Achilles took Briseis and each of the girls was treated with honour and in time came to love their captors.

Now the father of Chryseis was the most powerful priest of Apollo in the land and he grieved for his daughter. He said prayers at the temple of Apollo and asked the god what to do. 'The Greeks worship Apollo as I do,' he thought, 'surely they will return her to me if I ask them in the name of Apollo to do this.'

When the Greek leaders, Menelaus and Agamemnon, heard the old priest's pleas, Agamemnon was angry. He had come to love Chryseis and would not consent to return her. In vain the priest offered a rich ransom for his daughter and in vain he pleaded in the name of Apollo, the god whom they both worshipped. Agamemnon would not give in.

The High Priest returned to his city and prayed once more to Apollo.

'The Greeks have scorned me, even though I asked in your name,' he said. 'Send some sign of your displeasure that will show the Greeks that the gods are not mocked.'

Apollo heard him and sent a terrible plague to the plains of Troy. Only the Greeks were struck down with this and they began to sicken and die. Agamemnon took council with his priests and asked them what to do, for he knew that soon the army would be so weakened that they would have to return to Greece.

'It is the wrath of Apollo,' the priests told him. 'When you refused to return Chryseis to her father you angered the gods. You must now obey the High Priest and give Chryseis back.'

Agamemnon knew that what they said was true, but he loved Chryseis and was loth to part from her.

'If I return Chryseis, I shall do it for the good of the Greek army, and not for myself,' he said. 'What will I be given in return? Surely I am entitled to a further part of the riches that we have taken from the cities of the plain.'

Achilles heard this and became very angry.

'You know full well that the riches we have taken have been shared out among the men long ago. You are not entitled to anything further. If you had not been so obstinate before, Apollo would not have been angered,' he shouted at Agamemnon.

At this Agamemnon became angry, too.

'Why should I give up Chryseis while you keep Briseis? I am your commander, I shall take Briseis from you by force and show you who commands here.'

'If you do this, we shall part,' Achilles told Agamemnon. 'I will not fight beside a man I do not trust.' And he turned on his heel and strode back to his tent.

Agamemnon sent Chryseis back to her father and the High Priest prayed again to Apollo, who stopped the terrible plague.

Still Agamemnon's heart burned with anger against Achilles, and he sent his soldiers to Achilles' tent to bring Briseis to him. When Achilles heard what had happened he flung down his sword and gathered his men about him.

'We shall return to our ships,' he told them. 'I will no longer fight for Agamemnon.' And they withdrew to the shore and camped by their ships. Achilles prayed to his mother, the goddess Thetis, and asked her to punish Agamemnon for what he had done. Thetis agreed to avenge her son, although she had to consult with Zeus first, for Zeus had promised to aid the Greeks.

Again the two armies faced each other on the plains of Troy, and this time, Paris, the cause of all the strife, came to the front of the soldiers and hurled abuse at the Greeks. When Menelaus saw Paris his eyes blazed with anger. The Greek king strode to the front of his army and drew his sword.

. When Paris saw this his courage failed and he ran back and hid behind the first rank of Trojan soldiers.

'You coward,' his brother Hector shouted at him. 'We are fighting this war because of your deeds, many of our soldiers have been killed and yet you are too afraid to face the man you have wronged.'

At this Paris was ashamed. 'You are right, my brother,' he answered. 'There has been too much bloodshed already. I will offer to fight Menelaus in single combat and the victor shall take Helen and he who loses shall make peace with the other.'

Hector strode forward and conferred with Menelaus. The Greek king agreed and a space was cleared between the two armies where the combat was to take place. The two men stepped forward, each arrayed in his gleaming battle armour. They faced each other and Paris was the first to throw his spear.

It flashed through the air and struck the shield of Menelaus full in the centre. Menelaus staggered, but the spear had not gone through the shield and he was unharmed. Then it was the turn of the Greek king to hurl his spear. As straight as the flight of a hawk it sped towards the shield of Paris, and this spear pierced the shield and wounded Paris in the shouder. Menelaus sprang forward and brought his sword down on the helmet of Paris. The sword shattered but Menelaus would not give up. He took hold of the red plume of horsehair on the crown of Paris' helmet and began to pull Paris towards the Greek ranks. Paris began to choke on the strap of his helmet and would surely have fallen had not the goddess Aphrodite swooped down and carried him away from the scene of the battle back to Troy. Imagine the surprise that Menelaus felt when his foe disappeared. He searched for him among the Trojan ranks, but no one knew where Paris was.

Agamemnon declared that Menelaus was the victor and that Helen should be returned to her husband, and a truce should be arranged. This was agreed, but once again the gods intervened. They were angry that Aphrodite had interfered and were determined that the truce should be broken. Pallas Athene disguised herself as a Trojan soldier and whispered in the ear of Pandarus, the greatest of all the Trojan archers.

'If you kill Menelaus now, you will win great glory, and the favour of all the Trojans.'

Pandarus was swayed by the Athene's words and fitted an arrow to his bow. He drew back the bowstring and let the arrow fly. It was true to its mark and struck Menelaus on his belt. The wound was not fatal but Menelaus fell at the feet of Agamemnon. The Greek soldiers gathered round him and carried him back to his tent on their shields and Agamemnon, full of fury at the treachery of Pandarus in breaking the truce, at once called his men to arms.

'Fight on, noble Greeks,' he commanded. 'The treacherous Trojans have broken the truce. Fight on, fight on to the death.'

For days the battle raged, but neither side could gain a victory. Now Agamemnon greatly missed the strength of his friend Achilles. He remembered that the Oracle at Delphi had said that only with Achilles fighting beside him would Troy be taken and he decided to send a message to Achilles to beg him to join them once more.

The messengers arrived at Achilles' camp.

'Return to the Greek army, Achilles,' they begged, 'Agamemnon will return the beautiful Briseis to you and when Troy is taken you shall have the lion's share of the spoils.'

Achilles would not listen, even though his greatest friend Patroclus, a soldier as valiant as himself, begged him to do so.

'I shall only return to the battle if the Trojans try to burn my ships,' he told the messengers. 'Return to Agamemnon and tell him this.'

The messengers returned and the battle raged on. Patroclus

grieved to see so many Greeks killed and begged Achilles to let him take a troop of men to aid the Greeks.

'Take my armour,' Achilles said, 'and the gods go with you.'

Patroclus donned the armour of Achilles and led his men into the fray. The Trojans were greatly afraid when they saw the battle helmet and breastplate of Achilles, for they did not know that Patroclus and not Achilles was wearing them. Patroclus rushed at Hector, who was leading the Trojans, and drove him back to the very walls of Troy. But at the height of the struggle, Apollo, still angered at the disrespect that the Greeks had shown to him, pulled the helmet from Patroclus' face. When the Trojans saw that it was not Achilles that they were fighting they redoubled their efforts, and Patroclus fell dying at the feet of Hector.

'It is not the Trojans, but the gods who have defeated me,' murmured Patroclus. 'I will be avenged.'

Hector stripped Patroclus of the battle helmet and the breastplate and left his body lying on the battlefield where it was found by the Greeks and taken back to the camp of Achilles.

When Achilles heard of the death of his friend, and was told that his armour had been taken by Hector his anger knew no bounds.

'I will be avenged,' he cried, and prayed to his mother Thetis, who went to Vulcan, the blacksmith of the gods. Vulcan made a golden breastplate and helmet and Thetis took them to her son.

The next morning Achilles led his men into battle. The Trojans fled before him and Achilles drove them back. At last he stood face to face with Hector and they fought hand to hand. Achilles' grief at the death of his friend gave him terrible strength and with one dreadful blow he killed Hector. He commanded that the body of his enemy should be dragged through the Greek camp.

When King Priam of Troy heard of this he sent messengers to Achilles to beg him to return the body of his son and Achilles relented, for Hector had been a brave soldier and had fought fairly. That night the two great soldiers were honoured, Patroclus and Hector, the bravest men of the two armies.

And still the Trojan war continued with neither side winning. The plains of Troy became a burial ground for the brave Greek and Trojan soldiers who had fallen there.

'Will this war never end?' Agamemnon asked his commanders. 'There must be a way to take Troy.'

It was then that Odysseus, the cleverest of all the Greek commanders, spoke up. 'We are equally matched in strength,' he said, 'but I have a cunning plan. We will take the city of Troy by stealth. Once

34

we are inside the walls of the city, the Trojan army will not be able to withstand us. This is what we will do . . .' and he told them his plan.

They would build a huge wooden horse. This horse would be hollow, with enough room inside to hide the commanders of the Greek army. Then they would leave this horse outside the gates of Troy and pretend to leave. The Greek army would pack up their tents and retreat to the ships and sail away; but not back to Greece as the Trojans would think, but only a little way out to sea, out of sight of the watching guards on the walls of Troy. One man only would remain and he would pretend that he had been left behind by accident. He would tell the Trojans that the horse was an offering to the gods, and that if the Trojans dragged it into the city they would never again be attacked by enemies. Once inside, the commanders would leave the wooden horse, open the gates of the city and light a beacon fire to recall the ships.

For the next few days, the Greek encampment echoed to the sound of hammers and saws. The Trojan guard watched from the walls of Troy as a huge horse was constructed. This horse was designed by Epeios, the cleverest of the Greek architects. When the horse was finished on the night of the third day, the Greek commanders crept inside and the Greek soldiers packed up their tents and sailed away, leaving the plain empty and windswept. One man slept by the horse. His name was Sinon, and he was a cousin of Odysseus.

At dawn the next day, the Trojan guards ventured out and came to where the horse stood. They roughly shook Sinon awake.

'What is this?' they demanded. 'Why have the armies left, and what is this great horse?'

Sinon pretended to be surprised.

'Alas,' he said, 'they have left me behind. I surrender to you, I shall tell you whatever you wish to know.'

Sinon was taken to Priam and the horse remained outside the walls in the blazing sun.

Priam questioned Sinon. 'Tell us the meaning of this,' he demanded.

'The Greeks have left,' Sinon said. 'They have given up all hope of conquering Troy. The horse is a gift to the gods; it will protect any city from battle.'

Priam was amazed, but he was a cautious man and he took council with his cleverest advisor Laocoon.

'How do we know that this is not a trick,' Laocoon said, and he thrust a spear into the side of the horse. A booming groaning issued forth from the horse's mouth, and the Trojans trembled in fear. And then the gods intervened for the last time. They, too, were tired of the constant battles and decided that justice must be done. Zeus sent two great serpents from the sea which attacked Laocoon and wrapped their silvery coils round him and strangled him.

'It is a sign,' said King Priam. 'The gods are angry with Laocoon for doubting and turning away the gift the Greeks left. Drag the horse into the city.'

So the wooden horse was dragged into the city and a celebration was held to mark the end of the fighting. Late that same night while the soldiers and people of Troy were asleep, the Greek commanders crept out of the wooden horse and flung open the gates of the city. Sinon had lit the beacon to recall the Greek ships and so the Greek army swarmed into the city and took it.

Menelaus regained his beautiful Helen and forgave her, for he realized that she had been bewitched by Aphrodite. Paris was slain, for no one would defend him. As for the city of Troy, it was razed to the ground, never to be built again. The destruction of this once proud city was so complete that for many years no one knew exactly where Troy had stood. But the tales of the soldiers and kings who fought in the Trojan wars have never been forgotten and are still told today.

PHILEMON AND BAUCIS

The Romans worshipped many gods. Like the Greeks they believed that the gods lived at Olympus, but they called them by different names. The father of the gods, called Zeus by the Greeks, was known as Jupiter to the Romans. Mercury, the Roman messenger of the gods, was known as Hermes to the Greeks. This story tells of two simple peasants and how one day they were visited by the gods.

It was the custom in Roman times to offer hospitality, shelter and food to any passing strangers. Any traveller who found himself away from home at night could be sure of a welcome at any house if he knocked at the door and asked for shelter. And so it was with the gods. They expected the same hospitality when they visited the earth. One day Jupiter and Mercury decided that they would leave the splendid palace at the top of Mount Olympus and come down to earth to mix with mortal men and women. Jupiter, the father of all the gods, liked to make sure that all was well with the men and women he had created. So he and Mercury disguised themselves as men and made their way to Phrygia. Night was falling and so they knocked at the door of the first house they came to. It was a splendid marble house with fountains in the gardens and statues on each side of the door. There was no response to their knock, so they tried again. They knew that there were people in the house, for they could see candles burning at the windows and could hear music coming from the courtyard. Still there was no answer to their knock and as they waited in the gathering darkness they realized that no one was going to let them in.

'Strange,' said Mercury. 'Surely it is the custom of these people to offer shelter for the night. Let us try the next house.'

The next house was much more splendid; there were large gardens, and even a lake. The windows of the house were brightly lit and sounds of revelry and merriment floated up from them. Jupiter knocked loudly at the door and stood back to wait for an answer.

A man poked his head out of an upper window.

'What do you want?' he asked in a surly voice.

'We are strangers to this country,' answered Jupiter pleasantly, 'and we have no lodgings for the night. Will you offer us your hospitality?'

'Be off with you,' shouted the man, banging the wooden shutters, 'we have no room for strangers.'

Jupiter was very angry, but Mercury persuaded him to try again at the next house, but there, much the same thing happened. And so it was with all the splendid houses in the town.

By now Jupiter and Mercury were becoming tired as well as angry. 'We will try once more,' Jupiter told Mercury, 'and if no hospitality is offered to us we will return to Olympus and think how we can punish these selfish humans.'

The last house in the town was very unlike any of the others they had visited. There were no gardens or statues or fountains or lakes, only a bare patch of earth where a goose was pecking at a few grains of corn. The house was wooden and the roof needed mending.

'These people are too poor to offer any hospitality,' said Mercury, 'they have hardly enough for themselves. We shall not find shelter or food here.'

'We shall see,' said Jupiter, and he rapped on the door.

The door was opened almost immediately by an old, but smiling woman.

'Good sirs,' she said, looking up at them, 'pray enter, it is a cold night and you look tired and hungry. We do not have any rich food, but you are welcome to share what we have, and the house is warm and a bed can be found for you.'

Jupiter and Mercury entered the humble cottage and looked around them. An old man sat at a wooden table and a small fire burned brightly in the hearth. He rose and bowed.

'Welcome to our little home.' he said to the two gods, 'A glass of wine will warm you while my wife Baucis prepares food.'

The old woman brought a flagon of wine and four glasses to the table and the gods sat down. The old man poured a glass of wine for each of them and they drank a toast.

'It is a wild night to be in the open,' he said. 'You are very welcome to stay with us.'

'Thank you,' said Jupiter, 'we shall stay, but may I have a little more of this excellent wine?'

'Indeed you may,' said the old man, looking a little worried. 'You may drink as much as we have, but I fear that there is only that flagon left.'

'It is still full,' said Mercury, and to the old man's surprise he saw that it was, even though they had already drunk four glasses from it.

'This is a strange thing,' he said to his wife, 'no matter how much wine I pour from the flagon, it is always full. These strangers must be powerful magicians. Wife, go and kill our goose, for we must prepare a feast for them.'

Baucis curtseyed to Jupiter and Mercury and turned to go out.

'Stay!' commanded Jupiter. 'Your hospitality shall be rewarded. We are not mortals but gods, and we shall provide the feast.'

At once the table was covered with bowls and dishes of meat and fruit. Silver and gold plates shone in the firelight and finest crystal glasses twinkled to the brim with fine wine.

Baucis and her husband Philemon were amazed. They fell to their knees.

'Of all the people in this town you were the only two who offered food and shelter, even though you were the poorest. For this you shall be rewarded and the others shall be punished,' said Jupiter.

From outside the sound of a great tempest rose. Floods washed over the countryside sweeping away all the houses until only the little wooden house of Philemon and Baucis was left, and this Jupiter changed into a beautiful marble temple.

'We will grant any wish you desire,' Jupiter told the old couple.

'We do not need riches,' Philemon told him, 'We only wish to live together in happiness and tend the temple you have created, but there is one wish that you could grant to us — I do not wish to live after Baucis is dead and she does not wish to die after me. May we both die at the same time?'

'It shall be so,' said Jupiter, 'but not for many years yet.'

So for the rest of their lives, Philemon and Baucis lived happily at the temple and when the time came for them to die, they both died at the same instant and Jupiter turned them into two trees, their branches entwined together. And the trees are still there, as is the temple to Jupiter.

DEMETER AND PERSEPHONE

Do you remember the story of Tantalus and how he killed and cooked his own son Pelops? Do you remember that Pelops was brought back to life by Clotho, who made him almost as good as new, except for his shoulder, which had been nibbled by Demeter? This is the story of Demeter and her daughter Persephone, and it explains why Demeter was so upset that she did not notice that the food that Tantalus had brought for the gods was, in fact, his own son Pelops.

Demeter was the goddess of the Earth. It was she who made sure that the corn of the earth grew in abundance. She looked after the fruit and flowers and sent the rain to swell the crops.

Demeter had one beautiful daughter called Persephone, whom she loved more than anything, and when she was not busy with her duties she would talk and sing to her daughter and look after her.

One day Persephone went down to earth to gather some wild flowers for her mother. She was sitting in the grass plaiting columbine and wild hyacinths together to make a necklace when Pluto, the dark god of the Underworld, saw her. Pluto was the loneliest of the gods. It was his duty to guard the souls of the dead. Although he was rich and powerful, his kingdom was dreary and sombre. No sun ever shone there and no laughter rang through the dim halls of his palace. Day in and day out, Pluto would sit on his throne, alone and silent or stride to the gateway of the underworld and stroke the three heads of his watchdog, Cerberus. No one ever came gladly to see him and he had never found a wife. Even when he came up from the underworld to visit the other gods they would shun him and turn away from his grim face. For many years Pluto had been in love with Persephone. He dreamed about her golden hair and laughing eyes, he looked longingly at her slender form and dancing feet. He had even asked Demeter if he might marry her lovely daughter, but Demeter had laughed scornfully and told him that she would never allow her daughter to speak to him, let alone marry him.

From a cave in the hillside Pluto watched Persephone. She was so lovely, so golden and young. He could bear it no longer. He burst from the cave, snatched Persephone up in his arms and fled back to the underworld with her.

That night, when Persephone did not return, Demeter was frantic. She wandered round Olympus asking all the gods if they had seen her daughter, but none of them had. The next morning Demeter began to search all over the earth for her daughter, wandering across Greece and the islands off its coast. She disguised herself as an old woman and asked everyone she met if they had seen a beautiful young maiden with golden hair and shining eyes, but no one could help her. At last Demeter came to Eleusis, a little village about fourteen miles from Athens. There she lived like a beggar, eating nothing but barley meal, water and wild mint. She never smiled, but grieved and mourned ceaselessly for Persephone.

Meanwhile Persephone was living in the dark underworld with Pluto, who had made her his queen. She missed the sunlight and the green grass and many a night she would sob and beg her husband to let her return to Olympus.

'I cannot let you go,' Pluto told her. 'You would never return and I would be alone again,' and he would call Cerberus to play with her, but she would put her hands over her face and weep for her mother.

All the time that Persephone was in the underworld, Demeter neglected her duties. The crops did not grow and the fruit did not ripen on the trees. Zeus saw that a famine was overtaking the land and he sent his messenger, Hermes, to find out where Persephone

was. Hermes searched high and low and could find no trace of Persephone on the earth. He knew that she was not on Olympus and he knew that she was not on earth. That left only one other place — Hades, the kingdom of the dead.

Hermes flew to the entrance of Hades and stroked the head of Cerberus. The dog could not speak, but recognizing that Hermes was a god, let him pass. Inside the entrance of Hades the river of Lethe flowed. It was wide and cold and the only way to the other side was in a little wooden ferryboat which was rowed by Charon, the guardian of the souls who passed over the river of Lethe into the forgetfulness of the underworld.

Charon was a tall and gloomy spirit who never answered any questions. Hermes did not need the ferryboat; he flew over Lethe and into the palace of Pluto. There he saw Persephone.

'You must return with me to Olympus,' Hermes told her. 'Your mother grieves for you so much that she will not tend the earth. Famine is sweeping the land and the corn and barley is dying.'

'But my husband will never let me go,' Persephone replied. 'Only Zeus is powerful enough to make him release me.'

'I shall return to Zeus and tell him where you are,' said Hermes. 'You must stay here for a little while but be sure that you eat nothing that Pluto offers you, particularly the golden pomegranates.'

'It is too late,' she said, 'I have already done so.'

Hermes was horrified. Anyone who had eaten the sacred pomegranates belonged to Pluto for ever.

'How many did you eat?' he asked Persephone.

'Only one, but I was so hungry and thirsty,' she answered.

Hermes sped back to Olympia to tell Zeus that he had found Persephone and what had happened.

Zeus sent for Demeter and told her that her daughter would be returned to her and he ordered Pluto to bring Persephone to the world of the living. Pluto was forced to obey.

'But she is still my wife,' he told Zeus, 'and what is more, she has eaten the sacred pomegranate and belongs to me.'

'But she only ate one, and so she shall only return to you for one third of the year.'

And so it is that for two thirds of the year, Persephone lives with Demeter and her mother is happy and cares for the world. But when the dark months come and Persephone goes to live with her husband, Demeter grieves and pines for her daughter. She allows the crops to die, only reviving them in the spring when Persephone returns again from Hades.

THE TWELVE LABOURS
OF HERCULES

When someone is very strong, he is sometimes described as being like Hercules. He was a great hero who was honoured throughout all of Greece for his exploits of immense strength. This is the story of how he came to be born, and how he came to perform the twelve deeds that he was best known for: The Twelve Labours of Hercules.

Zeus, the king of all the gods, decided that he would like a son who would be a powerful protector of both the gods and the mortals. To achieve this he came down from the lofty Mount Olympus to the city of Thebes and, disguised as Amphitryon, the husband of Alcmene, fathered a son. Alcmene, whose name means woman of might, was herself the daughter of Perseus. On the day that Hercules should have been born, Zeus swore a solemn oath that the descendant of Perseus, about to be born, would one day rule Greece. Unfortunately, his wife Hera, who was a jealous goddess, immediately caused the wife of Sthenelus, himself a son of Perseus, to give birth early to Eurystheus. At the same time she caused the birth of Hercules to be delayed. Having given a solemn oath Zeus was obliged to recognize Eurystheus as ruler of all Greece, and it was this rival who was to impose all the hardest tasks on Hercules throughout his life. Unfortunately, Hera was still not satisfied and sent two serpents to attack the infant Hercules. Hercules was already very strong, and grasping one monster in each hand, wrung their necks.

By the age of eighteen he had been instructed in wisdom, virtue and music, and had developed his strength to such an extent that he was able to kill a ferocious lion that was eating his mortal father's herds.

Shortly afterwards, Hercules defended Thebes against Orchomenus, and although he was successful, Amphitryon, his mortal father, was killed. Creon became king of Orchomenus and gave his daughter Megara to Hercules as a wife. Still Hera had not finished with Hercules and drove him mad. While suffering in this way he mistook his children to be those of his rival Eurystheus (which shows that he was rather jealous too) and massacred both them and their mother. He fled the country, and consulted the Oracle of Delphi to find out how to remove the stain of his crime. Unfortunately for Hercules, the oracle told him to go to Eurystheus and labour for him for twelve years. Hence the Twelve Labours of Hercules.

Hercules' first labour was to kill the Nemean Lion and bring the skin back to Eurystheus. First of all Hercules tried with arrows, but nothing would pierce the skin of the beast. So eventually he had to fight with his hands and finally strangled it. Hercules, however, did not give the skin to Eurystheus. He kept it for himself and made a garment of it, which made him invincible. Although the reactions of Eurystheus to this theft are lost in the mists of time, one can only assume that Hercules' garment protected him from his anger, since he was soon to embark on his next labour.

In a marsh near Lerna lived a hideous monster called the Learnaean Hydra. This enormous serpent had nine heads, and only left the marsh to eat the herds and crops. The breath of this monster was so poisonous that anybody it breathed on died.

Accompanied by his nephew, Hercules drove the monster from the marshes by using flaming arrows, and attacked it with his massive club. Unfortunately, the hydra exhibited the unnerving habit (apparently quite common to hydra) of growing two heads back in place of each one that was chopped off. Hercules told his nephew to set the neighbouring forest on fire and with the help of red hot brands burnt the serpent's heads. Hercules cut off the last head and buried it. He then dipped his arrows in the blood of the hydra, which made them deadly.

Hercules' next labour was to rid the territory of Psophis from the Wild Boar of Erymanthus. The beast devastated the land until Hercules managed to capture it and took it back to Eurystheus. Eurystheus, although he was very powerful seems to have lacked courage, since as soon as he saw the terrifying beast he was so frightened that he ran away and hid in a bronze jar. An addition to this story is that while on the way to capture the beast, Hercules was entertained by the Centaur Pholus, who opened a barrel of special wine. When the other centaurs smelt this wine, they attacked the house of Pholus. They were, however, no match for Hercules and his poisoned arrows and many were destroyed.

Eurystheus then sent Hercules to rid the marshes of Stymphalus of the terrible birds whose beaks, wings and claws were made of iron. There were so many of these birds that when they flew the light of the sun was blotted out. Their most unattractive feature was that they fed on human flesh, and obviously Eurystheus was hoping that they would eat Hercules. He was out of luck again, as Hercules, protected by his clothing made from the skin of the Nemean Lion, frightened the birds with great cymbals made of bronze, and then destroyed them with his poisoned arrows.

Eurystheus then decided on a change in campaign. If Hercules could not be destroyed, perhaps he could be set a task that was so impossible that he would fail. He therefore sent Hercules to bring back alive the hind who lived on Mount Ceryneia. Her main attractions were that she had hooves of bronze, and horns of gold. Hercules almost failed in this, since she was very swift and must not be killed. Sustained by his great strength he chased her for a year before he caught her on the banks of the river Ladon.

The next labour that Hercules performed is perhaps the best known — the cleansing of the stables of Augeias. He was the King of Elis and he owned many herds of cattle including twelve white bulls, sacred to Helios. One bull was called Phaethon and he shone like a star. These magnificent animals had, however, to live in a stable that was heaped with the manure of many years. Hercules promised to clean the stables in one day provided that Augeias would give him one tenth of the herd. When Augeias agreed, Hercules made holes in the walls of the building and diverted the rivers Alpheus and Peneius so that they rushed through the stables. Augeias was not a man of honour, and when the job was done, he went back on his bargain, giving as a reason the fact that Hercules was working for Eurystheus. Hercules was in his own way as unforgiving as Hera and eventually made Augeias pay for this dishonesty.

Hercules was on the island of Crete when the king, Minos, asked him to capture a bull which was terrorising the country. This bull had been given to Minos by Poseidon so that he could sacrifice it to him. Minos was too impressed with the bull and didn't sacrifice it, so Poseidon drove it mad. Hercules captured the bull and carried it on his back, as he was so strong, across the sea to Argolis.

In Thrace at this time lived Diomedes, King of the Bistones. He owned mares that he fed on human flesh. Together with a few volunteers, Hercules captured the mares, having killed their keepers. There was a fierce battle, but eventually the Bistones were defeated and, in a very bloodthirsty fashion, Diomedes was given to his own mares to eat. At the same time, as is generally believed, Hercules saved Alcestis from death. Admetus, her husband, had obtained from the Fates an undertaking that he would not die if some one would consent to die in his place. Hercules was passing by when he saw the unfortunate Alcestis about to be buried. He rescued her from death by defeating Thanatos, death itself, in a fierce struggle and so restored Alcestis to her husband.

Admete, daughter of Eurystheus, very much wanted to have the Girdle of Hippolyte, the Queen of the Amazons, for her very own. To this end Hercules was sent to fetch it. He set off with a number of other famous heroes and had a rather eventful journey, fighting the sons of Minos, and helping King Lycus to conquer the Bebryces. Eventually he reached the country of the Amazons, and at first it appeared that he would have no difficulty, as Hippolyte agreed to give him the girdle, even though it was the mark of her sovereignty.

However, Hera again decided to put a spoke in Hercules' wheel. She disguised herself as an Amazon and spread the rumour that Hercules was going to abduct Hippolyte. The Amazons attacked Hercules, and believing that they had betrayed him, he slaughtered them and their queen, and took the girdle.

Geryon was a triple headed monster who owned a herd of red oxen which were guarded by the herdsman Eurytion and the dog Orthrus. Eurystheus commanded Hercules to capture these oxen, which he did, having first killed Eurytion, Orthrus and eventually Geryon. Unfortunately the journey back was full of danger. Firstly Hercules had to kill the sons of Poseidon, who tried to steal the oxen and then he had to wrestle with Eryx, the king of the Elymans, to obtain the release of one of the oxen who had escaped and been put in the stables of Eryx. While in the hills of Thrace, Hera sent a gadfly to frighten the oxen and it was only with great difficulty that Hercules managed to herd them together. When he finally brought them to Eurystheus, the king sacrificed them to Hera.

Never one to give up, Eurystheus commanded Hercules to bring back the golden apples that the Hesperides, daughters of Atlas and Hesperus, guarded in their garden on the western edges of the world. To obtain information on how to reach the garden Hercules was lucky enough to capture the prophetic god Nereus, who told him how to reach it.

While crossing Libya, Hercules had to fight with Antaeus, who was the son of Gaea, Mother Earth. He was an enormous bandit who forced all travellers to fight with him. He had the useful power of being able to regain his strength by simply touching the ground with his feet. To overcome this Hercules held him up in the air with his arms and choked him.

Next, Hercules was attacked by the Pygmies. He overcame them by sewing them up in his lion skin.

In Egypt at that time the king was Busiris, who sacrificed a foreigner every year to put an end to a terrible famine. Hercules was unlucky enough to be selected as that year's victim and put in chains and taken to the temple. With his great strength he burst the chains, and slew Busiris and his son.

46

Continuing on his journey across Ethiopia he killed Emathion and replaced him with Memnon. The Sun gave him a golden boat which shone almost as brightly as the sun, and this he used to cross the sea, and finally arrived at the garden of the Hesperides. This garden was well guarded by the dragon Ladon. He killed this dragon and entered the garden. He persuaded Atlas, whose duty it was to hold the world up, to pick up the apples while he, Hercules, held the world on his shoulders.

When Atlas returned with the apples he was unwilling to take up his burden again and Hercules realized that unless he was careful he would be left with it. Therefore he pretended to agree that he would now perform this duty, but that to make himself more comfortable, he would need to rearrange his lion skin so that his shoulders would be protected. To this end he persuaded Atlas to again support the world while he adjusted the skin. However, as soon as Atlas did this Hercules scooped up the apples and ran away. This was perhaps rather dishonest, but totally understandable.

Finally, Eurystheus, feeling that he would never get the better of Hercules sent him off to fetch the guardian of the infernal gates of Hades, Cerberus. Firstly Hercules went to Eleusis, the most holy place in all Greece. Here he was initiated into the infernal mysteries. Guided by Hermes he took the passage which descends from Cape Taenarum through the earth to the underworld.

Eventually he came upon Theseus and Peirithous, who had unwisely ventured into the underworld. They implored Hercules to help them, which he attempted to do. Unfortunately a massive earthquake stopped him from rescuing Peirithous. Hercules had a busy time in Hades as the legends say that he removed the boulder that was crushing Ascalaphus, overthrew Menoetes, the herdsman of Hades and even wounded Hades himself. Hades agreed to allow Hercules to take the monster Cerberus, provided he could conquer him using only his bare hands. Such was Hercules' strength that this was accomplished and he dragged the animal back to show Eurystheus, who doubtless again hid himself in his bronze pot. Hercules then released the beast and sent it back to Hades.

So at last Hercules was freed, but do not think that he settled down and lived out his remaining years in peace and quiet. He had many more adventures while he lived and his death was the strangest of them all. He had put on a tunic which his new earthly wife sent him. It was soaked in the blood of a centaur that he had killed. She believed that it would ensure his lasting devotion, but it was an act of revenge on the part of the centaur. Hercules was devoured by inner pain, and pulling up trees he made his own funeral pyre. After some difficulty he persuaded Peoas to set light to the pyre and was rewarded with Hercules' bow and arrows. The flames crackled and burned but when they reached his body there was a tremendous crash of thunder and lightning and the son of Zeus disappeared from men's eyes. He was admitted to Olympus and was so reconciled with Hera that he married her daughter Hebe and thereafter lived the magnificent and blissful life of the gods.

ROMULUS AND REMUS

It was dark and windy that night; the River Tiber rushed down from the hills, swollen and dark with soil and mud from the mountains. A slender figure, buffeted by the wind, clambered down towards the banks of the river, clutching in her arms a wriggling bundle. Above the howl of the wind and the thunder of the river a cry could be heard, then another — two tiny voices raised in protest against the cold and the dark. Sobbing, the woman knelt down and gently placed the two babies in a crudely hollowed-out log boat, hardly bigger than the babes. Her tears fell on their faces. She tucked the bundle of shawls tightly round the children and then, with a sudden push, the little boat swirled out into the mainstream of the swiftly flowing river, spinning and turning until it was swallowed up by the darkness; and still above the roar of the wind and the water could be heard the cries of the two infants until that sound, too, faded away into the night.

Who was this woman who could condemn her babies to such a terrible death? What kind of mother could abandon her children to the cruel waters of the Tiber?

Rhea Silvia was no monster. She had been forced to do this dreadful thing. Even the waters of the flooded Tiber were better than the fate that would have befallen her children had they not been cast away in that frail little boat. Only two weeks before, when the twins had been born, their mother had known that their lives would be threatened; for Rhea Silvia was a royal princess, the daughter of the once proud King of Alba Longa. Her father, Numitor, had been stripped of his crown by his own son and Rhea had been impelled to become a Vestal Virgin, one of the priestesses of the temple of Vesta who were forbidden ever to marry. Amulius, her own brother, had urged upon her to abandon her father, to leave public life and join the silent throng of maidens condemned forever to live in the cold marble temple.

Amulius was cruel and ambitious. He knew that because he had taken the throne of Alba Longa by force, the people of that sunny land did not want him to be their king. They loved old Numitor, who had ruled them well, and they resented the usurper-son. He knew that the only way he could keep the power he had snatched from his father was by force, and he also knew that if ever his sister should marry, her children would have a better claim to the throne of Alba

Longa. For this reason he hid Rhea Silvia in the temple and imprisoned his father in a remote villa far away from his court.

And now Rhea Silvia had given birth to twin boys! Amulius was terribly angry. Not only had Rhea defied him, but she claimed that the father of her twin boys was none other than the great god Mars himself. Amulius felt threatened and frightened.

The very evening of the twins' birth Amulius had stormed into the temple of Vesta with two guards. He had dragged his sister out while the two guards carried the crying babies.

'I shall put the babies to the sword,' he told the weeping Rhea. 'They must die, they are too dangerous to me. If I let them live they may grow up to rise against me as I rose against my father.'

In vain had Rhea begged for the lives of her babies, but the only promise she could wring out of her brother was that she herself must destroy the children. That was why she had crept out at dead of night and placed the children in the little wooden boat and sent them swirling away down-river.

'Perhaps someone will see them and save them,' she thought. 'Perhaps the gods will watch over them and guard them — anything is better than a cruel death by the sword.'

So Rhea stood sobbing on the banks of the Tiber while her twin babies were carried away on the foaming waters.

The boat floated on for the rest of the night, the wild spray splashing the twins and the waves tossing the boat to and fro. Then, as dawn filled the sky a sudden eddy caught the boat and pushed it into a little creek. There it came to rest at the foot of a huge fig tree. Perhaps the gods had been watching over the babes, for this fig tree was sacred to them, and now the boat rested safely among its gnarled roots.

The babies were hungry and thirsty and their crying grew louder, so loud that it could be heard deep in the nearby wood.

A great grey she-wolf heard the cries and lifted her pointed muzzle towards the sound. Rising to her feet she loped through the wood towards the fig tree. The she-wolf had given birth to cubs the week before, but hunters had killed them. The cries of the twin babies reminded her of the mewing sounds that her little cubs had made and she padded forward to find out what was making the noise. When she reached the boat she stretched out her neck and pushed aside the shawls with her nose. The twins redoubled their screams. They were not afraid of the wolf, for they were too young to know that wolves were to be feared, but they knew that they were hungry and cold. The wolf looked down at the two tiny children

50

because she was hungry and still grieving for her lost cubs. She sniffed cautiously at the twins and then did a surprising thing. Instead of devouring the babies she gently picked them up in her mouth and carried them back to her den, and there she suckled them and cared for them.

The years passed and the twins began to grow up. At first they ran about on all fours like little wolf cubs, but they soon learned that their legs were too long and their arms too short to be comfortable like this and they began to walk like normal children. Gradually and with difficulty they learned to speak by listening to the shepherds and farmers who lived around the forest, but although they watched and listened they never showed themselves, hiding in the undergrowth and ferns like young wild animals.

As they grew taller and stronger they became bolder. Their wolf-mother had taught them how to hunt and they knew the lore of the forest better than any ordinary child could. At first they had thought that they were wolves, but they noticed that they were more like the shepherds that they watched in the meadows. They still loved their wolf-mother dearly, but now they stood taller than she and could do things that no wolf could.

Before they had reached their teens they were fearless and strong, and nothing frightened them. They had learned all that their wolf-mother could teach them and they decided that it was time to go out into the wide world. They came down from the woods to the surrounding villages and there they met a herdsman and his wife. Faustulus and Acca Larentia had never had any children and they welcomed the two boys into their home. They named them Romulus and Remus and loved them as if they were their own sons.

So Romulus and Remus grew up, and in time began to forget that the first mother they had known had been a great she-wolf.

Acca Larentia became mother to them and Faustulus became their father. They were sent to school as were all the young men of the village and there they learned about the history of the country where they lived. They heard about the cruel King Amulius, who ruled their land, and they learned that all who disobeyed him were punished by his troops.

Because the boys were so brave they soon became the leaders of all the youths of the district. Little knowing that Amulius, King of Alba Longa, was really their uncle they banded together with other young men to fight against his tyranny. Amulius soon heard of Romulus and Remus and sent an army against them. It was then, in the fields and valleys beside the wood where they had grown up, that Romulus and Remus fought with the King's troops and defeated them. Amulius was overthrown and Romulus and Remus released old Numitor and restored him to power.

As soon as Numitor met the twins he realized that they looked strangely like his daughter Rhea Silvia; he called her to him in secret and showed her the two young men and asked her if she noticed the resemblance. At last Rhea could tell her father of the secret that she had carried in her heart for all these years. She told him the story of how she had cast her twin babies away on that dreadful night twenty years before.

Inquiries were made and when it was discovered that Faustulus and his wife were only foster-parents to the twins, Numitor himself asked the twins what they could remember of their babyhood.

'I remember the forest and the valleys,' said Romulus.

'I sometimes dream of a dark cave . . .' said Remus.

'We often had nightmares about stormy rivers and rushing water,' said Romulus. 'Even now we do not really like the river when it is in flood . . .' and then it all came back to them.

52

'I remember a great grey she-wolf,' said Romulus. 'She was taller than we were, and she taught us to hunt and prowl through the darkness . . .'

They pieced the puzzle together and realized that they were indeed the grandsons of Numitor, saved from death by a she-wolf.

Numitor was delighted and took them to the temple of Vesta where they met their real mother.

'These are indeed your sons,' said Numitor. 'You little thought that you would ever see them again and now they have restored me to power and overthrown the very man who first threatened their lives.'

Romulus and Remus became the king's most trusted friends. They built a great city which spread across the seven hills and valleys beside the wood where they had grown up.

When they began to build the city the brothers could not decide what it was to be named. They resolved that they would each climb to the top of a hill and the one who saw the most birds would name the city. Romulus saw a flock of twelve birds and his brother saw only six, so the city was named after Romulus and was to become the greatest of all the cities of the ancient world. Romulus and Remus governed the city together, but as so often happens, they became jealous of each other and began to quarrel. Romulus believed that Rome could be made safer by building a wall around it but Remus disagreed.

'The power of Rome and its reputation is enough to guard the city,' he told his brother. 'You will only waste time and money by building such a wall.'

Romulus would not listen and one summer, while his brother was away, he ordered the wall to be built. When Remus returned he laughed at Romulus.

'This is a puny wall,' he sneered, 'it would not keep out a flock of sheep,' and to prove his point he leaped over the wall with one bound.

Romulus was so angry that he completely lost his temper. He drew his sword and killed his twin brother.

'Thus perish any other who leaps over my walls,' he proclaimed, but he also ordered the walls to be built higher.

Romulus grieved greatly that he had killed Remus in a fit of temper and resolved never to draw his sword in anger again. He welcomed strangers to Rome and encouraged people from foreign lands to come and live there. Rome prospered and became rich and powerful. So many men and soldiers came to live there that soon there were too few women and it became very difficult to find a wife.

Romulus thought of a plan. The neighbouring people were the Sabines and the Sabine women were said to be the most beautiful of all the women in Italy. The Sabine men guarded their women jealously and would not allow them to meet the Romans. Romulus declared that he would hold a fantastic festival and that all should be invited. Rome was famous for its festivals and the Sabine men relented and agreed to attend. They came in their hundreds, bringing their wives and daughters with them.

The festival was truly magnificent. Thousands of oxen and sheep were roasted over open fires, enormous pies and loaves were baked, hundreds of vats of wine were made, grapes and figs and peaches from the surrounding countryside were brought into Rome and the whole city was decorated with branches of sweet-smelling myrtle and laurel. Silken banners hung from the houses and the trees, and at night flaming torches made the darkness seem like noonday. Plays and concerts were performed, and magnificent games were held in the amphitheatres and squares where gladiators fought with wild animals, and contests of swordmanship and archery entertained the crowds for hours.

For seven days the Romans and the Sabines feasted. As you can imagine a great deal of wine was imbibed and soon many of the Sabine men became very drunk. On the last night they started to fall asleep, exhausted by the wine and the merriment; even a splendid display of fireworks failed to rouse them and so, when they were sure that the Sabines could not stop them, the Roman men kidnapped the Sabine women and hid them away.

When the Sabine men awoke they discovered that their womenfolk were missing. They searched for them for days and when at last they found them, most of the women said that they would rather stay in Rome. The Sabine men were forced to make a pact with the Romans and their King, Titus Tatius, became joint ruler with Romulus.

Still Rome prospered and grew. The first wooden houses were pulled down and marble and stone villas were built. The city spread all over the seven hills and even as far as the wood where Romulus and Remus had grown up. This part of Rome became known as the Lupercal, which means 'wolf's den' in Latin. Romulus gave offerings to the gods at the foot of the fig tree where he and his brother had been cast up in their little wooden boat; the fig tree remained but now it was surrounded by a vast marble temple and standing by the altar was a bronze statue of a she-wolf suckling two baby boys. A statue like this can still be seen in Rome today.

The years passed and Titus Tatius died, leaving Romulus to be the sole ruler of the mighty city. Romulus ruled wisely and well, always taking care that his laws were just and that everyone was treated fairly. He was loved by the Romans and when one day he disappeared his people were greatly grieved. He never appeared again and his body was never found; because of this no-one ever knew what had happened to him and the Romans began to say that the gods must have taken him to live with them. They remembered that Romulus and his twin were said to have been the sons of Rhea Silvia and the great God Mars and so they made Romulus into a god. They called him Quirinus and worshipped him as the founder of their city. One of the seven hills of Rome was named after him and a great festival was held each year where sacrifices were dedicated to the man who had made the city of Rome so powerful.

TARQUIN

For many years Rome had been ruled fairly and by laws that made each Roman citizen free and unfettered. And then came the reign of Tarquin. Tarquin the Tyrant was a man who saw Rome as his plaything and the people of Rome as his slaves. True, the people of Rome had elected Tarquin themselves, but this was a costly mistake. Soon all those who opposed the rule of this haughty man found themselves imprisoned. Their goods and chattels, houses and servants were taken from them and brought to swell the wealth of Tarquin.

The Senate, the ruling body of Rome, which once had the power to overthrow any tyrant, was weakened. Tarquin murdered or deposed any senators who opposed him and put in their place his chosen friends who he knew would obey him without question. No longer were the streets of Rome filled with merriment. At night the Romans hid in their houses afraid to venture out into the streets for fear of the roving bands of soldiers paid by Tarquin.

Not only did Tarquin rule Rome with an iron fist, he was also the ruler of all the Roman states. Before many years he had subdued all the rebel kings of the surrounding lands and made their kingdoms into slave states answerable only to him. All that is except for one. This was the state of Aricia, governed by Turnus Herdonius. This king would not give it to the Roman dictator and refused to pay the taxes that cruelly impoverished the other states.

Tarquin heard about this and laid a plan. He called a meeting at a temple to the goddess Ferentia, where he was to meet with the other princes of the region. When they were all assembled Tarquin was nowhere to be seen. Turnus saw his advantage and began to address the other princes.

'We have suffered greatly from the tyranny of this Roman Tarquin,' he told them. 'We always give in because while we are stronger than Tarquin and his armies when we are all together, while we are separate we cannot defeat him. Why do we not join together and free ourselves from his cruel enslavement?'

As Turnus spoke he saw the expressions on the princes' faces change and turning round, he discovered that Tarquin was standing behind him. Furious that he had been tricked into showing his hand Turnus left the meeting.

Tarquin called another meeting for the following day. There he bullied the other princes into attacking Aricia, and Turnus was as-sassinated, leaving Tarquin in full control. So once again, Tarquin was sole controller of all the Roman states.

The years passed and the people of Gabia decided that they had had enough of the cruel taxes that they were forced to pay. They rebelled and refused to pay any more taxes. Tarquin sent a great army against them, but he did not succeed in conquering them, for Gabia was surrounded by a high and impregnable wall and no one could breach it. After the battle a badly wounded man staggered to the gates of Gabia and begged to be let in. The commander of the Gabian army recognized him as Sextus, the son of the King of Rome. Sextus seemed to have been terribly tortured.

The prince of the Gabians took him in and cared for him. Sextus insinuated himself into the king's favour and soon the king ordered all his soldiers to obey Sextus. In reality Sextus was a spy for Tar-quin and when he had gained the trust of the Gabians, he betrayed

them. Having gained the confidence of the prince, he ruled in his absence and beheaded the best advisors and commanders. When the prince returned, Sextus pretended that he had uncovered a plot against the prince. Gradually Sextus took control of Gabia and delivered it into his father's hands and so Tarquin's rule continued.

In Rome, Tarquin began to build a great temple to the god Jupiter. Men were brought from all over the Latin States to work on this temple, and if they would not come willingly they were dragged there in chains and forced to work as slaves.

One day the skull of a man was found in the earth while the foundations of this temple were being constructed. Tarquin let it be known that this skull was the head of an ancient soothsayer and that the ruler of land on which it was found would rule the world. From that day to this the hill on which the temple was built was called the Capitol, which means 'the head' in Latin.

Until now, the people of Rome had believed that the reason that Tarquin had never been overthrown was that he was favoured by the gods, but now sombre omens began to occur. A great plague swept through Rome and Tarquin, fearing that this was a sign from the gods that he had angered them went to consult the Oracle at Delphi. He took with him his three sons, Titus, Arruns and Sextus (the man who had betrayed the Gabians and had received their kingdom in exchange). He also took his nephew, Lucius Junus. This nephew knew how much his cousins hated him and how jealous his uncle was of anyone who threatened him, so he had pretended to be stupid. He had been so successful at this that his nickname was Brutus the Dunce. Tarquin consulted the oracle and asked who would rule after him. The oracle replied:

'Whichever man first kisses his mother will be the power in Rome.'

The three sons of Tarquin took this to mean their mortal mother and hastened back to Rome, but Brutus pretended to trip and fall and while he was on the ground he pressed his lips to the earth, the mother earth that all Romans worshipped. So it was Brutus who became the ruler of Rome after Tarquin.

It was the treachery of Sextus that brought about the downfall of Tarquin and his sons. One day, while Tarquin, Sextus, Titus and Arruns were resting in their tent during a battle campaign against the Ardians, they fell to talking about the beauty of their wives. Collatinus, one of the most loyal of Tarquin's commanders, told them of the beauty of his wife Lucrecia. This so fired the imagination of Sextus that he sought out Lucrecia and carried her off by force, not caring that Collatinus had fought bravely and well for him

and his father. Lucrecia escaped and told Collatinus what had happened and then, overcome with the shame and disgrace, stabbed herself. At this Collatinus swore revenge against Sextus and his father. Brutus, hearing this, revealed what had occurred at the Oracle of Delphi.

'If Tarquin is overthrown, I shall be the next ruler of Rome,' he told Collatinus, 'I and shall rule fairly and well.'

Brutus and Collatinus returned to Rome and told the citizens what had happened. The Romans, angered at Sextus' treachery and tired of the tyranny of Tarquin, hailed Brutus as their new ruler. And so, when Tarquin returned to the city he found the gates of Rome barred against him. For the first time, all the people of Rome joined together and Tarquin and his sons were driven out into Etruria. Sextus was sent to Gabia where the Gabians executed him.

So ended the rule of Tarquin the Tyrant and for the first time for many years the Romans knew what it was to be free.

HOW THE WORLD WAS MADE

This is the story of how the world was made. It is a German story and has been told to German children for centuries.

Before the earth was born the universe was dark and terrible. It consisted of one huge, deep, steep-sided valley — an enormous ravine called Ginnungagap. There was only one spirit in the universe and that was Fimbultyr, who had never been born and would never die. Fimbultyr divided Ginnungagap into two halves. The northernmost half he called Niflheim and the southern half Muspelheim. Niflheim was cold and foggy, great cliffs of ice fell steeply down to where the river Hvergelmir burst out of the ice and flowed in twelve separate icy streams along Ginnungagap.

Muspelheim was as hot as Niflheim was cold. Sheets of flame flared upwards and the rocks melted in the heat. In the kingdom of Muspelheim lived the god of that place, Surtur. He was the only one capable of bearing the heat and fire of that blazing furnace. He would sit on a rock and watch the tongues of fire streaming away towards Niflheim.

Where the fire and the icy water met, a huge cloud of steam rose up and it was out of this steam that Ymir was born. He was a terrifying giant whose groans echoed up and down Ginnungagap. An enormous cow was also born from the steam. She was called Audhumbla and fed Ymir with her milk. Some time later, while Ymir was sleeping two giant children appeared from his arms. From the left arm sprang a boy and from the right arm, a girl. The children and grandchildren of these giants became a race of people called the Hrimthurses, dark, moody giants who inhabited Niflheim.

Later still, the great Audhumbla freed another god from one of the blocks of ice in that cold and desolate place. This god was Bure, and his son Bor had three further sons, Wotan, Hoenir and Loki. Wotan became the father of all the gods. After Wotan, Hoenir and Loki were born there were two races of gods and they fought over who should reign. Battle raged over Ginnungagap and finally the gigantic Ymir was slain. His wounds poured with rivers of blood and from these were born the children and grandchildren of Ymir. Wotan, Hoenir and Loki made the body of Ymir into the earth. They took his skull and made it into the heavens and placed a dwarf at each corner to guard it. The dwarf of the north was called Norder, the dwarf of the south was called Suder. The dwarf of the west was called Wester and the dwarf of the east was called Oster. The three gods then sprinkled the heavens with sparks from Muspelheim and made the stars. Now they could tell day from night and so the days, weeks, months and years were created.

The earth they called Midgard, but it was a dreadful place with great seas of blood from Ymir's wounds and although trees and grass grew there, there were no men. The three gods then created a man and a woman from two trees that grew along one of the beaches. Wotan turned them into humans and blew life into them, Hoenir gave them their sense and reason, and Loki gave them their shape, hearing, sight and speech. The man was called Ask and the woman was called Embla and from these two the whole German people are descended. Wotan took Ask and Embla and showed them Midgard. 'This is your land,' he told them. 'Here you will lack for nothing, you will find all you need to eat and drink, be happy and prosper.'

The centuries passed and the children of Ask and Embla multiplied throughout the land of Midgard. The gods, too, had married, and Wotan, the father of them all, had taken Freyja, the daughter of the god Fjorgynn as a wife. Freyja and Wotan had many children and their first-born son Thor ruled as king. The gods dwelt in Asgard at the centre of the universe in a magnificent palace called Valhalla.

Wotan looked down on the earth; it had changed greatly since he and his brothers had made it. The seas were now clear, the land was rich and the children, grandchildren, great-grandchildren and great-great-grandchildren of Ask and Embla looked after it faithfully.

'These humans that we have created have done well,' he told the other gods. 'I should like to build a bridge between Asgard and Midgard. Some of the humans are as courageous as gods, they fight bravely. When they fall in battle the Valkyries shall bring them to Asgard where the earth's heroes can share Valhalla with us.'

The Valkyries were a race of warrior maidens who lived with the gods. They rode magnificent horses which could fly through the air. They wore silver armour and watched over the soldiers of Midgard.

All the gods agreed and a great arching bridge was created that stretched from Asgard to Midgard. It was called the Bifrost and shimmered with colour. Only on certain days could it be seen, and then only when the Valkyrie maidens were carrying one of the heroes of Midgard to an eternal life in Valhalla.

Now that Asgard and Midgard were joined, a grave problem arose. There were races of giants living on the earth and they were jealous of the gods.

'If men can reach Asgard by climbing the Bifrost bridge, then the giants will try to invade Valhalla,' Wotan decided. 'We shall build a fortress at the foot of the bridge and Heimdall, our most faithful son, shall guard it.'

The fortress was called Himinbjorg and faithful Heimdall never slept. If danger approached he would summon the gods by blowing a golden trumpet that made the heavens shake and the stars shiver.

Wotan also protected the earth. He planted a giant ash tree called Yggdrasil, which was so enormous that the tips of its branches touched the top of the sky. Its trunk stretched through the heavens and its roots plunged deep into the earth. There were three roots. Underneath the first was Midgard, the land given to men by Wotan. Under the second root was Nastrand, the gloomy kingdom ruled by the dragon Nidhogg. He guarded the souls of men and women who had died — all except the souls of the heroes who had been taken to Valhalla by the Valkyries. Under the third root lived the giants.

Three rivers flowed under Yggdrasil, and close to the second river lived three maidens, Urd, Verdandi and Skuld. These maidens held the key to the future. They tended the tree of the world and watered it, for they knew that the safety of the world depended upon it. And since they were also the controllers of destiny they knew full well how important their task was. Their greatest enemy was Nidhogg the dragon, who continually gnawed at the roots of Yggdrasil, hoping to kill the life-giving tree and claim the souls of all the men and women who lived under its protection. From the third root flowed the river Mimir, which protected all the wisdom and knowledge of the world.

In the topmost branches of Yggdrasil lived a gigantic eagle, the deadly enemy of the dragon Nidhogg, watching with sharp eyes for any chance to kill the cruel guardian of Nastrand. And in the trunk of the mighty ash tree lived Ratasok the squirrel. This sly creature told Nidhogg everything that the eagle said and reported all Nidhogg's words to the eagle. As he ran up and down the trunk of Yggdrasil he stirred up rumours and trouble and kept the earth in turmoil.

The giants and Nidhogg hated the gods with a consuming and terrible hatred. They continually plotted to overthrow Asgard and would do anything they could to harm Wotan and his family. In the dark and sombre kingdom of Nastrand, as well as Nidhogg, lived three other monsters: Fenrir, who was an enormous wolf, Midgard the serpent and Hel, the goddess of death. These monsters were the children of Loki, the brother of Wotan, and Angrboda, one of the giantesses. They had been raised by their mother and her gigantic

64

family and from the day they were born they had been taught to hate the gods of Asgard. Loki, who knew how awful his children were, tried to keep them a secret from his brother, but while they were still young, Wotan found out about the serpent Midgard. Realizing that such a creature was dangerous to Asgard he took the serpent up to Asgard and threw him down as hard as he could into the sea. What Wotan did not know was that the serpent, Midgard, like all Loki's children, was half a god and could not be killed so easily. Instead of being destroyed, the serpent grew and grew until it circled the earth and began to squeeze tighter and tighter. It was so huge that when it was irritated it would lash its tail and cause storms and whirlpools. At last it grew so large that all feared it, and only Thor, the eldest son of Wotan and Freyja, was brave enough to be able to calm it. From that day to this the serpent Midgard twines round the earth, controlled only by the strength of Thor.

Fenrir, too, was growing as fast as his terrible brother. When he opened his mouth his jaws spanned the heavens. Naturally the gods found out about Fenrir and realized that he must be controlled, but who could govern such a creature? Even his giantess mother was afraid of him and no one but Thor dared to try to capture him.

Wotan called a meeting of all the gods. Everyone came except Loki, who hid in Nidhogg's kingdom.

'What are we to do?' Wotan asked the gods. 'This mighty monster will destroy everything and we are powerless against him. 'He is half a god and cannot be killed.'

Thor stood up. He was the handsomest of all of them with fair hair and broad shoulders; his arms were muscular and strong and he carried a great iron hammer.

'We must trick the monster,' he said, 'and I have a plan.'

Thor shouted down from Asgard so that Fenrir could hear him.

'You may think that you are stronger than the men of earth, and it is true,' he bellowed, 'but you are not as strong as the gods of Asgard.'

Fenrir heard Thor and began to laugh. The mountains trembled and the rivers stopped flowing at the sound of Fenrir's voice.

'Nonsense,' replied the wolf, 'nothing is stronger than me!'

'We do not believe you,' shouted Thor. 'Prove it to us. If we can bind you with chains that you cannot break, will you admit defeat?'

'Certainly,' replied Fenrir, 'no chain could ever hold me.'

So Thor, who was an excellent blacksmith, went to his anvil and, using his mighty hammer, forged the strongest chain he had ever made. Each link was as large as the trunk of an oak tree. Thor took it down to Fenrir and bound the wolf up.

Fenrir smiled evilly and took a deep breath, then another and another and each time he breathed in he swelled up until at last, with a cracking and rending sound the chain snapped.

The gods were appalled, for the strength of Fenrir was greater than they had ever dreamed.

'We will try once more,' announced Thor, and Fenrir, who was feeling very smug about his success, agreed. This time Thor did not make the chain, but went secretly to the three maidens who held the key to the future — Urd, Verdandi and Skuld. He asked them to make a chain that would keep the earth and Asgard safe from the terrible Fenrir. The three maidens worked fast and when their chain was completed they dipped it into the river Mimir which held all the wisdom of the world. Then they took it to Thor.

Thor looked at it in amazement. 'This is no use,' he said, holding it in one hand, 'this would not hold a kitten, let alone a wolf as strong as Fenrir.'

'Try to break it, mighty Thor,' said the three sisters. 'It is not only a chain of iron that can hold strength enough to bind Fenrir.'

Thor took the chain and tugged at it as hard as he could. The veins stood out on his forehead and his shoulders creaked with the strain and yet, for all his strength he could not break it.

Once again Thor went to Fenrir.

'One last try,' he said to the wolf, 'and then we will admit that you are the greatest of all the gods.'

But Fenrir was wary; the chain that Thor held out seemed slender and fragile, and he suspected trickery. 'How do I know what sorcery you have used in this chain?' he asked.

Thor looked innocent. 'I have used no sorcery,' he said; and this was true, for Thor himself had not made the chain.

'I do not trust you,' snarled Fenrir. 'To prove good faith I shall ask for a sign of trust. One of you must put his right arm in my jaws, and keep it there while you bind me; if no one will do this then I shall know that you are trying to trick me.'

The gods looked at each other in horror. It seemed as if Fenrir had outwitted them, and then Tyr, the god of war, stepped forward and thrust his right arm between the sharp teeth of the monster wolf.

Quickly Thor bound Fenrir with the chain the three wise maidens had made. Then he stood back.

The great grey wolf again breathed in as he had before but the chain held. He strained all his muscles but the chain still held. He squirmed and wriggled and struggled but it was to no avail — the chain was unbreakable. In fury he snapped down on the arm of Tyr

66

and severed it at the elbow. Tyr shuddered but smiled bravely.

'What is the loss of an arm compared to the end of the world,' he said, and that is why Tyr, the god of war, has only one arm.

The gods had conquered and Asgard and Midgard were safe. They took the bound body of Fenrir and tied his tail to a huge boulder at one end of the Bifrost bridge and pinned the jaws of Fenrir to the other end with a silver sword. Where the sword pierced Fenrir's jaw a river was born, poisonous and yellow, called the river Wan. And so Fenrir was enslaved, stretched across the Bifrost bridge until the end of eternity, guarded by the gods of Asgard, for should he ever free himself his anger would be terrible to behold.

THE SIDH OF IRELAND

The Sidh are the spirits of Ireland; their name is pronounced 'shee'.

Wonderful tales are told of them and Irish songs recount the history of these magical people. Here are just a few of these stories.

The king of all the Sidh was called Dagda. He had many, many sons and to each of them he gave a kingdom and taught them how to rule it. These kingdoms lay around the hill of Brug na Boinna and inside the top of the hill stood the castle of Dagda himself. Unfortunately, when Dagda had divided his kingdom up amongst his sons, the oldest son, Angus, had not been there and Dagda, in the hustle and bustle of the occasion, had forgotten all about him. When Angus returned he heard what had happened and went to his father.

'Oh, father,' he said sorrowfully, 'have I done anything to displease you? All my other brothers have received a kingdom and now there is nothing left for me.'

Dagda was horrified. 'My son,' he said 'you have never displeased me, you are the wisest and bravest of all my sons. I must be growing old, for I had forgotten all about you. I do not know what to do. I will give you anything you ask for, but I cannot take away a kingdom from any of your brothers.'

'So be it,' said Angus. 'I only ask that you allow me to govern Brug na Boinna itself for a day and a night.'

Dagda kept his promise and from that day onwards Angus became the king of all Ireland, for after all, eternity is made up only from days and nights.

Before the Sidh ruled Ireland it was a miserable land, cold, poor and barren, ruled by a race of monster-spirits called the Fomorians. The Sidh had seized the land from the Fomorians and had brought beauty and peace to it. First Brigit and Cairpre brought poetry and song and music. Then Diancecht brought health and well-being, planting herbs and berries that could be used to cure illnesses and pains. The magical blacksmith Gribnoum and his brothers Creidne and Luichne, both skilled in working with wood and ivory, brought the arts of carving, furniture making and forging and the land blossomed and flourished, and that is why Ireland is so beautiful today.

From time to time, all the Sidh gathered together at Brug na Boinna to reminisce about the old days.

At these gatherings each Sidh had to tell a tale and here are some of them. The first is the story of the lovely Deirdre.

'I remember the old days well,' said Deirdre, one of the most beautiful of the Sidh maidens. 'I was young then, and even more beautiful than I am now. I was walking along a valley in County Leinster when I came across two young men playing at hurling. The taller of the men was so beautiful that I fell in love with him at once and knew that I should pine away if I could not stay with him for ever. But he was a mortal and could not see me, and I knew that unless he came into my fairy palace of his own free will I could never show myself to him. I went down to the lake and found the jawbone of a great pike that was washed up on the shore. This I strung with my own golden hair to make it into a harp and then I returned to where the young men were still playing. I began to pluck the strings of my harp and sing magical songs. The young man, whose name was Aedh, followed the sound of my music until he reached the entrance to my fairy hill wherein my palace lay. I entered, still playing the harp and Aedh followed me. Once inside I ceased to be invisible and he saw me and in turn fell in love with me. What happy days we had then. I showed him all the delights of our fairy kingdom, taught him to ride the Tuatha de Danann, our fairy horses who can fly on the wind, and to hunt with Bran and Sceolan, the hunting dogs. We bathed in the inland seas of Ireland and for three years we were happy. But Aedh was only mortal and at last began to long for his own people. I tried in vain to hold him to me with spells and enchantments, but one day he slipped away from me and sought the help of Saint Patrick, who took him back to his father, who was King of Leinster. Ah, I still remember him and how happy we were, if only he had stayed with me and had never grown old.'

So Deirdre's tale ended and another of the Sidh took her place.

'Speaking of hurling,' said Finvara, the king of the Sidh people of Connaught, 'do you remember the match we played against the Sidh people of Munster? It was like this. As you know, when the Sidh play at hurling there must always be two humans present. We had chosen Paudyeen O'Kelly and little Donal to go with us and we set off for a place called Moytura. There the Sidh of Munster were waiting for us and the hurling match began straight away. The people of Munster soon began to get the better of us, and then, Paudyeen O'Kelly joined in. To be sure he was strong for a mortal and soon the Sidh of Connaught were winning again. And what did the people of Munster do then but turn themselves into a swarm of flying beetles and begin to gobble up every growing thing between Moytura and the sea. Of course you all know what the Sidh of Connaught did to stop that. We

turned ourselves into a flock of doves and began to gobble up the
beetles in turn. That is why to this day the scene of the great hurling
match is called Pul-Na-Gullum, the 'place of the doves'.' Finvara sat
down to loud applause and Brigit, the wisest of the Sidh, stood up. It
was Brigit who had brought poetry and learning to Ireland. Her
name meant 'fiery arrow' and the left side of her face was stern and
frightening while the right side was beautiful to behold.

'I tell the tale of how the Sidh came to live under the green hills of
Ireland,' she began, and the host of Sidh sat back with a sigh, for this
was one of their favourite stories.

'After I and my sisters and brothers had brought our gifts to
Ireland, the fame of this lovely land of ours spread across the world.
It came to the ears of the Milesians who at that time were living in
Spain. These were the descendants of Mil and were led by his son
Ith. The Milesians were the first men to reach our land. At first we
fought them fiercely, for we did not want to share our land with
anyone, but they were almost as powerful as we were and in the end
we were forced to ask Ith to decide how the land should be divided.
Ith told us that we were all brothers and should live together peacefully. At first we tried, but our people felt cheated and at last several
of them banded together and killed Ith. The Milesians were cast into
confusion by this and returned to Spain, carrying with them the skin
of Ith. There they gathered together a great fleet of ships and set out
again to regain the land that Ith had told them to share.

'Our people waited at the seashore to try to defeat this fleet with
enchantments and at first this worked. Three times the Mils tried to
land and three times the fleet was driven back. We had sent our most
powerful sorcerers, Banba, Fodla and Eriou to fight the people of
Mil and it was they who guarded the coast with spells.

'But the Milesians had a powerful sorcerer on their side too. His
name was Amargen, and he managed to find out the secret names of
our sorcerers and so broke the enchantment. The Mils landed and
made camp. They sent messengers to bargain with us, but we would
not give in and prepared to go into battle. Strangely the Milesians
would not fight. We heard later that Amargen had told them that his
magic showed that the time was not yet right. So they returned to
their ships and sailed a little way out to sea. At once our sorcerers
called up a great storm and the winds drove the ships of the Milesians far round the coast, but here the magic of Amargen conquered,
and the Milesians discovered a landing place that was not guarded.
They landed and at once the Sidh hurried to do battle. This took
place at Tailtiu and the people of the Sidh conquered. Our king

70

made a treaty with them because they had fought so bravely and at last peace returned to Ireland. The years passed and the men of Mil and the people of the Sidh lived happily together.'

Brigit looked round at the people of the Sidh. 'Do you remember some of the marvellous magic we had in those days?' she asked. 'Do you remember the spear that the great fighter Lug carried? It was tipped with gold and hafted with ivory. Its aim was true and it flew straight to its mark, but the most magical thing of all was that it made its bearer invisible. And do you remember that cauldron you once had, Dagda?' she asked, turning to the king of all the Sidh.

'I do indeed,' answered Dagda, 'and a wonderful thing it was too and most useful to me with so many sons. It never emptied and no matter how many people ate from it it always held more. There was nothing that the cauldron could not provide,' King Dagda sighed. 'I also remember the magic stone Lia Fail. Whoever stood upon it became the king of Ireland.'

'Yes,' said Brigit, 'I remember too the gift I gave to the people of the southern part of our land. That too was a stone, and anyone who kissed it gained the power of poetry and the ability to tell wonderful stories. That stone I gave to one of the Milesian kings.'

'There is one gift we have never lost,' said Dagda, 'and that is the gift of music. The gift that you brought to us all.'

At that the Sidh took up their instruments and began to play. The music of the Sidh was like no other music in the world; it could do many things. It could fill the heart of the listener with joy and happiness. It could bring back memories of childhood and youth so that the old felt young again. It could charm the birds from the sky and soothe the fishes. It could conjure up gentle rainstorms that would water the ground and cause the crops to grow. It could make the sun shine down so that the fruit ripened on the trees and the corn grew golden in the fields and it could soothe the hearts and minds of men so that when their last dark journey drew near they fell into a gentle slumber and did not fear the approach of death.

As the strains of the music died away, the last storyteller rose to his feet. His name was Froech.

'I will tell the last tale,' he said. 'It is to do with the power of our music and how through this I gained the hand of my wife. When I was young I fell in love with the daughter of the Milesian king of Connacht. I went to ask for her hand in marriage, but her father had promised her to a nearby prince. I begged and pleaded as did his daughter, but the king would not give in. I went to see the prince who had been promised her hand and begged him to release her from her father's promise, but even though he knew that she would never be happy with him, he still refused. At that I took out my harp and began to play. I played a song of war and battle that put fear into the heart of the prince and then I played a song of peace and tranquility that showed him how much better it was not to fight. Then I played a song of love, so that all who heard it could under-

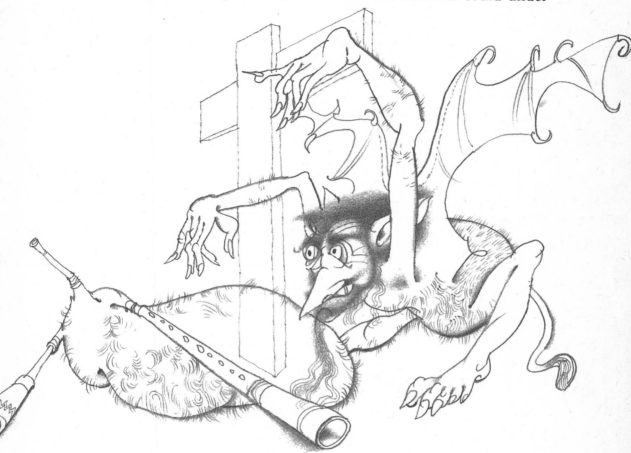

stand how much I loved the king of Connacht's daughter. At last I played a song of sleep so that all who heard it became drowsy and while they slumbered I crept away with my true love and returned to my castle under the green hills of my kingdom. All their life the people of Connacht remembered my music and they never tried to regain their princess.'

Froech sat down and played the same song of love again, and all the Sidh heard how much he loved his mortal bride and understood then why she had never wished to return to the land of men, as did so many of the mortals who came to live in their fairy kingdom.

VAINAMOINEN

Once upon a time in a far off land called Kalevala, there lived two brothers. The oldest was called Vainamoinen and the youngest Ilmarinen. They were both handsome men, tall and strong with broad shoulders and wide smiles, but Vainamoinen earned his living as a musician, whereas Ilmarinen had taught himself to be the best blacksmith in Kalevala. It was said that there were no instruments that Vainamoinen could not play and that there was nothing that Ilmarinen could not make. Besides being a great musician, Vainamoinen was also wise in the ways of healing. He could make medicines from the herbs and fruit which grew in his native land, he could set broken bones and heal wounds, advise mothers on how to help their children to grow up strong and healthy, and even cure the animals that came to harm in the forests and on the plains of Kalevala. The two brothers lived together in perfect harmony, each helping the other and spending their days in happiness and usefulness.

At last the two brothers decided that it was time that they each found a bride.

'I have heard of the beauty of the daughter of Queen Louhi of Pohjola,' Ilmarinen told his brother. 'They say that the Aino is the loveliest of all the princesses of the north.'

Vainamoinen had also heard of Aino, but had heard other things about the dismal and harsh land of Pohjola.

'They also say that Queen Louhi is a cruel and greedy queen,' he replied. 'You must take care when you visit her kingdom.'

'You are only jealous,' Ilmarinen retorted. 'I know that you too wish to marry the beautiful Aino. You are only trying to put me off so that you can win her.'

It was true that Vainamoinen wanted to marry the princess and when he saw that he could not dissuade his brother they each decided to journey to Pohjola and see which of them the lovely Aino would choose.

The next morning Ilmarinen harnessed his horses to his sleigh and set off across the snowy lands which lay between Kalevala and Pohjola.

Vainamoinen wandered down to the seashore and looked out across the grey waves. As he stood there he heard a sad voice wailing and crying. He hunted for the source of this mournful sound and discovered a little boat lying on its side in the sand dunes. The boat's

sails were ragged and torn and the paint that covered the wooden hull was faded and peeling.

'Here I lie, useless and tattered,' the little boat sobbed. 'Once I sailed across the wide seas to distant lands, journeyed through storms and sunshine to golden shores and strange islands; but now I lie rotting in the sand dunes, with no one to sail in me, and no one to care for me.'

'All your troubles are over,' Vainamoinen told the little boat. 'I shall care for you and mend your sails. Together we will sail across the sea to Pohjola.'

Quickly Vainamoinen pulled away the torn sails and made a new set from an old red cloak. He repainted the sides of the boat with bright blue paint and polished up the little boat's anchor. Then he pulled the little boat down to the edge of the sea where the waves danced and chuckled.

'I will serve you faithfully, Vainamoinen,' said the little boat, 'and if I can help you in any way you may be sure that I will.'

Together they sailed away across the sea to Pohjola and when they arrived they met Ilmarinen.

'Well met, brother,' called Vainamoinen. 'Together we shall try for the hand of the lovely Aino, and may the best man win.'

Pohjola was a terrible place. The houses were small and mean, and even the castle of Queen Louhi was made of wood. The land was poor because very few crops grew there and the animals were thin and weak.

The queen and her daughter sat in the highest room of the castle round a small fire that smoked and crackled. They were guarded by two fierce wolfhounds, Lukki and Halli. These dogs never slept and if any stranger entered the kingdom they growled and barked to warn their mistress. The two dogs were growling now.

'We have visitors,' said Queen Louhi. 'I shall ask the fire what they want of us.' The queen picked up one of the logs lying beside the smoking fire and threw it into the feeble flames.

'If the log weeps blood it means war, and if the log weeps water it means peace.'

The log hissed and crackled and a clear, amber liquid flowed out.

'It weeps honey, mother!' said Princess Aino. 'What does this mean?'

'It means that suitors come to seek your hand,' answered Queen Louhi, 'suitors from the far off land of Kalevala.'

Vainamoinen and Ilmarinen entered the chamber and bowed low before the queen and her daughter.

'All hail, Queen Louhi,' said Ilmarinen. 'I have heard of the fabled beauty of your daughter and I come to woo her.'

'All hail, Queen Louhi,' said Vainamoinen. 'I too have come to woo your daughter.'

Queen Louhi looked sharply at the two young men and then at her daughter. Aino's eyes were modestly cast down and a faint blush stained her cheeks.

Queen Louhi saw how she could turn the situation to her advantage.

'Sit down, young sirs,' she told them. 'This is a most important choice for my only daughter. Tonight we will eat together and perhaps you, Vainamoinen, would play for us on the Kantele you carry.'

Vainamoinen played for them on the stringed Kantele, and the sound of his voice and the sweet music of the strings floated round the chamber and up to the roof with the smoke from the fire. As he played he looked at Aino, but her eyes never met his. She looked only at Ilmarinen or at the floor, and she said nothing. Her mother was silent too, but Queen Louhi was silent because she was plotting, whereas Aino was silent from shyness.

In the morning, Queen Louhi called the two brothers to her. She had spoken with her daughter and knew full well that Aino preferred Ilmarinen, but she did not let the brothers know that Aino had already made her choice.

'My daughter cannot decide which of you she wishes to marry,' she said, 'and so I shall set each of you a task. The one who completes the task first shall gain the hand of Aino.'

She handed a wooden spindle from her spinning wheel to Vainamoinen.

'You must take this spindle and turn it into a ship; but this must be no ordinary ship. It must be a magnificent ship as long as a fir tree is tall, a ship which will sail by itself, with no sailors to guide her and no wind to blow her along.'

She turned to Ilmarinen and handed him a small golden ring.

'You, Ilmarinen, must take this ring and turn it into a grinding mill; but this must be no ordinary mill. It must have three sets of grindstones; the first must grind flour, the second must grind salt and the third must grind fine gold.'

The brothers prepared themselves for their tasks. Ilmarinen went to his sleigh and took out his tools. His task was difficult to be sure, but he, Ilmarinen, the greatest blacksmith in all Kalevala, would surely be able to undertake it.

Vainamoinen was worried. He was a wonderful healer and

a splendid musician, but what did he know about ships? He wandered down to the seashore and sat down in his little boat.

'Why do you look so sad, Vainamoinen?' asked the little boat. 'Is there any way I can help you?'

'I fear not,' replied Vainamoinen. 'I must take this spindle and turn it into a fine ship which will sail with neither wind nor crew, or I shall never marry the lovely Aino.'

'I cannot do this for you,' said the little boat, 'but I know of a giant who could help you. The only way you can fulfill your task is by using three magic words and the only person in the whole world who knows those words is the giant Antero Vipunen. He sleeps some way from here, and the way there is hard and dangerous. To reach him you must endure three torments. The first is a path covered with hundreds and hundreds of sharp needles, each needle pointing upwards to pierce the feet of the bold traveller who would dare to walk there. The second is a path covered with thousands and thousands of sharp swords, each sword pointing upwards to pierce and cut the feet of the brave traveller who would dare to walk there. The third is also a path, this time strewn with the blades of hundreds of thousands of axes, each blade sharpened like a razor, and each one pointing upwards to cut and slash the feet of any daring traveller who tries to walk there. Only when you have walked along these three paths will you reach the meadow where Antero Vipunen lies slumbering.'

Vainamoinen shuddered when he thought of those three paths. He went to his brother and asked him to make him a pair of steel boots that would protect his feet from the needles, the swords and the axes.

'Please help me, brother,' begged Vainamoinen. 'I also need a tiny golden box to keep the three magic words in.'

'I shall make no boots for you, and no golden boxes,' Ilmarinen told his brother. 'I am far too busy to waste time helping you. I must finish the mill before nightfall.'

Vainamoinen set off. When he reached the first path he wrapped his cloak round his feet and so avoided the sharp points of the needles. When he reached the second path he made rough shoes from the branches of a fallen tree and so avoided most of the sharp sword points, but when he reached the third path the blades of the axes cut through the wooden shoes he had made and cut into his feet. Vainamoinen struggled on and at last reached the meadow. There he paused and made a salve from the sweet herbs that grew among the rich green grass of the meadow, spread this on his feet and the cuts healed.

There ahead of him in the long waving grass was the sleeping giant Antero Vipunen. This giant was as tall as the tallest pine tree, as broad as a long-boat and as hairy as a grizzly bear. He snored and grunted in the sunshine. Antero Vipunen had been asleep for three hundred years, but this was no more than a nap to him.

Vainamoinen walked bravely up to him and drove his sword into the giant's hand. Antero Vipunen twitched his fingers as if no more than a gnat had stung him.

Vainamoinen stood by the giant's ear and shouted as loudly as he could.

'Wake up! Wake up!' but the giant did not stir.

Vainamoinen went back to the axe-path and pulled up one of the axe heads. Quickly he tied it to a long stick and walked back to the giant. Antero Vipunen lay with his mouth open and Vainamoinen crawled into the giant's mouth, down the long red throat and into Antero Vipunen's stomach. There he began to hack at the inside of the giant with his axe.

This time Antero Vipunen awoke.

'Ooh! Oh! Ouch!' he roared. 'How my stomach hurts. I must have eaten something which disagreed with me.'

Vainamoinen chopped away inside the giant's stomach.

'Aargh! Ooooh!' yelled the giant.

'Can you hear me?' Vainamoinen shouted.

'Who is there? groaned the giant. 'It sounds as if you are inside me.'

'Indeed I am,' answered Vainamoinen, 'and I shall chop away at your stomach unless you tell me the three magic words.'

'Never!' roared the giant.

'Oh yes, you will!' shouted Vainamoinen and swung the axe as hard as he could.

'Stop, stop, please stop!' yelled the giant.

'Only if you tell me the words,' shouted Vainamoinen.

'Very well,' said the giant.

So Vainamoinen crawled out of the giant's stomach and the giant whispered the words to him.

'Remember,' said the giant, settling himself down to sleep again, 'you may use the words only once. After that they lose their magic, so use them wisely.'

The giant lay back, but just before he fell asleep he sneezed and the sneeze was so strong that it carried Vainamoinen over the path covered with axes, over the path covered with swords and over the path covered with needles and back to the wooden castle.

Evening was falling and Ilmarinen was still working away at the mill.

Vainamoinen smiled to himself and prepared to chop the spindle into three pieces so that he could use the three magic words on them. As he swung his axe he felt an odd trembling in the earth and the axe seemed to twist in his hand. Instead of cutting the spindle, the axe embedded itself in Vainamoinen's leg, just below the knee. It was a terrible wound and blood began to pour from Vainamoinen's leg onto the ground.

'Help me, help me,' he called to Ilmarinen. 'I cannot stop the blood, even I cannot heal this wound. The axe must be enchanted. Only you, my brother, who are the master of all the axes in the world can help me now.'

Ilmarinen was horrified to see the wound in his brother's leg. He began to chant a spell, a spell that should heal the wound.

'Axe, axe, heal this cut,
Stop the blood from flowing.
Axe, axe, heal this wound,
While the wind is blowing.
Axe, axe, heal this hurt,
Before the moon is glowing.
Axe, axe, heal this wound,
Before the stars are showing.'

But the wound went on bleeding and the axe did not heal it. 'You are right,' said Ilmarinen, 'the axe is enchanted. Only Queen Louhi could have made such a spell, but I can undo it.'

'Come iron, come steel,
Come steel, come iron,
By the fire that made you,
By the hand that forged you,
Heal this wound.'

Ilmarinen chanted these words and stretched out his hand towards the axe. The axe twisted again on the ground and then sprang upright and the dreadful wound on Vainamoinen's leg was healed.

'Thank you, my brother,' said Vainamoinen. 'Without you I should be dead. In gratitude I shall give you the three magic words of Antero Vipunen. It is obvious that Queen Louhi wishes you to marry her daughter and I shall not stand in your way.'

Vainamoinen told Ilmarinen the three words. Ilmarinen swung his great hammer and shouted the first word. As the hammer struck the completed mill the first set of millstones started to grind out fine white flour.

Ilmarinen swung his hammer again and shouted the second word. The mill began to grind out fine white salt from the second set of millstones.

Ilmarinen swung the hammer the third time and shouted the third magic word, and the mill began to grind out fine gold from the third set of millstones.

So Ilmarinen gave the magic mill to Queen Louhi and won the hand of the fair Aino. The two brothers and Aino returned to Kalevala.

Sadly the very next year the beautiful Aino fell ill. For many days she lay quiet and still, the roses in her cheeks faded and her lovely eyes closed. Vainamoinen tried as hard as he could to heal her, but none of his medicines worked, and then, one cold night, just as the moon rose in the sky, Aino died, leaving Ilmarinen and Vainamoinen to grieve for her.

The years passed and the brothers grew older. Neither of them married, they were happy with each other's company, but they were very poor. One evening a traveller came to their door, and, as was the custom in Kalevala, they invited him in and offered him food and drink.

'We only have a little,' they told the traveller, 'but you are welcome to share it.'

After they had eaten and listened to Vainamoinen play wonderful tunes on his Kantele, the traveller told them of his voyages.

'. . . and the richest land I ever visited was Pohjola,' he related to them. 'There they have a magic mill which they call the "Sampo". It is a marvellous machine that grinds not only fine white flour, but fine white salt and pure gold. It has made the queen so rich that she can buy anything. But she still cannot buy happiness or a kind heart. She is the cruelest queen in the north.'

Vainamoinen and Ilmarinen listened in amazement.

'Just think . . .' murmured Ilmarinen, 'that is our mill. We have made Pohjola rich.'

'Yes,' said Vainamoinen, 'and your beautiful Aino has been dead all these years and yet still her greedy mother has the mill. The mill is rightfully ours.'

When the traveller had gone, the two brothers put on their cloaks and walked to the seashore. There Vainamoinen's little boat was moored, with its blue paintwork still bright and its red sail untorn.

'Take us to Pohjola, little boat,' said Vainamoinen. 'We go to claim our magic mill, the Sampo, which has ground out riches for the queen for all these years.'

The little boat set sail with the two brothers, across the oceans to Pohjola. They had not gone very far when ahead of them they saw a smooth grey island.

'How strange that an island should have no grass or trees,' said Vainamoinen.

'That is no island,' said the little boat. 'That is a huge fish. Chop off its head.'

Vainamoinen did as he was told and they carried the head of the great fish with them all the way to Pohjola. When they landed they walked to the nearest village. Although Queen Louhi was rich, her people were still poor, and so the brothers cooked the great fish-head and shared out the meat amongst the villagers.

'We see that you are a musician,' said the villagers. 'The jawbone of that fish would make a wonderful Kantele.' They picked all the meat from the jawbone of the fish and from the spines in the fins they made strings. Vainamoinen strung the Kantele and began to play. As he drew his fingers across the strings the music that poured forth was truly magical.

The brothers journeyed on until they came to the castle of Queen Louhi. The old wooden castle had gone and in its place stood a magnificent castle made from ivory, with a roof of pure gold and golden trees and flowers in the garden round it.

Queen Louhi knew that they were coming, for her two hounds, Halli and Lukki, had been growling and barking. As she had done before the first visit of the two brothers, she threw a log onto the fire.

'If the log weeps blood it means war, and if it weeps water it means peace,' she said. The log wept tears of blood.

'War is coming to Pohjola,' she said. 'I must guard the magic mill very carefully.' She commanded one thousand soldiers to guard the mill day and night and she unleashed her two fierce hounds and allowed them to roam round the castle so that they could chase and catch anyone who tried to steal the mill. When the brothers entered her throne room she told them,

'You need not think that you can steal my mill, it is well guarded. Even though Aino is dead, the mill is mine and I shall never let it go.'

But Vainamoinen was crafty. 'Oh, Queen Louhi,' he said, 'we have not come to steal your mill, but merely to play and sing to you. To be sure, Ilmarinen would love to see the mill he made so many years ago. May we look at it?'

Queen Louhi could not resist the chance to gloat over the mill and she commanded the soldiers to bring it to the chamber.

'Guard it well,' she said. 'The brothers are only to look at it.'

The mill was brought and Queen Louhi showed the brothers how it still ground out flour, salt and gold.

'I shall sing a song in praise of the magic mill,' announced Vainamoinen and he took up his Kantele and began to sing.

The music that Vainamoinen played was so beautiful and magical that soon all the soldiers fell into a deep slumber. The queen slept and even her two great wolfhounds slept. Quietly Vainamoinen and Ilmarinen took up the mill and crept away to their little boat and sailed away with it across the sea towards Kalevala.

They had not been gone long when Queen Louhi awoke. She saw that the mill was gone and in a terrible fury she called upon the powerful god Ukko, who controlled the wind, storms and sea.

'Avenge me, O Ukko,' she demanded. 'Vainamoinen and Ilmarinen have stolen the magic Sampo, the mill which grinds flour, salt and gold.'

Immediately Ukko caused a great storm to arise. The storm rushed across the sea and tore at the red sails of the little boat.

'Throw the mill overboard,' begged the little boat, 'for I cannot sail in this storm with the mill on board.'

The brothers would not and the boat rocked about madly. The boat heeled over to the right and the millstones which ground out flour were smashed. Then the boat heeled to the left and the millstones that ground out gold were smashed. At this the brothers tossed the broken mill over the side and the little boat made its way safely to the shores of Kalevala.

From that day to this, the magic Sampo has remained at the bottom of the sea. It grinds no more flour and no more gold, for only the wheels that grind salt are left. Day and night they grind away, never ceasing and never slowing. And that is why the sea is so salty.

KING ARTHUR

Long ago, when the green land of Britain was covered with great forests, and wolves and bears roamed wild in the countryside, there lived a powerful king. His name was Uther Pendragon and he was the bravest of all the kings of Britain. His closest friend and advisor was an old man called Merlin.

Now Merlin was no ordinary man. In the days when the old magic had not died there were many great wizards and Merlin was the greatest wizard who had ever lived. Because he knew so many magical spells and was so very wise in the ways of the world, King Uther Pendragon always asked Merlin for advice and help. King Uther's wife was the beautiful Ingerne, Duchess of Tintagel, and when they had been married for about two years, Ingerne gave birth to a baby boy. They named him Arthur and Merlin was present at his christening.

'Sire,' said Merlin, holding the baby in his arms. 'This child will grow up to be the greatest king that Britain has ever known. Would you allow me to bring him up to be a good and wise king?'

'We can bring him up ourselves,' said Ingerne, for she did not want to lose her baby.

'To be raised in a royal household is not always the best training for kingship,' Merlin told them. 'What will your child know of the people he will one day reign over if all he sees are castles and palaces? How will he know how ordinary people live, what they need and what they lack if he always has everything he wants? Let me take him and put him where he will learn all he needs.'

So Uther Pendragon and Ingerne agreed, for they knew that Merlin was the best person to help their son to learn to rule wisely and well. Thus Merlin took the baby away and for many years no more was heard of little Prince Arthur.

In those days, the country of Britain was made up of many different kingdoms, each ruled by a different king. Uther Pendragon was the most powerful of all the kings, but his lands were often threatened by the people of the North who were greedy for Uther's lands and possessions. When Uther fell ill the men of the North formed a huge army and sailed southwards round the coast of Britain to overthrow the dying monarch.

Merlin went to Uther and advised him.

'Sire, only you can lead your armies into battle,' he told Uther.

'The soldiers trust you and will fight fiercely if you are there, but if you are not, then they will surely be overthrown.'

Uther left his sickbed and rallied his men round him. He knew that he had only a few weeks to live but even so he was determined that his men should not know how near he was to death. The two great armies met at a place just outside St Albans, a town close to London. The Northmen believing that Uther's army had lost heart without their king to lead them were amazed when they were met with fierce opposition. The battle was short but decisive — the Northmen were soundly beaten and fled back to the north. Almost the last thing that Uther heard was the cheering of his soldiers and the joyful sound of victory trumpets.

The king was dying. He sent for Merlin and made his last wishes clear. His son Arthur was to become king and Merlin was to be chief advisor to the crown. But where was Arthur? He was a young man by now and almost old enough to rule, yet no one knew where he was, and Merlin would tell no one what had become of the heir to the throne. When he was asked he would answer,

'All will be made clear in time,' and he would say no more.

The winter after the death of Uther Pendragon a strange stone appeared outside one of the largest churches in London. Buried in this stone, so that only the richly carved hilt could be seen, was a great broad sword, and carved round the stone in clear letters was the legend: WHOSOEVER PULLS THE SWORD FROM THE STONE IS THE RIGHTFUL KING OF BRITAIN.

'But Arthur is the rightful king of Britain,' the people said. 'Why does he not pull the sword from the stone?'

Months passed and still Arthur did not appear. People began to believe that like his father, he was dead.

Many knights came to London to try to take the sword from the stone, but none succeeded and strife began to break out in the land. There was no one to rule and some of the knights tried to take the crown by force, but they failed.

The following summer, a great tournament was held in London and knights and soldiers came from all over Britain to take part. One of these knights was Sir Hector, who brought his two sons with him. Sir Hector's elder son was Kay, a young man of eighteen. The younger son, who was only just sixteen, was not yet allowed to carry arms, although he was fully trained in the arts of horsemanship and combat. Because he was not allowed to join in, the younger son was acting as squire to Kay and Sir Hector. He looked after their horses and took care of their armour and weapons. Sir Hector and Kay took

86

part in many of the tournaments, particularly the single combat contests where two men fought each other on foot with swords and shields. During the first contest, Kay's sword broke and Kay sent his brother to fetch his other sword.

The young lad darted away as fast as he could, for the place where they were staying was a long way away from the tournament ground, and he did not want his brother to miss any of the contests. As he ran through the streets he passed the churchyard where the magic stone stood. The young man did not stop to read the inscription; all he saw was a sword that no one seemed to want. He vaulted over the churchyard wall and took hold of the hilt of the sword. With one smooth pull he drew the sword from the stone.

It was a beautiful sword, as sharp as a razor and well balanced. Kay's brother ran back to the tournament as fast as he could, pleased that he could return so quickly. He was in such a hurry that he did not notice the amazed look on the faces of the people who had seen what he had done.

'He must be the rightful king . . .' said one man.

'But he seemed not to know what the stone said . . .' said another.

'The inscription said that only the rightful king could take the sword,' said another.

The news spread through London and people began to make their way to the tournament ground to see the boy who had pulled the sword from the stone and proclaim him their king.

Sir Hector and Kay were just as amazed when they saw the sword.

'Where did you find this?' they asked. 'Don't you know what this sword is?'

Sir Hector fell to his knees before his younger son.

'Sire . . .' he said.

'Oh get up, father,' said his son, 'don't be silly . . .'

'Arthur,' said Sir Hector, for that was the boy's name, 'the time has come for me to tell you the secret that I have kept in my heart for nearly sixteen years. Although you have always thought that I was your father, you are not, in fact, my real son. When you were a tiny baby, the wizard Merlin brought you to me. He would not tell me who your real parents were, but he asked me to bring you up as if you were my own child. He told me that you must be taught all the arts of a knight as well as honesty and duty. He said that you must be treated as any other boy even though you had a high destiny to fulfil. I see now that Merlin knew all along that you were the rightful heir to the throne of Britain.'

'And so I did,' said a deep voice.

Turning round, Arthur saw a tall, white-haired man. It was the wizard Merlin.

'Your real parents were Uther Pendragon and Ingerne, King and Queen of Britain,' said Merlin. 'You are truly the rightful king. It was only in this way that I could ensure that you would gain the throne. If the people of Britain did not believe you to be the king, they would not allow you to rule them. Now all can see that you, and only you, could draw the sword from the stone. Other men have tried and failed; other men have tried to take the crown and have failed. You will not fail, for you are the true son of your father.'

A great cheer rose up above the tournament ground, and the people there fell to their knees and hailed Arthur as king.

And so Arthur took the crown and led his people into battle. He had ruled for several years when the sword vanished. It had gone as mysteriously as it had arrived.

That evening Merlin took Arthur to a quiet and secret lake, high up in the Welsh mountains. A small rowing boat was moored at its edge but there were no oars.

'Get into the boat,' Merlin told King Arthur, 'and do not be afraid of anything that may happen to you.'

Arthur did as he was told and as he seated himself, the boat began to move smoothly out into the lake. When it reached the centre of the lake it stopped. All around Arthur the lake shimmered in the moonlight, as still as a mirror. Then, without a sound, and without causing a ripple, a slender white hand rose from the waters. The hand held a sword.

'Take the sword,' Merlin's voice whispered.

Arthur reached down and took the sword. Faintly through the water he thought he could see the face of a beautiful woman, but as he grasped the sword the hand sank back under the lake again and the face disappeared. The little boat moved back to the shore bearing Arthur and his precious gift.

'This is the sword Excalibur,' Merlin told the king. 'It is a magical sword and may only be carried by you. It will protect you in battle and while you wear it you will never be wounded.'

'Who was the beautiful woman I saw under the water?' asked Arthur.

'That was the Lady of the Lake,' answered Merlin.

All his life Arthur carried the sword Excalibur, and as Merlin had said, he was never wounded.

Some years later, Arthur married the beautiful daughter of King Laodegan. Guinevere was said to be the loveliest lady in Britain and for many years she and Arthur were happy together. When the wedding was celebrated, knights and kings came from all over the kingdom bearing rich gifts for the happy couple. Of all the wedding presents that Arthur and Guinevere received, the most wonderful was a huge wooden table, richly carved and painted. The table was completely round and could seat one hundred and fifty knights. It was a present from Queen Guinevere's father Laodegan, and with it came one hundred knights, all sworn to the service of King Arthur.

This table became famous as the round table of legend. Only the bravest and noblest knight was allowed to sit there and because the table had no top or bottom, no knight could claim that he was more important than the others. When Arthur had decided who was to be allowed to sit at the round table, he held a great feast and for the first time the knights were all seated together. Suddenly, during the feast, the room became dark and on the back of the chairs where each knight was sitting, their names appeared in golden letters. Sir Lancelot of the Lake, Sir Gawain, Sir Bors, Sir Hector, Sir Perceval, Sir Galahad, Sir Pinel, Sir Kay, Sir Bedivere: these and all the other knights saw their names written in glowing letters and knew then that many adventures awaited them.

90

ROLAND

Roland was the nephew of Charlemagne, the king of France who had conquered all of Spain apart from Saragossa. He was a great favourite of the king, who prized valour and courage in battle above all things, for Roland had already proved himself to be both heroic and noble.

Oliver was Roland's closest friend and companion-in-arms; in fact they were soon to become brothers, for Roland was engaged to be married to the beautiful Aude, Oliver's sister. Roland's only enemy at this time was in fact the Count Ganelon, his own stepfather, who was jealous of Charlemagne's high opinion of Roland, and had sworn he would bring about the downfall of his stepson.

Nobody suspected Ganelon of treachery. Charlemagne was deeply worried about the bad tidings he had received from Spain. The Saracen king, Marsilion, had sworn an oath of allegiance to Charlemagne and had promised to follow the Christian faith. But, little by little, Marsilion had become less humble, enlarging his kingdom and acquiring greater riches and possessions, whilst setting fire to the Christian churches one by one and having mosques erected in their place. This news was a thorn in the side of Charlemagne. In the meantime those Spaniards who had remained devoted to the Christian faith were begging Charlemagne to come to their aid. He answered their pleas, leading his army even as far as Saragossa itself where crosses were replaced on the roofs of the houses. Marsilion wept to see the downfall of his domain.

He sent messengers to Charlemagne bringing valuable gifts to try to stop the fighting. But Charlemagne's advisers were divided as to the meaning behind these symbols of peace; Roland and Oliver wished to continue the war as they felt that Marsilion was a cruel man and was likely to betray them at the first opportunity. The archbishop Turpin and the Count Otto shared their views, but Ganelon and his friends thought that they should be reasonable.

'Why could the Christians and Muslims not come to some peaceful agreement?' he asked. 'Surely Marsilion as such a great leader is a man of his word and we should therefore take this peace offering.'

He was thinking of the fabulous jewels and riches belonging to Marsilion.

Roland was annoyed at his stepfather, for he was sure that Marsilion would deceive his uncle yet again. He suggested that if an ambassador were to be sent, then who better than Ganelon himself since he was so sure of Marsilion's good faith. Now this made Ganelon extremely angry but at the same time fear grew in his mind. It was common knowledge that Marsilion had executed previous ambassadors and he was determined that this time he would be revenged upon Roland. An evil plan grew in his mind.

He was certain that Roland had only made the suggestion so that he would inherit his stepfather's property if he were to be murdered. Ganelon did not understand Roland and thought he was as grasping and mean as Ganelon himself. He laid his plans.

He visited Marsilion and was treated with great kindness and hospitality, for Marsilion could see through him and realized that Ganelon could be very useful against the Emperor to whom he was so close. On his return Ganelon informed Charlemagne that Marsilion was an honest man and would not betray them. He was prepared to promote the Christian faith as well as making yearly payments of gold as a mark of his trust, if Charlemagne would withdraw most of his troops except for those in occupation. Charlemagne saw no reason to disbelieve this story. The plot was laid perfectly; Charlemagne even appointed Roland to command the rearguard as Ganelon wished.

Retreating back to France over the plains of Roncevaux, Roland was carrying as ever his famous sword 'Durandal' and his horn 'Oliphant', which was so loud and piercing that it always drove terror into the hearts of his enemies. It was a clear day and as Roland was riding along he perceived a cloud in the distance on the horizon behind them. He wondered at first what it could be and then finally it dawned on him that it was a vast army of Saracen horsemen galloping very swiftly in their wake. It was by now obvious that they were intent on battle and that Marsilion's promises were as empty as the winds rattling across the plains. Charlemagne was very far away from them, moving ahead back to France, but he could even now be summoned by the earshattering blasts from Roland's horn Oliphant. Oliver, the ever faithful and wise comrade, urged Roland to call for help before it was too late, for they were outnumbered ten to one. But Roland was a warrior brave and valiant and the lust for battle was flowing through his veins as he heard their cries. He wished to punish Marsilion for his lies and deceit, though nobody as yet realized the hand that Ganelon had played.

The sun rising over the flat, featureless landscape glinted on the glowing, golden helmets of the Saracen hordes, making their tall spears flash and sparkle in the early morning light. Their black hair flowed in the wind of their passage as they rushed ever nearer to start the assault. Roland grouped his men as best as he could to face the onslaught and they waited to meet the enemy, for escape in those empty lands was impossible.

Leading the Saracens was the nephew of Marsilion, Aldarot, charging forward bearing the flag of Marsilion. The cry of 'Allah! Allah!' echoed down the plain as the two armies clashed together. The air was thick with lances and spears which flew to meet their mark. As the men fought one against the other their horses stumbled and fell, some ending their masters' lives as they rolled over and crushed them. The luckier soldiers were able to scramble to their feet and snatch a sword or even a dagger out of a sheath to slash at any part of the enemy that was not protected by armour. The cries of war and death soon filled the surrounding area as men stricken with many terrible wounds staggered and fell on to the bare, dry plain which was to be their final resting place on this earth. Lances were broken in two and the flags and standards which had been borne so proudly over the land were ripped to shreds by swords and torn by

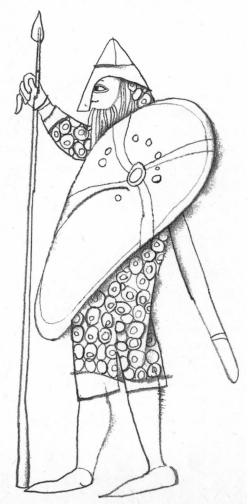

battling men lurching this way and that. Soon they had all fluttered to the ground to be trampled underfoot. Roland skilfully parried any blow that came his way and found that he was soon very close to Aldarot, who was battling with a fervour that overcame almost all. But not Roland. Roland raised his sword above his head. It had been blessed by the Archbishop Turpin so that it would never fail him against the pagans, and brought it down with all his strength against Aldarot's sword which shivered and finally shattered into two pieces on the ground. Roland raised Durandal again and pierced his enemy's neck so that Aldarot swayed for a long moment, staring at Roland with rapidly glazing eyes, he finally fell heavily, shuddered once and died.

Marsilion was both furious and despairing when news was brought to him of the death of his nephew; furious that Roland had outwitted them again and despairing because Aldarot had been very close to him. He screamed for revenge against his enemy, threatening his commanders with a horrible death if they failed in their duty to slaughter Roland. He then despatched into the fray his own son, trusting that he would succeed where all the others had hitherto failed. His son was never seen again, his head hewn bloodily from his shoulders by the mighty sword of Oliver.

Roland stood there, his sword and hands covered with the blood of his enemies, and surveyed the battle scene. Things were going badly for him and his friends. They were now encircled by the murderous Saracens. Marsilion himself had launched into the attack, having spent even his own son in the feud against Roland, and was now forging ever closer through the sea of black and gold Saracen heads to the small knot of fighting men that surrounded Roland. By now even Roland could see that battle was overcoming them. Mortally injured or murdered Frenchmen outnumbered the living at this stage. He decided to sound his horn Oliphant to summon Charlemagne to avenge them at least, if not to rescue them. However now it was Oliver who was against the sounding of the horn.

'How may we sound the horn when help will come too late?' he gasped. It was the Archbishop Turpin who finally decided the matter. And so Roland at last sounded a tremendous blast from his horn that could be heard thirty leagues away within Charlemagne's earshot. However, so hard had he blown that the effort burst a blood vessel in his temple. The battle continued, but the French were fading fast. Oliver was pierced by so many wounds that the blood running into his eyes blinded him. Such was his anguish and terror that he was lashing out at anyone who approached him, whether friend or foe. And so it was that the faithful Oliver delivered a fatal wound to his friend Roland, whom no-one else had been able to touch.

Horns were blowing wildly in the distance. Charlemagne was charging back to the battle, and on hearing their horns and wild cries the Saracens lost heart and turned tail after a final attempt to kill Roland. Archbishop Turpin was dying on the battlefield, his body dismembered and barely recognizable. Roland was left alone, for no pagan hand was able to destroy him. Knowing that death was near he attempted to smash Durandal against a rock, rather than have it fall into enemy hands. And it was while he was doing this that his soul finally passed away.

Charlemagne wept when he saw the bloodshed that had been wreaked on his men and he became distraught when he found the remains of Roland and Oliver, swearing revenge would be taken against Marsilion.

At last the bodies were returned to Aix-la-Chapelle where the dreadful news was broken to the lovely Aude, Roland's fiancée. On hearing of her lover's and brother's death she fell down and died of a shock and a broken heart.

So ended the tragic tale of Roland and Oliver, two of the bravest knights to fight for Charlemagne.

LUG THE WARRIOR HERO

In the old days, when Ireland was ruled by the people of the goddess Danu, there were many great hero gods. The greatest of all these was Lug, for he was not only a mighty warrior but also the wisest man in the world. The Tuatha De Danann, as the people of the goddess Danu were called, were a peaceful people. They would fight fiercely to protect their lovely island if anyone tried to come there and invade them. This tale tells how the Tuatha De Danann, helped by Lug, defended Ireland against the Fomiori.

The King of the Tuatha was called Nuada of the Silver arm, because he had one arm entirely made of silver. His real arm had been chopped off at the Battle of Mag Tuired and his silver arm had been made for him by Dian Cecht the healer.

Nuada was holding a great feast at Tara for all his warriors and advisors. The entrance to the castle was guarded by a door-keeper who had been told that only people who were skilled at some craft or other should be allowed to enter. On the night of the feast a handsome young warrior followed by a troop of soldiers strode up to the door-keeper and demanded entrance.

'And who might you be?' asked the door-keeper.

'I am Lug Samildanach, son of Cian and Ethne and grandson of Balar of the Fomiori, and I wish to join the army of Nuada of the Silver Arm,' replied the young man proudly.

'What skill can you offer in the service of Nuada of the Silver Arm?' asked the door-keeper. 'Only those who are skilled may enter.'

'I am a blacksmith,' replied Lug.

'Then you may not enter,' said the door-keeper. 'We already have a blacksmith called Colum Cualleinech.'

'But I am also a wheelwright,' the young man responded.

'Still you may not enter, for we have a wheelwright called Luchta mac Luachada,' answered the door-keeper.

'I am also a harper and a champion,' said Lug.

'Still you may not enter, for we have a harper called Abcan mac Bicelmois and a champion called Ogma mac Elathan.'

'I am also a hero,' persevered Lug.

'Still you may not enter, for we have a hero called Bresal.'

'I am a soldier and a fighter,' Lug went on.

'Still you may not enter. In Dagda is our fighter. We have no need of you,' replied the door-keeper.

'I am a magician and a sorcerer,' continued Lug.

'Still you may not enter, we have magicians and sorcerers,' answered the door-keeper.

'I am a doctor and a poet.'

'Still you may not enter, we have a doctor and a poet in Tara already.'

'And do you have one man in Tara who can do all these things?' asked Lug.

'I will ask the king,' replied the door-keeper and he went into the hall and told Nuada about the young man who wished to enter.

'This is indeed a clever man,' Nuada said. 'Take all the chessboards of Tara out to him and we shall see if he is as wise as he claims.'

The chessboards were brought out and Lug played a hundred games of chess and won them all.

'Let him enter,' commanded Nuada of the Silver Arm. 'For never has so wise, strong and brave a man come to my court.'

And so Lug joined the band of soldiers and heroes who were to fight against the Fomiori.

Nuada then held a council of war to decide who should lead the Tuatha Dē Danann into battle. Lug was chosen because he was the wisest and cleverest of them all.

The following morning, In Dagda, the greatest of the Danann fighters, went early to Connacht to meet the war goddess Morrigan. She was a terrible creature with iron fingernails and teeth and hands that were so strong that she could splinter a tree trunk as easily as you could wring out a cloth. She was washing herself at a ford by the river and In Dagda came and stood beside her.

In Dagda was Morrigan's favourite warrior and they fell to talking about the coming battle. In Dagda cunningly flattered Morrigan, telling her that she was the most beautiful of all the goddesses and that he loved her more than the sun and moon. Morrigan asked him to kiss her, for she knew full well that she was hideous and that everybody recoiled from her. In Dagda swept her into his arms and kissed her soundly, even though her iron teeth cut his lips badly and her iron fingernails scratched him through his chain-mail armour. In return for the kiss, Morrigan told In Dagda how the battle could be won.

At noon, the battle began. The two enormous armies faced each other across a gentle valley and the sun gleamed on their lances and spears. At the back of the army of the Danann waited Dian Secht the healer. He would take the slain from the field of battle and bathe them in an enchanted spring which would bring them back to life, although they would never speak again. The king, Nuada, had decided that Lug was far too important to be allowed to fight and had told him to stay at the top of the hill and watch and advise.

A horn gave the signal for the battle to start and the two armies surged together. The valley rang with battle cries and the clashing of steel against steel. In Dagda was in the thick of it, swinging his enormous battle club, while Nuada's silver arm flashed above the struggling bodies. Lug, watching the battle, became so enraged that he forgot his orders and charged down to the fighting.

The armies struggled back and forth; first the Tuatha De Danann seemed to be winning and then the Fomiori seemed to gain the upper hand.

The leader of the Fomiori was none other than Lug's grandfather, Balar the Dreadful. This chieftain's right eye was covered with an iron eyelid that was only raised during battles because his eye was so horrible that it killed anyone it looked at. Four Fomiori warriors raised the eyelid and Balar began to gaze about him. The destruction was terrible: soldiers from the people of Danann began to fall in their hundreds as Balar slowly turned his head from side to side. Then Lug loaded his sling with a smooth granite stone and whirled the sling round his head. The air hummed and whistled as the sling turned and at its furthermost point Lug let the stone fly — straight into Balar's eye. It struck Balar with such force that his eye was driven right through his head and looked backwards on the army of the Fomiorians.

And this was how the Fomiori were beaten. Thousands of them were slain by the gaze of Balar and the others were driven into the sea. Balar's head was buried so that his terrible eye would never again look on the living; for even though Balar was dead, his eye still stared blindly up at the sky and threatened to kill the stars.

After the battle, Morrigan declared peace throughout Ireland and for one hundred years after this there was no more fighting.

THE TWILIGHT OF THE GODS

Nearly all the myths from the northern lands tell of the ending of the rule of the gods. In Iceland this is called Ragnarok, which means 'The destiny of the gods' and in Norway and Sweden it is called 'Ragna Rokkr,' which means 'The twilight of the gods.' You have heard many myths about the strength of Odin and Thor, of Loki's cunning and cleverness and of the giant's ceaseless struggle to over-throw the gods of Asgard. But the gods were not always fair and it was their treachery in betraying their word that eventually brought about their downfall. This is how it came about.

The beautiful land of Asgard had been protected by a series of impregnable walls which had been built by a giant who had de-manded as payment the hand of Freyja. The gods had promised the giant that he would marry Freyja when the walls were finished but had broken that promise. Because the gods could not keep their word, strife began to break out all over the world and in all the lower regions of Niflheim treachery and malice became commonplace. This terrible state of affairs was made worse by Loki, who betrayed Baldur, one of the best loved of all the gods. Baldur, who spread happiness and peace wherever he went, began to be troubled by strange dreams. He went to Thor and begged that the other gods should protect him and they agreed. The gods made everything in the earth promise never to betray or harm Baldur. All the animals, trees, plants and men of the earth agreed. All that is, except one, the little mistletoe plant which had been thought too young to take the oath. Only Loki knew this. One day, when the gods were laughing and joking and playing a game of hurling everything they could at Baldur to test his invincibility, Loki secretly collected a branch of mistletoe and persuaded Hod, a blind god, to throw the mistletoe branch. This pierced Baldur through the heart and killed him. This enraged the gods and, knowing that it was Loki, with his love of malice that had caused this thing to happen, chained Loki up. Loki escaped, and, filled with bitterness against the gods, joined forces with the demons and giants of earth to fight against the gods. One of Loki's children was the terrible wolf Fenrir, who the gods had chained up many years before in order that Fenrir should not de-stroy the universe. Now the children of Fenrir were growing and one of them became so strong and powerful that it chased after the sun and ate it up, leaving nothing but a dull red glow in the sky. Worse

was still to come. Heimdall, the god who guarded the Bifrost bridge, the pathway from the earth to Asgard, had his sword stolen by Loki and was tricked into allowing the giants to begin to march on Asgard without sounding his great battle horn. Fenrir finally escaped and began to chew at the roots of Yggdrasil, the sacred ash tree which guarded the universe. Two monstrous boats appeared, driven forward by the waves created by the writhing body of the serpent Midgard. On one, the giant Hrym rode and on the other sat Loki, accompanied by his gigantic son Fenrir. The fire giant, Surt, attacked from the south and when they all reached the Bifrost bridge and marched over it the heat from the fires that Surt caused made the Bifrost bridge crack and splinter in two.

The two armies faced each other, the giants and Fenrir on one side and the gods, led by Odin on the other. As the battle began, Odin charged at Fenrir, his sword upraised, but Fenrir opened his huge mouth and swallowed Odin. Vidar, one of Odin's sons, soon avenged his father by standing on the wolf's lower jaw and holding the beast's muzzle open with his right hand, stabbed Fenrir in the heart, through the throat.

Midgard the serpent, who had wound itself round the earth all those years ago, now rose out of the ocean and threatened Thor. He crushed its head with the magic hammer Mjöllnir, but alas, the poisonous breath of the serpent Midgard overcame the god of thunder and Thor, too, fell dying. Loki and Heimdall fought hand to hand and each killed the other. Only Tyr, one of the bravest gods, who had lost his right arm when the gods had first chained Fenrir, was left on the battlefield. It was to the dog of the underworld that Tyr lost his life, but not before he had mortally wounded Garm.

The battle was over. No gods were left to protect the earth. The giants were victorious and swarmed over the lands, destroying them and setting them on fire. After the fire the seas rose up and flooded everything. The old universe was gone and in its place was a wasteland, with no living thing moving in it.

And was this the end? No. Out of the destruction of the old world grew a new one, one that was ruled by gods who kept their word, gods who preferred peace to war and gentleness to battle. But that is another story.

THOR'S HAMMER

Thor was the favourite son of the great god Odin. Even when he was young he showed such strength that his mother had had to make him a teething ring of iron because he chewed through his silver one as soon as it was put into his mouth — and that was before his teeth had even started to grow! When Thor reached full adulthood his power was legendary, as was his most famous possession, a magical stone hammer. This hammer was called Mjöllnir and never missed anything that it was hurled at. What was even stranger, it always returned to the hand of Thor and then shrank until it was tiny enough to hide in Thor's sleeve. Yet the moment Thor drew it out, it grew to its full size immediately, ready to be hurled at the next god or mortal who angered Thor. Not that many gods or mortals dared to anger this god of thunder, since his temper was as legendary as his strength.

Thor had a brother called Loki and hardly ever have two brothers been bōrn who were so different. Where Thor was burly and tall, Loki was slender and of middle height. Where Thor was open-faced and ruddy-cheeked, Loki's face had a closed and secretive look and his cheeks were pale. Where Thor's voice was loud and jolly, Loki always spoke softly and hissed like a snake when he said words with an 's' in them. Where Thor was fast to act but sometimes slow to think, Loki had a quicksilver mind and weighed up everything he did before he acted. Nevertheless, the two brothers were fond of each other, and often, when Thor needed advice, it was to Loki that he turned. And when Loki needed the help of his brother's huge strength, he turned to Thor.

One day a dreadful thing happened in Asgard, the kingdom of the northern gods. Thor strode out of his castle Bilskirnir, and shouted in a voice that made the roofs and mountains of Asgard shake,

'Where is my hammer — Mjöllnir? Who has stolen my hammer?'

The gods were horrified. They had been feasting and carousing the night before and had gone to their homes in a very jolly mood indeed. Thor had been the jolliest of all, and had stumbled several times on the way back to Bilskirnir. His snores had rumbled through the night until even the gentle Freyja, the best loved and most peace-able goddess in Asgard, had finally complained. Even Odin could not wake his snoring son, so the gods had returned to their beds and pulled their wolfskin blankets up round their ears.

'The dragon Fafnir would not have woken Thor last night,' said Loki. 'Let alone a sneak thief who must have crept into Bilskirnir while Thor slept. But who would dare to do such a thing?'

Thor, of course, had no idea. He strode about, shaking his fists and roaring until the trees of the forest that grew at the edge of Asgard trembled so much that all their pine needles fell to the ground, leaving the branches spindly and bare.

'Enough of this roaring and fuming,' said Loki. 'This will do no good, we nust think what to do. No mortal could have entered Bilskirnir, so some giant from the realms of Niflheim must be the culprit. Leave this to me, my brother, I shall seek him out.'

Loki went to the goddess Freyja. She was sitting by her spinning wheel, spinning fine wool into cloaks for the Valkyrie maidens and humming one of the more gentle war songs to herself.

'O, lovely Freyja,' Loki began, 'most beautiful of all the goddesses, would you lend me your magic cloak of eagle's feathers, that I might fly to the realm of giants to seek the hammer of Thor?'

'Of course, dear cousin,' replied Freyja in her sweet voice, 'and all success to your venture.'

Loki donned the cloak and sped on the winds to the dreary kingdom of Niflheim. There he met the giant Hymir.

'Tell me, dear Hymir of the wise head,' said Loki flatteringly, 'have you heard anyone speak of the great hammer of Thor lately?'

'Er . . . no . . . er . . . er . . . the hammer of who?' asked Hymir, who could never remember names.

'Then tell me if any of your number have seemed particularly happy today,' Loki went on.

Hymir scratched his head with his club which had an iron spike sticking out of it and rolled his eyes round in his head,

'I heard tell that er . . . er . . . Thrumm . . . no, Thremm . . no, that's wrong . . . Thrymm, that's it! that's it . . . Thrymm was singing this morning and he hasn't been heard to sing for four thousand years or so. He's your man,' and Hymir wandered off, still scratching his head and murmuring 'Threem . . . Throom, no that's not it . . . Thrymm! That's your man!'

Hymir was right. Thrymm had indeed stolen the hammer and had hidden it eighty leagues below the ocean, under the coils of the serpent Midgard, which was why the hammer could not return to Thor's hand as it usually did when it was away from its master.

Now Thrymm was one of the ugliest of all the giants. He never cut or combed his hair or beard so he looked like a great mountain covered with dried bracken. His teeth were long and yellow and his fingernails curved and black. He only ever wore one suit of clothes which was so dirty that when he took it off it stood up by itself. But in spite of all this he had a romantic nature and longed for a beautiful bride. He was passionately in love with the lovely Freyja and pined for her day and night. He knew that in the normal way of things there was no chance that Freyja would accept him and this was why he had stolen Thor's magic hammer. He hoped that the gods would persuade Freyja to accept him as a husband in return for the hammer.

'I shall return the hammer to Freyja on our wedding day,' he told Loki, 'as is the custom at our weddings. After that she may do with it as she chooses.'

It was the custom in those lands for the new husband to give the bride his most precious possession before they were married and Thrymm's most precious possession was the hammer he had stolen from Thor.

Loki returned to Asgard with the news and went straight to Odin, the father of the gods.

'Thrymm is quite serious about this,' he told Odin. 'Unless Freyja promises to marry him we shall never regain the magic hammer, and that would be a terrible thing. You must speak to Freyja.'

With a trembling heart Odin went to see Freyja, the gentlest of all the goddesses. She was sweeping the floor of the great hall of Valhalla with an ebony broom and singing her favourite battle song. She stopped when she saw Odin.

'Welcome, dear brother,' she said, 'and what can I do for you today?'

Odin twisted his beard round and round in his fingers and shuffled his feet in his battle boots.

'Sister Freyja,' Odin began, 'you know how important Thor's magic hammer is to all of us . . .'

'I do indeed,' said Freyja. 'Without it we should all have been defeated many times.'

'Well,' Odin went on, 'it's like this — the giant Thrymm had stolen it and will only give it back on one condition.' Here Odin paused and looked at the peaceful face of Freyja.

'And what might that be, dear brother?' asked Freyja, polishing one of the great cast-iron candelabra that stood at the side of the hall.

'I don't think you are going to like this, dear sister,' said Odin. 'Thrymm says he will only return the hammer if you consent to marry him.'

A dreadful silence fell on the hall as Freyja looked at Odin in disbelief. 'What!' she said. 'What did you say?' and the sound of her voice blew out half the candles in the hall.

'If you consent to marry him,' muttered Odin, glancing behind him and working out the distance to the door.

'Marry him!' said Freyja. 'Marry Thrymm! That ugly, unwashed, ignorant giant ... me, the gentlest of all the goddesses to marry Thrymm!' She picked up the nearest candelabra and broke it over her knee.

'Me! The goddess of beauty and motherhood to marry that horrible creature who never scrubs his teeth or his fingernails!' And she picked up the broom and began to hit Odin about the head and shoulders. 'Me! The goddess of learning and gentleness to marry that ...' here Freyja ran out of breath and words and shook her fists over her head. Her neck swelled up with rage so much that the heavy gold necklace that she always wore snapped and clanged to the floor.

'Well, don't think, don't do anything except go back to Thor and tell him that he might as well marry Thrymm himself because I won't.' And with that Freyja swept out of the hall and slammed the door behind her so hard that the rest of the candelabra fell down with a crash and all the battleaxes and shields and battle pennants that hung from the roof hurtled to the floor.

Odin picked himself up, disentangled his horned helmet from three battle pennants and a candelabra and went back to see Thor.

'She says no,' he told his favourite son. 'She says that if you want your hammer back you'll have to marry Thrymm yourself.'

'Just a moment,' interrupted Loki, who had been trying to calm his brother, 'that's a marvellous idea!'

'What do you mean?' growled Thor. 'Are you trying to make fun of me?'

'Certainly not,' said Loki, putting a prudent distance between himself and his brother. 'Think about it for a moment. You know that a bride is always veiled until the marriage is over, and you know that Thrymm is not the cleverest of giants. You also know that the bride must receive as a wedding present the most precious thing that the groom possesses. Now what is the most precious thing that Thrymm possesses?'

'My magic hammer,' replied Thor, grinding his teeth.

'Well then,' said Loki, 'why don't you pretend to be Freyja? You can dress up in her long blue cloak and grey veil and borrow her golden necklace. As long as you say nothing, how will Thrymm know that it is you and not Freyja? And once you have the hammer, there will be no question of a wedding anyway.'

'That's not a bad idea,' said Odin, 'but you'll have to go with Thor, for who knows whether he'll control his temper or not . . .'

So it was decided that Loki should send a message to Thrymm to say that Freyja had consented to be his wife and that she would soon be arriving for the wedding feast. Freyja willingly gave Thor her blue cloak and grey veil and golden necklace and Loki dressed Thor up and took him down to Niflheim where Thrymm was waiting.

All the giants were there. There was Hymir the thick-witted, and Surt, the giant of fire who wore a blazing crown and sat by himself for fear of scorching the other guests. There was Suttung, who knew the secret of the marvellous wine that the gods and giants loved, but who was always drunk because of this. There was the giantess Grid, who carried a girdle, gloves and magic wand that made her the strongest of all the giants; and there were many many more, most of them very merry from the wine that Suttung had brought with him.

Fortunately the hall where the wedding feast was to be held was dark and gloomy, as were most of the giant's dwelling places and Thor's disguise hid him well. Loki and his disguised brother were seated at the places of honour, next to Thrymm, who had plaited greasy red ribbons into his hair and beard and looked even more horrible than usual.

'Here is your bride,' announced Loki as they entered.

Thrymm took the hand of his supposed bride eagerly, but was surprised to find it gnarled and rough.

'What is this?' he asked Loki. 'My bride's hand feels strangely rough!'

'Ah! Well...' said the quick-witted Loki, 'er ... yes, that is because she has been sewing her bridal clothes for the last three days without ceasing and the needle has pricked her fingers so much that they have become roughened.'

The feast began and rich food was placed before the guests. To Thrymm's surprise his bride ate more than all the other giants, and not only at eating did the bride prove to be the greediest but at drinking too! Flagon after flagon was drained and plate after plate of food disappeared beneath the veil of the bride.

'This is surely a strong appetite for a bride,' Thrymm remarked, looking suspiciously at Loki.

'Ah! Well...' replied Loki, 'it is, um ... not surprising to me, er ... um ... after all, she has been so busy preparing herself for the wedding that she has had no time to eat for three days.'

The feast continued and Thrymm became more and more curious to see his bride. At last he could bear it no more and attempted to lift the grey veil. He only caught a glimpse of the face beneath and reeled back, amazed at the ruddy complexion and blazing eyes that he saw.

'Is this the face of the gentlest of all goddesses?' he asked Loki.

'Ah! Well...' replied Loki, 'er ... yes ... it is no wonder that she seems flushed and bright-eyed. For the last three days she has had no sleep because she was so excited by the idea of her forthcoming marriage, she was so overcome that it has given her a fever.'

At this Thrymm decided to delay no longer.

'Let us be married,' he roared.

'First the Bride-Gift,' insisted Loki. 'At so important a wedding all the customs must be obeyed.'

'Very well,' Thrymm agreed, and he commanded that the hammer should be brought from a side chamber where he had hidden it after bringing it from beneath the oceans.

Two servants carried it in and the other giants withdrew to a respectful distance, as did Loki, who knew exactly what was about to happen.

Ceremonially the hammer was laid across the knees of the bride. 'Now will you be mine?' demanded Thrymm of his bride.

'No,' replied the bride, 'but you shall be mine!' And casting off the veil and the cloak Thor swung the mighty Mjöllnir round his head and struck Thrymm as hard as he could.

At the first blow, all the greasy, red ribbons fell from Thrymm's hair and beard.

At the second blow, all Thrymm's yellow teeth fell out.

At the third blow, all Thrymm's black fingernails fell off.

And at the fourth blow, Thrymm was driven deep into the earth never to be seen again. Not that any of the giants saw this happen, for they had all fled from the hall after the second blow.

So Thor regained his hammer and Freyja remained free, and it is said that Thor carried the red ribbons and yellow teeth and black fingernails back to Freyja as a present — but it is also said that Freyja was not very pleased about it.

THOR, LOKI
AND THE ENCHANTER

Here is another adventure of Thor and his brother Loki. It shows how even the gods themselves may sometimes be deceived.

One day, Thor felt the need for adventure. He and his brother Loki left Asgard and came down the Bifrost bridge to earth. There they met two young peasants.

'We are off to seek an adventure,' Thor told the young men in his jolly booming voice, 'would you like to come with us?'

The two young men, who had no idea that Thor and Loki were gods, agreed and the four of them set off for Niflheim and the land of the giants. They marched along at a good pace and soon came to an enormous forest. This forest was so huge that even after three days of travelling they had still not come through it. On the third night Thor decided that they should rest and the two peasants were delighted, for they were amazed at the strength of their companions and had not liked to complain of tiredness.

'We must find shelter,' said Thor, 'for we shall be cold when we stop marching.'

He looked around and saw a house just ahead of them in a large clearing. A very strange house to be sure, but it seemed empty and would give them shelter.

They entered the house through its enormous doorway and found that there were five long narrow rooms leading off the central chamber.

'This will be fine,' boomed Thor. 'There is a room for each of us and one for our sacks of food.' Each of them made themselves comfortable and settled down to sleep. But sleep was difficult that night, for all through the hours of darkness they heard rumblings and groaning and the earth shook and quivered.

'How did you sleep?' Thor asked the others in the morning. 'I had a most disturbed night. Perhaps we should go on and find somewhere quieter to rest.'

They picked up their sacks of food and set off through the forest again. They had not gone very far when they came across the biggest giant any of them had ever seen. Although all of them had seen many giants in their time they were each amazed that anyone so big could live on the earth.

The giant was lying on his back snoring and wheezing and they understood now where the strange sounds that had kept them awake the night before had come from. They walked all round the giant and marvelled. Just as Thor was about to tap the giant lightly with his hammer to wake him up the giant stirred and stretched and stood up. He towered over them.

'Good morning,' he said, and his voice made the trees shake and the grass flatten as if in a gale. 'I am the giant Skrymir. I recognize you,' he said, pointing at Thor. 'You are Thor, the god of thunder.'

The two peasants were as amazed by this as they had been by the giant.

'No wonder they needed no rest in three days' marching,' one whispered to the other. 'We have been journeying with the gods!'

Skrymir stretched again and then looked around him.

'Where is my glove?' he asked. 'I must have dropped it.'

The four travellers then realized that they had spent the night inside the giant's glove. They led him to it and Skrymir asked if he might join them on their journey.

'Indeed you may,' answered Thor. 'But we shall stop early tonight, for we are all tired. You may carry our food sacks.'

They marched on and on and when night came Skrymir immediately lay down and fell asleep. Thor and his companions tried to open the sack of food, but Skrymir had tied it so tightly that even Thor could not loosen the drawstring that held the neck of the sack closed. This irritated Thor so much that he picked up his hammer and hit the sleeping giant on the head as hard as he could. Skrymir stirred in his sleep. 'The flies round here are very irritating,' he said and fell asleep again. This made Thor even angrier and again he swung his hammer at the giant's head, almost snapping the handle with the force of his blow.

'Mmmmm . . .' mumbled the giant. 'The night moths seem to be alighting on me.'

Again Thor swung his hammer and this time the hammer sank into Skrymir's head.

'Mngngngng . . .' muttered the giant, 'bird's eggs must be dropping out of the trees. I think I shall never get any sleep here.'

The giant rose and said to Thor and his companions, 'I shall be off now but if you go on to the castle over there, you will find giants far stronger than me. I am but a babe compared to them.'

The giant left and Thor, Loki and the two peasants journeyed on to the castle. The castle gateway towered over them and by the side of the gate was a vast iron bell. Thor rang it and demanded entrance.

A great voice boomed out at them.

'Whoever enters here must first prove his strength,' the voice roared. 'We will have no weaklings here.'

The voice belonged to Utgardaloki, the master of the castle and one of the most powerful magicians of that place.

'It is Thor. The god of thunder, and Loki, his brother, who rings,' Thor bellowed back. 'We will match our strength with any of you.'

Loki stepped forward. 'Throughout Asgard I am known as the mightiest eater of the gods,' he announced. 'I challenge any one of you to an eating match.'

At that a thin, red-headed giant called Logi stepped out and behind him two giants each carrying an enormous plate heaped high with joints of meat. There must have been meat from at least sixteen oxen on each plate. Loki sat down and started to eat and in no time had emptied the plate, leaving only the clean bones. Imagine his surprise when he looked at his opponent's plate and found that the thin red-haired man had eaten not only the meat but the bones and plate as well.

'I am the fastest runner on earth,' announced one of the peasants who had been journeying with Thor and Loki. 'I am Thjalfi the swift. Match me with one of your clumsy giants.'

At this another giant stepped out. His name was Hugi and he looked so weak and frail that Thor began to laugh. Utgardaloki gave the signal and Thjalfi and Hugi began to race. Although the peasant ran as fast as the wind he could not catch up with Hugi.

'And now it is my turn,' announced Thor. 'First I challenge anyone to outdrink me.' For Thor could drink more than any god or human.

An enormous drinking horn was brought out of the castle and Thor took a deep breath and raised it to his lips. He took three great gulps from the horn but to his amazement, when he put it down the level in the horn was only a little lower than before.

'I am also the strongest of all the gods,' he boasted, 'give me another test.'

'If you can lift my cat up, then I shall believe that you are the strongest,' said Utgardaloki. He whistled and a small grey cat slunk out of the castle. Thor grinned and bent down to lift the little animal, but no matter how hard he tried he could only lift one paw of the cat from the ground.

'One last test,' Thor demanded, 'and then I shall admit defeat.'

'Very well,' said Utgardaloki. 'You must wrestle with my old nurse Elli and we shall see who wins.'

An old, wrinkled woman came slowly out of the castle and stood before Thor.

'Are you afraid to wrestle with an old woman?' she demanded. 'No, by the Bifrost Bridge!' retorted Thor, and rushed at her. They grappled together and slowly but surely, Elli forced Thor to his knees.

Thor and Loki were ashamed and amazed.

'Never have I been beaten before,' said Thor. 'These are indeed mighty giants.' They turned to go when Utgardaloki stopped them.

'Stay a moment,' he said. 'I will explain why you were defeated. I would never dare to let you in, for you are truly the strongest gods of all. When you met Skrymir in the forest it was none other than myself. When I lay down I covered my head with mountains to protect myself. You may see what damage you did.'

Thor looked at the mountain range in the distance and saw huge trenches and valleys had been gouged out of it.

'When Loki tried to outeat Logi, he failed because Logi is none other than fire, and fire consumes everything. Thjalfi has been beaten by Hugi because Hugi is thought, which runs faster than anything. The drinking horn that Thor could not empty is always full because the other end is dipped into the sea, and by lowering the level of the horn, Thor has caused the first tides to appear. The cat is none other than the serpent Midgard, which is coiled round the centre of the earth and by lifting one paw, Thor has caused gigantic earthquakes. Finally the old nurse, Elli, is really old age, and no one can defeat age. So you see, your strength is amazing.'

Thor was furious when he found out that he had been tricked. With a mighty war cry he rushed at Utgardaloki and raised his hammer to smash him into the ground. But the magician was too quick for him and in a twinkling the castle and the giants disappeared, leaving only the sighing trees of the forest and the rushing winds of the plain.

MARGOT THE BLACK

This is the tale of a terrible queen. A woman so evil that she willingly made a pact with the Devil. A woman so wicked that she was prepared to give away another life to gain what she wanted.

Margot, daughter of Sambor, Duke of Pomerania, was said to be so beautiful that few men could look at her without being overcome by her loveliness. Certainly King Christopher of Denmark fell in love with her and married her without knowing that her beauty hid a heart as hard and cruel as winter.

Soon the people of Denmark began to hear tales of her cruelty, tales of her greed and wicked ways. It was even said that she could call up the Devil. She was never known as Queen Margot, only as Margot the Black.

In the reign of King Christopher, Denmark was often at war. The frontiers could not be defended well and fighting constantly broke out along the borders of the land. King Christopher asked his queen for help. She agreed, but warned the king that she must be allowed to do whatever she wanted or she could not help him. Weakly the king agreed.

That night Margot the Black conjured up the Devil. She made a bargain with him.

'If you build a wall for me,' she told Satan, 'I will give you anything you want. The wall must be high and strong, with iron gates — it must stretch across the borders of our land and keep out any enemies of Denmark.'

'If I do this for you,' said Satan, 'what will you give me in return?'

Margot the Black was wise in the ways of evil and knew that the Devil liked nothing better than the souls of innocent people.

'I will give you the soul of the first living thing to pass through the iron gates,' she said. She pricked her finger and signed her name in her own blood and so the pact was sealed.

That night was the blackest night ever known in Denmark. People locked themselves in their houses and peered timorously through the shutters. Strange noises filled the land and terrible figures were seen against the clouds. The smell of sulphur crept into the houses and a dull red glow was noticed over the borders of Denmark. In the morning a huge wall with just one iron gate stood stern and harsh against the sky. The Devil had fulfilled his part of the bargain and now waited for Margot to pay the dreadful price.

Margot the Black stood on the ramparts of the terrible wall and watched for the first unwary traveller. About midday a travelling merchant came into sight, and Margot chuckled. Here was her hostage. Here was the innocent soul she had promised to the Devil.

'Open the gates,' she called down to the guards, 'welcome the poor traveller in.' The guards obeyed, although they were surprised that their wicked queen should show such hospitality. As the great iron gates creaked open the weary merchant spurred his horse on. But before he could pass through, his little dog, who had been running beside his horse, darted ahead and so passed through the gates first. The Devil was furious, but the bargain had to be kept. He had been promised the first living thing to pass through the gates and so he had to be content with the dog and not the merchant. He vowed then never to deal with Margot the Black again. Margot, too, was furious, for she knew that she could never call on Satan again and her power would from that day never be so strong.

But that is not the end of the story. When Margot the Black died her ghost came back to haunt the ramparts of the great wall. Every night she could be seen, dressed in a great black cloak, riding on a white charger with her raven hair blowing in the wind and a crown on fire round her head. The wicked spirit of the woman who made a pact with the Devil has no rest and it is said that even today her ghost still haunts the ruins of the wall.

BIG KAMINIK

This story comes from the frozen lands of the north. Eskimo mothers have told it to their children for many years, and in Greenland, where this tale comes from, the children often skip to the words of the song that was once sung about Kaminik.

Once upon a time there lived a fisherman and his wife. They lived in the village of Norssit which in those days was near to the sea. Today, the same village is found high up in the mountains. Now, you may say that a village cannot possibly change its position, but this is just what happened and this is how it came about.

The fisherman and his wife had one child, a boy that they called Kaminik. The years passed and while the other children of the village grew tall and strong, little Kaminik never grew any taller than he had been when he was three, even though he was nearly twenty years old.

Because he was so small he was afraid of almost everything and spent a great deal of his time hiding away from the fierce husky dogs that pulled the villagers' sledges over the icy lands round the village. When he did creep out from his hiding place, the village children would dance round him and sing this song:

Poor Little Kaminik

You don't grow so quick

We are growing tall

You stay very small,

and they would make snowballs and throw them at him and chase him back to his mother and father's house where he would hide again.

His father, too, used to say to Kaminik,

'You are so small; all the other village boys help their fathers when they can. They go out with them fishing and hunting for seals and whales, but you cannot help me. You're far too small and not even as strong as the kitten that plays by your mother's hearth. You will never grow up into a man.'

This made Kaminik very sad and he decided that he would leave the village and go out into the world where no one knew him and no one would tease him. His mother made a kayak for him out of sealskins and sadly waved goodbye as her son set out across the icy seas.

Kaminik steadily paddled his kayak through the waves and as he looked back he could see the shore and the village growing smaller and smaller until they disappeared into the mist. All that day and night he paddled on, through seas that grew colder and colder. Enormous icebergs towered above him and on one of them he saw a gigantic seagull, four or five times bigger than himself. Kaminik was very frightened.

'This is a strange part of the world,' he thought to himself. 'Even back at the village, where everything seemed bigger than me, I never saw a seagull as big as that!' He paddled on as fast as he could. He was growing very tired by now, and then, ahead of the prow of his little boat, he saw an island.

'I shall rest here,' he said to himself, but before he had reached the shore of the island, it began to move. Kaminik looked in amazement as first an enormous head and then an enormous body rose up out of the middle of the island! It was the Giant Akitinek. The giant stretched and yawned, and his yawn caused huge waves that very nearly upset Kaminik's little kayak. Kaminik cried out in fear and the giant heard him. Reaching down, the giant took up Kaminik and his kayak in one huge hand.

'What have we here?' boomed the giant, peering down at Kaminik. 'A little man I declare! I shall take you home to show my wife,' he said and began to wade through the sea, carrying Kaminik carefully. When the giant reached the mainland of Greenland where he lived, he walked ashore and strode over the mountains, until he came to his house.

'Here you are, my dear,' he said to his wife, placing Kaminik and his kayak on the table, 'I have brought you a present.'

Akitinek's wife was almost as large as her husband, but even though she was so much bigger than he was, Kaminik could see that she had a kind face.

'Oh,' said the giantess, clasping her hands together, 'he is so sweet. I have always wanted a little boy of my own. We shall bring him up as our son. What do you think of that, little man?' she asked, but Kaminik did not reply, he had fallen sound asleep in his kayak.

So Kaminik stayed with the giant Akitinek and his wife and was very happy with them. The giants were always very gentle with him, but at first Kaminik was often frightened, for in the land of the giants everything is big and the houseflies seemed like big birds, and the spiders like large dogs. Soon though, Kaminik noticed a strange thing. The spiders and the flies seemed to be getting smaller, and so did Akitinek and his wife. Kaminik could not understand it and then one day, Akitinek said to him,

'Well well, my little adopted son, you seem to be growing up at last.'

It was true. Kaminik grew in leaps and bounds, and soon he was as tall as Akitinek and just as strong. He could catch seals and whales with his hands and once, he even wrestled with a huge polar bear and overcame it. Akitinek and his wife watched all this with pride. One day, Akitinek said to Kaminik,

'It is many years since you have seen your real parents. Would you like to journey to Norssit to see them again?'

'I would, adopted father,' answered Kaminik.

Together they made an enormous kayak for Kaminik. It was so large that it took the skins of a hundred seals to cover it. Each blade of the paddle that Kaminik used was as big as a double bed, and its handle was as long as a fir tree is tall. Akitinek's wife loaded the kayak with food, for Kaminik's appetite was now so huge that he would eat a whole ovenful of loaves at one sitting and still be hungry for more. She also put many presents in the kayak for Kaminik's parents.

'Promise that you will come back,' begged the giantess. 'We have come to love you so much and you are now so huge that you will not be comfortable living with ordinary people.'

'I promise to return,' said Kaminik, 'for I am happy here, but I wish to see my village again and surprise all those who once laughed at me for being so small.'

Kaminik set off. What had seemed such a long journey when he was small now took only half a day. He arrived at Norssit just as the men had returned from a fishing expedition. Kaminik could see his father unloading the fish from the boats and his mother standing at the doorway of their house. Kaminik stood up in his kayak and called out a greeting to them. You can imagine how amazed the villagers of Norssit were to see such a giant.

'Do you not remember me?' called Kaminik, and he sang the song that they had taunted him with so many years ago.

'Poor little Kaminik
You don't grow so quick
We are growing tall
You stay very small.'

And then he laughed and laughed until the houses shook and all the husky dogs that had once frightened him so much ran away and hid under the sledges. Kaminik took the presents to his parents and told them all that had happened to him. That night they feasted and made merry and in the morning Kaminik said farewell to them all.

Before he left he did a strange thing. He carefully lifted up all the houses of the village of Norssit and placed them on the top of the mountain.

'Why are you doing this?' the villagers asked him.

'It is to keep you safe,' he told them, 'for when I launch my kayak, the waves that it makes would drown the whole village if it was not high up and away from the sea.'

Then Kaminik launched his kayak and it was just as he said. The waves rose up and up until they covered the place where Norssit had once stood.

And that is why the village of Norssit is now found high up in the mountains instead of by the sea, and that is the end of the tale of Big Kaminik who was once the smallest man in Greenland.

THE LIVING DEAD

This is a strange and mysterious tale about two graveyards, a rich merchant and the spirits of the dead. It all begins on the borders of Lithuania and Germany at a little village called Ragnit. This village was known as 'Ragnit of the two Cemeteries', for close together to the west of the village lay two graveyards; one was the German cemetery and the other was the Lithuanian cemetery.

Ragnit was a happy village, surrounded by beautiful countryside and close to the swiftly flowing river Niemen. Why then, during the stormy months of the autumn did the people of Ragnit hide inside their houses and bolt the doors and bar the windows? Why did they lock up their dogs and cats and tie their horses up in the stalls in the barns and stables? Why did the cattle in the fields and the pigs in the sties crouch low into the straw while the chickens clucked and fussed and hid their heads under their wings and didn't look out until morning? Because on those dark and stormy nights the spirits of the dead travelled between the two graveyards to visit each other.

For the rest of the year the people of Ragnit went about their business in the normal way, no one minded being out after dark at all, but when the winter months came, up would go the shutters and locks would be put on all the doors. One day, a rich merchant came to live in Ragnit. There was no house splendid enough for him so he decided to build one himself. He chose a plot of land that lay directly between the two graveyards for, he thought to himself,

'Here I have space all round me, no one can look into my windows, no one will cross my land or walk over my flowerbeds.'

The villagers looked at each other and nodded wisely, but they said nothing to the rich merchant because he was still a stranger to them, and they took many years to accept strangers into their midst.

Soon the splendid house was finished and the merchant moved in and furnished it richly. The summer months passed and all was well and then, autumn came and with it the first night of the storms!

The merchant heard the wind howling round the house and went outside to see that his horses were safely in the stable. As he stepped out of the house a great gust of wind rushed across the land and his house fell in a heap at his feet. The merchant was amazed and angered.

'That was a fierce wind,' he thought, 'but even so my house should not have fallen down.'

He rebuilt the house, but it was no use. The next stormy night came and down fell his house again. This happened three times and at last the merchant decided that he must go and ask the wise man of the village why it was that only his house fell down during the stormy nights while all the other houses of Ragnit stood firmly through the strongest gales.

The wise man of the village had been born between the first two strokes of midnight on the night of All Hallows, and all people born at that moment have 'second sight' and can see things that ordinary men and women cannot.

'Come with me,' said the wise man to the merchant, 'I will show you why your house falls down on stormy nights.' They walked to the heap of rubble that had once been the merchant's house.

'You see, over there, and over there,' said the wise man pointing first to the German Cemetery and then to the Lithuanian Cemetery. 'Those are the resting places of the dead of our village. But they do not always rest, on stormy nights they fly up from their graves and visit each other, just as they used to do when they were alive. Now look around you and see if you can see any other houses.'

'Why, I cannot,' said the merchant. 'Only that old barn over there.'

'That is because the people of the village know very well that they must not build anything that would stop the dead from visiting each other. Farmer Hans built that barn, but the corner stuck out into the pathway of the dead and look what they did to it.'

The merchant looked, and could see that the corner of the barn had been cut off as if an enormous pair of shears had cut it away.

'If you wish your house to stand, you must build it away from the pathway of the dead,' the wise man told the merchant. 'Only then will it stand in peace.' And that is just what the merchant did. He built his house right away from the two cemeteries, as did all the other villagers of Ragnit, and for all I know, are doing so still.

TILL EULENSPIEGEL

Till Eulenspiegel was a most mysterious character: he was said to have been born in Germany about 1300. He was thought to be the son of a peasant and many amusing stories were told about him. He was rather like Simple Simon of the nursery rhyme, silly and seemingly stupid but very cunning when he wanted to get his own way. Stories of how he had tricked noblemen, innkeepers, tradesmen and clergymen were written down in a book that was published in 1519 which was later translated into English under the name of 'The Marvellous Tales of Master Tyll Owlglass'. Even before this he became so famous that as far away as England, in the fourteenth century, the English poet Chaucer retold one of Till's adventures as part of the Summoner's Tale, one of the Canterbury Tales.

Hundreds of songs and plays were written about him and paintings of some of his most famous exploits were made, and can still be seen today.

No one really knows for sure whether Till actually existed, but there is museum to Till Eulenspiegel at Schoppenstedt in Germany and a tomb at Molln where he is supposed to be buried. This is probably the most peculiar tomb in the whole of Germany. The strange thing about it is that instead of being buried lying down as everybody was in those days, Till is supposed to be buried upright, and what is even more peculiar, no one knows whether he is buried standing on his feet or on his head, a fitting memorial to a man who spent his life fooling people. The gravestone above the tomb is carved with these words:

In 1350 these words were written,
When Till Eulenspiegel was sheltered here.
All you who pass here
Always think,
That what has happened to me,
Will one day happen to you!

And on the top of the tombstone on the left is a carving of a wise owl, and on the top at the right is a mirror. This is a pun on the meaning of his name, 'Eulen,' which means owl and 'spiegel,' which means mirror.

WISE LIBUSE

Today, Prague is one of the greatest cities of Europe, but it was not always so. In the olden days when Prince Krok ruled Bohemia, the city of Prague did not exist. There was only a small town called Vysehrad near to where Prague is now. This is the story of Princess Libuse of Vysehrad, and how the city of Prague was founded.

Krok of Bohemia had three daughters. The oldest was called Kazi and had long blond hair and green eyes. She was tall and graceful and could play the harp like an angel. The second daughter was called Teta and was round and plump with a lovely smile. She could embroider so well that butterflies would alight on the flowers that she had made from silken threads because they thought the flowers were real. The youngest daughter was called Libuse. She was the merriest of the sisters and could call the birds of the air down to her where they would flutter about her head and sing to her. All the sisters were beautiful and very clever and all of them knew a great deal about magic. This was not the sort of magic which brought harm to people, but the sort which helps the crops to grow and cures illness and brings happiness and laughter to the land. The three sisters gave advice freely and helped everyone they could. Libuse was the sweetest of the sisters and the people loved her. They flocked to the great castle of Vysehrad to ask for her help and listen to her wise words.

When Krok died the people of Bohemia chose Libuse to be their princess and in a magnificent ceremony at the biggest church in Vysehrad she was crowned and declared to be the ruler of all Bohemia.

For several years Libuse ruled her people wisely and well. Bohemia was a happy land and everything prospered because it was guided by such a clever ruler; but after several years people began to murmur and mutter.

'Libuse is very beautiful,' they said, 'and still not married. It is time she chose a husband.'

They went to the princess and asked her why she had not married.

'I have never found any man I can love,' she told them. 'My country is my first love.'

So the years passed and although many suitors came to court Libuse, none of them gained her hand.

At that time there were several noblemen in Bohemia who were quarrelling about who owned the lands round Vysehrad. They simply could not agree and so they went to Princess Libuse to ask her to decide. The princess thought about the matter carefully and then gave her judgement; she awarded the land to the poorest of the noblemen. This led to a great uproar.

'Now see what becomes of us when we are ruled by a woman,' said the noblemen who had lost their lands. 'It is time we had a man on the throne. He would not be so soft.'

When Libuse heard this she was very angry, but she hid her anger. 'Are you sure that you wish to be ruled by a man?' she asked them. 'Do I really care for you so badly? You think that I am too gentle. Very well, come to the castle tomorrow morning and I will tell you the name of the man I will marry.' That night Libuse went to the temple of the pagan god that she worshipped.

'Great Perun!' she prayed. 'Tell me what I must do. '

For many hours she prayed, but no answer came to her. Then, just as dawn was breaking, the voice of the god Perun spoke. Libuse listened and bowed her head.

'It shall be so,' she said, and returned to the castle where her people were waiting.

Once again she asked them if they really wanted to be ruled by a king.

'It is easy to choose a king, but what will you do if he is cruel and wicked. He holds the power of life and death over you. Your lands and houses will belong to him and not to you. Now you are free, but how do you know that the man who I marry will not be stern and harsh? Once you have chosen the king you cannot put him away easily. Think again, my people, are you not content as you are?'

But the Bohemian people would not listen to their princess.

'Tell us the name of our king,' they demanded. 'Tell us the name of the man you will marry.'

'Very well,' sighed Libuse. 'He is called Premysl. He lives in a village called Stadice, which lies by the River Belina.' 'How will we recognize him?' they asked.

'He is a tall man, with golden eyes. He works in the fields and his plough is pulled by two white bulls and he eats from a table of iron. Go and ask him to be your king. Take royal robes with you so that he may be royally dressed when he comes to take the crown.'

'How shall we find the way?' they asked.

'Take my two white horses and ride to the south from here. When you reach the valley of the River Belina you will see Stadice at the foot of the mountains.'

126

What wise Libuse did not tell them was that Premysl had been chosen by the god Perun, and that her magic had shown her that he would become a great ruler and king, the founder of a line of kings and queens of Bohemia.

The messengers set out and soon reached Stadice. In a huge field outside the village they found Premysl ploughing the land with a great plough pulled by two white bulls.

The messengers fell to their knees before him and told him that he had been chosen to be the king of Bohemia.

'Very well,' said Premysl, 'but before I come with you we will all eat together.' Premysl unyoked the two bulls and turned them loose.

'Go back to where you came from,' he ordered, and the messengers watched in amazement as the two bulls rose into the air and disappeared.

From his pocket Premysl took a long loaf of bread and broke it in half. One half he thrust into the ground and the other half he put back into his pocket. With a mighty heave he turned his enormous plough over so that the blade was uppermost making a rough iron table and on this he put the half loaf and some cheese from his pocket. He walked over to a nearby spring and brought back water and then the messengers and Premysl ate a hearty meal. After they had finished, Premysl dressed himself in his new robes.

'I am nearly ready,' Premysl told the messengers. 'Let me see what the future holds.'

He turned to where he had planted the half loaf and there, in its place, grew a strange tree. It had three branches covered with leaves and fruit, but two of the branches were withered while the tallest one was laden with heavy fruit.

'This means that I shall be the founder of many royal dynasties, but only one will prosper,' Premysl said.

Before they left for Vysehrad Premysl put his old pair of wooden shoes into his pocket.

'This will remind me and my children and my grandchildren that we are all descended from humble peasants; even though we will be rulers from now on, we must never become vain or haughty,' he said.

So Premysl married Libuse and ruled the country justly. It was Premysl who founded the city of Prague and made it rich — so rich that it became known as the Golden City. He never forgot that he was once a humble peasant and even today, the coat of arms of Vysehrad bear a picture of the wooden shoes that Premysl carried with him.

ALBERT
THE GREAT MAGICIAN

In the year 1193, in the little town of Lauingen in Germany, a boy was born who was one day to be known as one of the wisest men who had ever lived. He was born the son of the Count of Bollstädt and was christened Albert. When he grew up he became a monk of the Dominican order and studied at Paris and Cologne. He wrote thirty-nine books and was famous all over Europe for his learning and scholarship. When he gave a sermon, people would come from miles around to hear the great man speak and listen to his wisdom. Famous men, such as Thomas Aquinas, studied with him and learned from him. History books speak of him as Albert the Great, Count of Bollstädt.

Albert was not only learned in academic subjects, but knew a great deal about the occult sciences. It is said that he could predict the future, could conjure up bodiless heads who would speak to bystanders and tell them what would happen to them in life. It was believed that he could speak strange incantations and change icy winter into warm summer in less than a second.

Even more miraculous than this, he once held a splendid feast for King William of the Low Countries. When the royal guest arrived he was startled to find that the table, although laid with wonderful crystal glasses and silver and gold plates and cutlery, had not a scrap of food or wine on it.

'I see that we shall go hungry tonight,' the king remarked.

'Not at all, sire,' replied Albert the Great, 'I have a marvel to show your majesty.' He turned to his servants. 'Draw the tapestries over the windows,' he commanded, 'light the sconces and throw herbs into the fire.'

The servants obeyed and the room was lit only by the flickering light from the sconces set round the walls. The sweet smell of herbs rose from the fire and Albert's guest watched in amazed silence as the magician took out a long ebony wand. He drew a huge circle round the table and made sinuous movements in the air with his arms. The fire flared up and there, on the table, a marvellous meal appeared. Haunches of venison on silver salvers, roast meats and chickens, and salmon surrounded by succulent vegetables, fresh peaches and cherries — a meal truly fit for a king.

One of the strangest tales told about Albert the Great is how he humbled a king. This is what happened: One summer, a young man made the acquaintance of Albert the Great. This young man was an idle fellow who had wasted his father's fortune. He flattered Albert and pretended friendship with him. One evening the two were drinking together when the young man lifted his glass and said to Albert,

'My dear friend, today I am poor, but if ever I should become rich and powerful, I shall never forget you.'

Now soon after this the young man came into a fortune, and what was more, became first a Count, then a Duke and finally a King. Everything he touched prospered and he became immensely wealthy with several large palaces, hundreds of acres of land and servants by the thousand. News of this came to Albert the Great.

At this time, Albert had fallen on hard times. Although he still kept his house, he had very little money and at times was forced to beg through the streets for a living. He remembered the promise that the young man had made to him and decided to visit this king who had once sworn never to forget his old friend.

The journey was hard and long and when Albert arrived and asked for an audience he was kept waiting for many hours. At last he was ushered into the throne room.

'Sire,' he said, bowing before the splendidly dressed monarch, 'you are wealthy and well fed, while I am poor and hungry — can you spare alms for an unfortunate brother?'

'Certainly not,' the haughty king replied. 'A fine thing it would be if I had to concern myself with all the poor of the world. If I gave alms to every beggar I might just as well give up my throne.'

'So be it then,' said Albert, 'as surely as you are holding that glass.'

The king looked at the poor beggar in horror and the glass slipped from his grasp and shattered on the marble floor.

'Now perhaps you remember me,' Albert the Great said sternly. 'Do your promises mean so little to you, and is your heart so proud that you have no room in it for kindness and charity?' In a twinkling the grand palace was gone and the king found himself sitting on a crude wooden bench in the house of Albert the Magician.

'What has happened?' asked the bewildered king. 'Where am I?'

'Brought down by your pride and haughtiness,' Albert told him. 'You think that you have been king for three years, but it has all passed away in three seconds. Your ingratitude has cost you your kingdom.'

This was only one of the wonderful stories told about Albert the Great. He lived to a ripe old age and when he died the townspeople of Lauingen built a monument in honour of their most famous citizen.

THE DRAGON GUELRE

In France, between the rivers Rhine and Meuse, there is an area called the Gueldre. You may say that this is a strange name for a region and so it is, but the reason for the name is even stranger.

Long ago this part of France was plagued by the most awful dragon. To be sure there were many dragons in those parts, but this one was particularly horrible. It was covered in slimy scales and had glaring red eyes. Its teeth were as long as barbers' poles and the spike on its tail was so sharp that it mowed the grass in the meadows when the dragon swished it about. But what was particularly fright-ful about this dragon was the noise that it made. When it heard anybody coming it would roar, "GUELRE, GUELRE". This may not look frightening when it is written down, but you try saying it aloud in a gruff voice and then imagine that sound magnified sixteen thousand times! The dragon frightened the people so much that no one ever dared to try and kill it. Indeed, they were so terrified of it that they would not go anywhere near its lair in case they heard the dreadful noise it made.

Since the dragon's lair was near the best grazing land for miles about, the cows could not graze and became thinner and thinner and the people became poorer and poorer. This state of affairs would have lasted for ever had not one brave man decided that the time had come to do something about it. This man was called Leopold von Pond and he was the son of the local landowner.

'I am going to fight the dragon!' he told his father. 'I have read a story where a tiny mouse defeated a great lion because it was not afraid. I shall do the same.'

Leopold von Pond buckled on his armour and sharpened up his lance until it was so sharp that it could cut the breeze into little pieces. Then he set off on foot because it was not too far to the dragon's lair and anyway his horse refused to come out of the stable. As he neared the lair the noise of his armour clanking woke the dragon up.

'GUELRE, GUELRE, GUELRE!' roared the dragon, and the sound was so horrible that even the brave Leopold shook and shiv-ered inside his chain mail.

'GUELRE, GUELRE!' roared the dragon again, puffing out clouds of evil-smelling smoke and sulphur. Soon the air was so full of smoke that the dragon could not see what Leopold was doing, which was just as well, because Leopold had crept up behind the dragon and was about to stab him with his razor-sharp lance.

One thrust and it was done.

'GUELRE . . . GUEL . . . GU . .' moaned the dragon and then no more was heard. Brave Leopold von Pond had killed the dragon and the people could live happily ever after. In thanksgiving the people of the region built a splendid castle for Leopold on the very spot where he had killed the dragon. The king knighted him and gave him the title of Count of Guelre and ever after the region was known as the Gueldre in honour of the brave knight who had delivered the countryside from terror.

THE PIED PIPER
OF HAMELIN

The town of Hamelin was in an uproar: there were mice and rats everywhere! Rats in the houses, rats in the barns, rats in the streets, rats in the palace and the Mayor's office. Mice ran about all over the place. They hid in the pantries and kitchens, eating everything they could find. They hid in the wardrobes and made nests among the clothes, they scampered about in the Council Chamber and their squeaking made it difficult for the Mayor to be heard.

'Something has got to be done!' announced the Mayor, brushing a cheeky mouse from his hat where it was eating the feather. 'This state of affairs simply cannot be allowed. I haven't had a wink of sleep for three weeks and my wife tells me that as soon as she bakes any bread the mice and rats queue up outside the kitchen and when her back is turned, they rush in and devour it all.'

'That's right, that's right,' said Adolphus the Corn Merchant. 'I have put padlocks on all my storeroom doors but it's no use, the rats chew their way through the walls and raid the corn and barley. If this goes on we shall starve in a few weeks.'

'Look at my cloak,' said Bartholomew the Tailor, 'the mice have nibbled away all the fur from the edge and last night began to eat the silk lining. We shall have nothing to wear if no one rids us of these pests.'

'Worst of all,' said the Town Clerk solemnly, 'several rats have eaten three books of the laws passed by the Council and unless we stop them no-one will know what to do or how to behave.'

'We will offer a reward to whoever can rid us of these creatures,' said the Mayor. 'How much do you think would be suitable?'

'Not too much,' said the Town Clerk.

'One hundred crowns and not a penny more!' said the Mayor.

A large notice was nailed to the Town Hall door and the people of Hamelin waited to see who would come and save them. Not a single person arrived and in desperation the Mayor and the Council raised the reward to five hundred golden crowns, and sent the Town Crier of Hamelin out into the countryside to tell everyone about it.

And then, in May, a strange man arrived at the Town Hall.

'Well,' said the Mayor, looking scornfully at the man's tattered clothes. 'What do you want?'

'I am the Pied Piper,' responded the tattered man. 'I can rid you of

the plague of rats and mice. Is it true that there is a reward of five hundred golden crowns?'

'It is,' said the Mayor, 'but I don't believe that you can do it.'

'Oh, but I can,' said the tattered man, 'but you must promise that I shall receive the reward if I succeed.'

'Of course, of course,' said the Mayor, but already his crafty mind was working out how to cheat the Pied Piper.

The Pied Piper strode out of the Town Hall and took a thin reed pipe from his pocket. Putting it to his lips he began to play a strange tune. The sound of the flute curled round the houses like wisps of smoke. To the amazement of the citizens of Hamelin, the rats and mice began to pour out into the streets. As the Pied Piper walked along, still playing his pipe, the horde of rats and mice followed him, out of the town, across the countryside and away from Hamelin.

The next day the Pied Piper came back to Hamelin, but not a single rat or mouse followed him. He marched up to the Town Hall and demanded his reward.

'The reward was offered to the person who would rid Hamelin of all the rats and mice,' said the Mayor. 'It will not be given if one single rat or mouse remains.'

'That is so,' said the Pied Piper. 'The reward is mine.'

'Then what is this?' asked the Mayor, taking from his pocket a tiny, terrified mouse (a mouse that he had caught the day before and hidden away so that he could cheat the Pied Piper).

'No reward for you,' said the Mayor. 'This little mouse proves that you have not done what you claimed.'

The Pied Piper looked steadily at the Mayor. 'I will give you one month to reconsider,' he told him, 'and if, when I return, you do not deal with me fairly, then I shall take my own reward, and it will be something that you cannot afford to lose,' and he turned on his heel and left.

'Ha!' said the Mayor, 'what can a ragamuffin like that do?'

The month passed and the Pied Piper returned.

'Will you give me my reward?' he asked.

'No,' replied the Mayor.

'Very well then,' said the Pied Piper.

Once again he took out his pipe and began to play the haunting tune. This time it was not the rats or mice who followed him, but all the children of Hamelin. They followed the Pied Piper away from Hamelin and not one of them ever returned. So the town of Hamelin paid a far greater price than they expected, and all because of the greed of the Mayor.

THE FAITHFUL WIVES
OF WEINSBERG

There is a town in Germany called Weinsberg, dominated by the ruins of a large castle which is called The Castle of the Faithful Wives. Here is the story of how it got its name.

In the middle of the twelfth century King Conrad III laid siege to the castle because his life-long enemy, Duke Welf of Bavaria, had sought refuge there. The siege went on for month after month.

Every day a messenger of the King would ride up to the foot of the castle wall and call out, 'Duke Welf! Your King demands that you surrender to him.'

And each morning the messenger received the same reply; 'Tell your King to go to the Devil.'

The Duke knew that winter would soon be upon them and that his supplies would not be able to last until spring, but still he refused to surrender, until one morning when his commander came to him and said, 'Sire, we have two days' food left. The well is running dry. We must surrender'.

'Never!' cried the brave Duke, but he knew that what had been said was true.

With sorrow in his heart he awaited the King's messenger the next morning, and when he heard the cry, 'Duke Welf! Your King demands that you surrender,' the Duke replied, 'Very well, but I ask for safe conduct for my men and their wives and myself and my wife back to our own castle in Bavaria. If this assurance is given, I will surrender.'

The messenger rode back to the King and repeated Welf's message. 'I agree,' the King said, 'that the womenfolk may return to Bavaria in safety. And with them they may take anything that they can carry on their backs. But the men, I will put to the sword.'

The message was duly presented to Duke Welf. The Duke listened horrified and was about to shout his refusal when his wife, who was at his side, stopped him, and whispered something to him.

'But, my dear!' he gasped with surprise. 'To accept these terms means certain death for me and my men.'

'Accept the terms and I will never again ask you for anything.'

'If I accept them, I will not be here for you to ask,' the Duke replied.

But the Duchess was so insistent that, with a heavy heart, the

Duke shouted to the messenger below. 'Very well. Tell your master that I accept. The women will leave at dawn tomorrow. Tell your King that I trust him, and that they will be allowed to return to Bavaria with all that they can carry on their backs.'

Word spread around the castle that at dawn, all the women were to leave with whatever they could carry on their backs. The night was spent in frenzied preparations and tearful farewells. Many of the wives declared that they would rather remain and die with their husbands, but the Duchess was adamant.

And so, at dawn the following morning, the courtyard was filled with weeping women carrying bundles and baskets on their backs. They stood waiting for the Duchess to lead them from the castle.

But when she appeared from her chambers, a puzzled gasp went up from the women and their husbands, for she was carrying nothing. And the Duke, who was at her side, was wearing, not his heavy armour, but a light doublet and hose.

As the sun's rays crept into the courtyard the Duchess cried to the women, 'Put down your possessions and do as I do.'

And to the men she cried, 'Take off your armour!'

The men and women, mystified, did as they were bid.

'Page,' the Duchess commanded, 'open the door. And, brave women, do as I now do and prepare to carry your most precious possession out of this place.' Having said that she bent down and her husband gently climbed upon her back. She almost stumbled under his weight, but somehow she managed to straighten herself and carry him through the open gates. The other wives did likewise.

Within minutes a very strange procession was to be seen winding its way out of the castle gates and past the astonished eyes of the King and his army.

When the King saw the faithful wives struggling to keep straight under the weights they were carrying, he was impressed. He turned to his brother and said, 'Would that our womenfolk would be so faithful. They could have carried fine cloths, precious jewels, gold and silver. But, no. They carry their menfolk.'

'But these are your enemies,' his brother protested. 'You must kill them or you will live to regret it.'

'But I gave my word. I said that the women could have safe conduct back to Bavaria along with whatever they could carry. I did not specify what that should be. If a King's word cannot be kept, then it is a sorry world we live in.' And he sent his messenger to tell the women that their faithfulness had so impressed him that they could put their men down and continue their journey home in safety.

ONDIN AND THE SALT

In Austria, many hundreds of years ago, there lived an old fisherman called Friedl. He lived in a large house on the banks of a large lake, with his daughter, Gunde. Friedl was very old and could not handle his fishing tack very well, so it was left to Gunde to do most of the fishing. Every morning, she would row out into the middle of the lake and spend the hours hard at work. When she returned home, her father would inspect the morning's catch and no matter how many fish she had caught, he was never satisfied.

Friedl was much too mean to pay for a servant, so poor Gunde spent the rest of the day cleaning and cooking, but she did not really mind because she loved her father dearly.

As well as being hard working, Gunde was also extremely beautiful, and many men from far and near had asked Friedl for her hand in marriage. But each time Friedl refused. Who else would do his fishing, clean his house and cook his meals? If Friedl allowed Gunde to marry he would have to pay three servants to do her work.

Gunde was not upset. Although she had liked all the men who had asked her to marry them, she had not yet been in love.

One day, however, a handsome young hunter came to live in the forest. His name was Antoine and as soon as Gunde saw him she fell head over heels in love with him. And as soon as he set eyes on Gunde, he fell hopelessly in love with her. The happy couple spent hour after hour walking through the forest and along the shores of the lake, talking about the future and how happy they would be when they were married.

Gunde and Antoine decided on a day when Antoine should come to the cottage and ask Friedl for Gunde's hand. On the appointed day, Antoine duly turned up, his heart beating wildly.

Now, Antoine was as brave as any man and better-looking than most, but he was poor — as poor as poor could be. So when Friedl asked him if he would be willing to pay for the servants that he would need to replace Gunde, Antoine could only shake his head. 'Then go,' said Friedl. 'Come back when you are rich enough and then you may marry Gunde, but until then I forbid you to see her.'

Gunde was an obedient child and did mean to stop seeing Antoine, but her love for him was so strong that occasionally she would slip out of the house to meet her lover. 'One day you will be rich,' she would say comfortingly to him, 'and Papa will have to let us marry, then.'

But Antoine knew that no matter how hard he worked in the forest, he would never be able to afford to pay for three servants. And he grew sadder and sadder.

One night after one of their meetings when the two lovers had talked and talked about what life would be like when they were married, Antoine was unable to sleep, so he decided to go fishing. The day had been very cold and the moon shone down from the cloudless sky. Stars twinkled and glittered from the velvet blackness and as Antoine walked to the lakeside he could not help but be filled with wonder by the beauty of the night. When he arrived at the water's edge, he cast his line and sat under an old oak tree and began to think of his dear Gunde.

After a few minutes, the line tightened and the rod was almost snatched from his hands. Antoine stood up and began to pull in the line. But the fish was not going to give in easily. 'It must be enormous,' thought Antoine as he struggled to land the monster. It took a long time and every ounce of his strength, but at last he managed it. He gave a huge tug and suddenly the monstrous fish came from the water.

Only it was not a fish. It was unlike anything Antoine had ever seen before. It was like a little green man with long hair. It had arms and legs, but where its hands and feet should have been, there was webbing, just like a frog.

'Who are you?' asked Antoine, more afraid than he showed.

The little creature muttered something incomprehensible, and as he spoke two great tears rolled down his cheeks. 'I meant you no harm,' said Antoine. 'Are you hungry?'

The little fellow nodded.

'Then come with me back to my house and I will give you something to eat.'

Antoine held out his hand and the little thing took it in his webbed hand and the two made their way through the forest to Antoine's cottage. They ate a little fish and drank a little wine and soon the little man was smiling and happy. Antoine was now feeling sleepy and he said to the little fellow, 'Go, sit by the fire and sleep.' But the little man was afraid of the flames. Antoine had to coax him into a chair. When he held out his hands to the heat, the little man did the same, and the look of fear vanished and a smile spread across his strange little face. Within a few minutes he was sleeping peacefully and Antoine left him and went to bed.

140

The next morning, Antoine expected the little man to be gone. But no, there he was sitting by the embers of the fire. 'Do you have a name?' asked Antoine for the umpteenth time. The little green creature nodded.

'Then do tell me what it is. If you are going to stay here, I must know what to call you.'

The little man croaked something that Antoine could not make out. It sounded like 'Ondin'.

'Ondin?' he enquired and the little man nodded.

From then on, Ondin followed Antoine like a dog. When they went hunting, he would run hither and thither through the undergrowth and fetch the game that Antoine had caught. He was a very inquisitive little creature and loved to look at everything in sight. When the two went near the lake, the little man jumped up and down with great joy. Water was obviously his element, but when Antoine asked him if he wanted to return to his beloved water, Ondin shook his head and jumped up into Antoine's arms.

One day, about a week later, as the two were crossing the forest a herd of deer passed by. Ondin became very agitated and ran into the undergrowth to hide from them.

'Poor thing,' thought Antoine, 'he is obviously afraid of the fine stag,' and followed him to try to comfort him. He found Ondin sitting by a small stream, shivering with fear.

'It's all right,' said Antoine. 'No one is going to harm you,' and he stooped down to pick Ondin up. But as he did so he lost his footing and slipped on a patch of smooth rock. In his panic to right himself he dropped Ondin into the water. A few seconds later, the little green creature came to the surface with such an expression of distaste on his face, and with such a spluttering and spitting that Antoine thought he was having some kind of fit.

Ondin managed to clamber back onto the bank, still spitting and shaking.

'What on earth is the matter?' asked Antoine.

The little man pointed at the water and spat again.

Antoine knelt down with a puzzled expression on his face and scooped up some of the water from the stream into his cupped hands. When he sipped the water an even more puzzled expression came over his face. For the water was salty and they were many miles from the sea.

In those days, salt was one of the most valuable things that there was, and people who were lucky enough to own salt mines were very rich indeed. Antoine ran home as fast as he could and picked up

a spade. He returned to where Ondin was still sitting, and began to dig as quickly as his muscles would allow him. He had only gone down a few inches when the spade hit something hard. He threw it to one side and began to clear the loose earth away with his hands. Within a few instants he was looking at a beautiful white vein of pure salt. As he dug wider he could see that the salt vein stretched for a great distance and went as deep as he could imagine.

He hugged Ondin and said, 'Now I will be rich and Friedl will have to let me marry Gunde.'

The man and the strange creature made their way back to the hut where Antoine washed and put on his best clothes. He cleaned Ondin, too, and together they went into town to register their claim on the salt vein.

Word of Antoine's good fortune soon spread around the town, and wherever he went, people crowded round him to congratulate him.

'It is all his doing,' Antoine would say pointing at Ondin. 'If he had not fallen into the stream, I would still be a poor hunter.'

Antoine bought himself a suit of fine cloth and a pair of beautiful leather boots. The next morning he was up bright and early and put on his new clothes. With Ondin at his side, he rowed across the lake to Friedl's house. Gunde saw him from her window and rushed to meet him.

'I have come to ask for your hand in marriage again,' said Antoine as the two embraced.

'But you know what Father said. You must pay for three servants to do my work, if he is to allow me to marry you.'

'That is no problem now,' said Antoine. 'Thanks to this little fellow here, I am now a rich man and could afford thirty servants.'

'What is it?' asked Gunde, nervously recoiling from the little green man.

'My dearest friend, my faithful companion,' said Antoine and explained how he had caught Ondin when he had been fishing after their last moonlight meeting.

'Then I hope that you will be my friend, too,' said Gunde and bent down to kiss the little creature. 'For if Father allows us to marry, I shall owe all my happiness to you.'

Ondin had never been kissed before and he drew back from Gunde's lips.

Antoine laughed and coaxed him to allow Gunde to kiss him.

The happy lovers went inside the cottage and, of course, Friedl had no alternative but to give his permission for the wedding.

Two weeks later the forest echoed to the sounds of laughter and merrymaking. The churchbells pealed joyfully across the lake and everyone agreed that the bride was the most beautiful they had ever seen. Antoine looked so handsome in his fine new clothes that all the women were envious of Gunde. And even Ondin looked smart. Gunde had made him a beautiful suit of green silk which he wore, with tremendous pride. And this time when Gunde bent down to kiss him after the wedding, he did not recoil. He decided that he quite liked being kissed by such a pretty lady, and every night from then on when Antoine and Ondin returned from their salt mine, Gunde would kiss, first, her handsome husband, and then, her favourite little green man.

And the three of them lived happily ever after.

And today, in the Austrian mountains salt is still mined. But it could have lain there undiscovered, if not for an unhappy lover who went fishing one night when he was unable to sleep.

WILLIAM TELL

At the beginning of the fourteenth century, the country that is known today as Switzerland was ruled by the Archduke of Austria, Albert I. Albert was also the overlord of Germany, and, not content with ruling Switzerland, Germany and Austria, he wanted to extend his empire as far as possible. His greedy eyes looked towards Bohemia and he would also have loved to extend his rule to Italy in the south. He wanted his empire to stretch from the Mediterranean to the North Sea and from the Caspian Sea to the Atlantic.

As his empire grew, he found it almost impossible to rule single-handedly, so he appointed governors to rule in his place. Being a greedy, cruel man himself, his friends tended to be as greedy and cruel as he was and it was these friends whom he appointed to positions of power throughout his empire.

But throughout the empire there was much discontent. Troops of Austrian soldiers were often ambushed in mountainous areas by nationalist patriots who resented the Austrian rule. And for each ambush, the emperor would imprison, without trial, as many men, women and children as there had been soldiers.

Also, expanding an empire is a very expensive business. Soldiers have to be paid. Supplies have to be paid for, too. Horses are required, boots and uniforms must be purchased. And even bribes must be funded somehow. As Albert enlarged his empire, he needed more and more money and so taxes were raised higher and higher.

In one area of Switzerland there lived a hunter called William Tell. He hated the Austrians passionately, and tried to have as little to do with them as possible. He was proud of being Swiss and looked forward to the day when the Austrians would be forced to retreat and hand back the country to the Swiss.

At this time the area in which William Tell lived was ruled by an Austrian baron called Gessler. Gessler was as cruel as the emperor, he was proud to serve, and much more cruel than most of the other governors. Not only was he cruel, but he was as ambitious as his emperor. Just as Albert wanted to rule all of Europe, Gessler wanted to rule all of Switzerland, and Gessler would go to any ends to please his master. If twenty Austrians were ambushed, then Gessler would imprison twenty men, women and children. If the emperor demanded one thousand extra schillings in taxes, then Gessler would go and collect two thousand five hundred — two thousand for the emperor and five hundred for himself.

The people hated Gessler.

One day Gessler decided on a new way of pleasing his emperor. There was, after all, a limit to the number of people his prisons would hold and it was not possible to collect taxes once all the peasants' money had been taken. So he erected large poles in the market squares of each village in his domain, and on each pole he set an Austrian cap.

He then ordered that every Swiss subject who passed the hats had to salute them. It was, he declared, the Austrian emperor that they were really saluting. There would be a large fine imposed on anyone who failed to salute, but as the peasants had no money and could not pay the fine, they all did as they were ordered and saluted the token 'emperor'.

Now William Tell, being a hunter, did not come into the town very often, and when he did he made his visits as short as possible so as to avoid any contact with his Austrian overlords.

One day, however, his wife had to go to market to buy salt and William and his son went with her to protect her on her trip. They arrived at the market place at exactly the same time that Gessler arrived in the village on his annual tour of inspection.

Tell walked past the pole without even noticing it. 'Guards!' roared Gessler. 'Arrest that man.'

Six burly soldiers surrounded Tell and forced him down onto the ground.

Gessler then ordered that Tell be brought before him, and the soldiers obeyed.

'Why do you not salute your emperor?' demanded Gessler.

'I see no one I recognize as emperor here,' replied Tell from the ground where he had been thrown.

'The pole and hat represent your emperor.'

'Sir,' replied Tell with a grin on his face, 'the emperor must be fatter than that, considering the money that he gathers from us poor people in taxes.'

'Impudent wretch!' yelled Gessler, his plump face turning a deep shade of angry red. He lashed out with his foot and kicked Tell on the side. 'As you are obviously a fool, I will give you one last chance. Rise to your feet and salute your emperor.'

'I repeat, Sir,' said Tell, 'I see no one here that I recognize as emperor.'

By this time, Gessler's fury was boiling over.

146

'Guards,' he commanded. 'Bring that boy over to me. The one who is crying for his father, for he must be this man's son.'

'Leave my son alone,' shouted Tell. 'He has done nothing.'

'The father's crime is enough to justify punishing the son,' sneered Gessler. 'But *I* shall not harm him. I shall be merciful.'

The guards brought the child before the Governor.

'Do not cry, child,' smiled Gessler. 'I shall not harm you ... But perhaps your father will.'

'I shall never harm so much as a hair on my son's head,' shouted Tell.

'No?' The smile on Gessler's lips grew wider. 'You are obviously a hunter, Sir,' he said. 'And as a hunter you must be a good archer. Let us see just how good. Guards! Tie the child's hands behind his back and bring me an apple.'

The crowd who had gathered around murmured to each other as the soldiers did as they were told. An apple was brought to Gessler, who stepped forward and placed it on top of the boy's head. Turning to Tell he shouted. 'Let us now judge for ourselves just how good a shot you are, Sir. Come, with one arrow you must shoot the apple off your child's head.'

The crowd gasped with horror.

'If you fail,' continued Gessler, 'you and your wife and your son will never see the sun shine again, for I shall have you cast into the deepest dungeon in my castle.'

'And if I succeed?'

'If you succeed, then this time you shall go free. You see,' he said, turning to the crowd, 'I am a merciful man, am I not?' And he laughed at their silence.

Very carefully, Tell put an arrow into his crossbow. For what seemed like several minutes he carefully aimed. The crowd stood in hushed silence. A bell pealed from far away across the valley, and that was the only sound heard.

There was a loud swish as the arrow left the bow and flew through the air. The crowd gasped as the apple on the child's head split neatly into two halves and the arrow thudded into the tree behind.

Gessler was furious. The crowd was jubilant and cheered and cheered and cheered.

'Silence,' boomed Gessler. 'Silence. I demand silence.'

Eventually, the tumult lessened and Gessler called to Tell, 'Very well, you win this time,' and turning to the guards he ordered them to release the terrified child.

'Hold,' shouted Gessler as father and son ran towards each other.

'You drew two arrows and yet I said you only had one chance. What was the other for?'

'Had I missed, and so much as shaved a hair from my child's head, the second arrow would have found your heart, as sure as one day Switzerland will be free.'

On hearing these words, the crowd broke into a tumultuous cheer.

'Silence,' roared Gessler. 'Guards, arrest that man. Send the people back to their houses. Order a curfew.'

The guards pulled William Tell to the ground and dragged him towards the lake. 'Take him across the lake to my castle,' yelled Gessler. 'I will come too.'

Tell was bundled aboard a rowing boat. Six soldiers took the oars and Gessler sat in the bows calling the strokes. The boat headed out to the centre of the lake. Half way across, a sudden storm blew up. The mighty waves crashed around the little boat. It tossed upwards and downwards in the heavy waters. It almost overturned, righted itself and then almost overturned again. The soldiers panicked and Gessler's face turned purple, then red, then blue. 'Help!' he screamed at the top of his voice, the spray crashing into his panic-stricken face.

'Stay still,' shouted William Tell, who knew the lake and its behaviour as well as he knew his own hand. 'Give me an oar.'

'Do as he says,' pleaded Gessler.

Tell's hands were hurriedly untied and an oar was thrust into them. Seeing his chance, Tell stood up and spun round, swinging the oar round his head. The soldiers tumbled to the bottom of the boat and in the melee, Tell leaped overboard.

He dived downwards and downwards, for he knew that if he could hold his breath long enough, the underwater currents would carry him to safety. With a tremendous effort, he managed to do this and a few minutes later, his lungs nearly bursting, he was washed up on the shore near to the jetty where they had set off. He hid until nightfall, and then made his way deep into the forest.

From that time onwards Swiss resistance to Austrian rule intensified and today, Switzerland is a free country where the name of William Tell is still spoken of wherever people who love freedom are gathered together.

FAITHFUL FLORENTINE

There was once a ruler of the principality of Metz in Germany called Alexander. He was a deeply religious man and he decided to go on pilgrimage to the Holy Sepulchre in far-off Jerusalem.

His betrothed, Florentine, could not accompany him so she made him a pure white shirt to wear on his journey.

'Wear this always,' she said to him as he was about to set off. 'No matter what happens it will remain as pure and white as my love for you. I will remain faithful to you no matter how long you are away. And when you return, the shirt will still be as fresh as it is now.'

She kissed her dear love tenderly and Alexander set off.

But things did not go well for him, for when he crossed the border into Turkey, he was taken prisoner by the Saracen. He was put to work in the palace gardens, forced to dig the soil, and pull the hoe and the plough. The work he did was dirty, but no matter how dirty his hands and face became, his shirt remained as white and fresh as it was on the day that his beloved had given it to him.

Naturally this did not go unnoticed and Alexander was hauled before the Saracen to explain the mystery.

'There is no mystery,' he said. 'My faithful betrothed sewed this shirt for me and it will remain as pure as this as long as she is faithful to me.'

'No woman could remain so faithful for so long,' replied the Saracen, refusing to believe Alexander's story, but Alexander was so adamant that at last the Saracen was convinced.

He sent for his most handsome guard and commanded him to journey to Metz to search for Florentine. The guard did as he was commanded and several weeks later, he arrived in Germany.

He went straight to the Castle of Alexander and sought an audience with Florentine. As soon as he saw her he fell in love with her, for she was as beautiful as she was pure.

'Your grace,' he said to her, 'I come from the mighty Saracen to tell you that Alexander is his captive.'

Now Florentine was a very brave woman and she refused to show any emotion in front of the soldier.

'You will never see him again,' said the soldier, who was as handsome as Florentine was beautiful. 'Come, marry me and together we will rule Metz.'

'Never,' replied Florentine. 'As long as my dear Alexander lives, I shall never be unfaithful to him.'

The soldier stayed for several weeks and every day he asked Florentine to be his wife, and each time he received the same reply.

He saw how hopeless his suit was, so he set off early one morning to return to his native land.

Florentine watched him leave from her window and as soon as he was out of sight she summoned her maid. 'Bring my harp, and bring me the pageboy's best clothes.'

The startled maid did as she was told. A few minutes later Florentine rode out of the castle disguised as a minstrel. Her long hair was tucked into a silken cap and her pageboy's best clothes fitted her to perfection. Day after day she followed the soldier, keeping out of his sight at all times.

As he neared the Turkish border one night, the soldier stopped at an inn to spend the last night before he returned to the Saracen.

Florentine, too, stopped at the inn a few minutes later and asked for a room.

After supper, Florentine took out her harp and began to play a sad tune. The soldier was so moved by it that he demanded that the harpist be brought before him. When Florentine stood in front of him, he did not recognize her; so good was her disguise. 'Play, minstrel,' the soldier said and Florentine did as she was commanded.

'Tomorrow we will journey together,' the soldier said. 'You will play before my master, the Saracen. Be ready to leave at dawn.'

And so, at first light, Florentine and the soldier set off to cross the border into Turkey.

A few hours later Florentine was standing before the mighty Saracen, her heart aching. For, in the garden beyond the throne, she could see her dear Alexander toiling in the hot sun. His hair was long and filthy. His hands were rough and red, but his shirt was as pure as it had been so long ago.

Florentine began to play songs of forgotten love and parted sweethearts. So sweetly did she play that the Saracen felt a lump swell in his throat. She continued with her haunting songs until the Saracen could stand it no longer. 'Bring the German to me.'

When the servants brought Alexander into the throne room, he looked at the pageboy and did not recognize her as his beloved Florentine.

'Alexander,' said the Saracen, 'the songs of this youth have so moved me that I am giving you your freedom. Return to your own land and your faithful betrothed.'

With a happy heart Alexander set out on his journey. He had not gone far when he was overtaken by the pageboy with the harp. 'Sir,' said the lad, 'may we journey together, our paths lie in the same direction.'

And so the faithful Florentine and the unsuspecting Alexander

journeyed across Europe. As they neared Metz, the page stopped and said, 'Sir, here our paths separate. Give me something to remind me of our journey.'

'Anything you desire,' said Alexander, 'for it is to you that I owe my freedom.'

'A corner of your shirt is all I want,' replied the page.

'Anything but that,' said the surprised Alexander. 'Gold, jewels, land, but not that.'

But the boy insisted and eventually Alexander agreed with a heavy heart. The boy took a knife from his bad and cut a band of cloth from the hem of the shirt. 'Thank you, Sir,' he said. 'And now we part.'

Alexander rode on and arrived at the castle before Florentine. 'Bring my betrothed to me,' he ordered.

'Sir, she has not been here for many a week,' said the servant. 'A soldier came and she left the same day as he. He was so handsome.'

With a heavy heart Alexander retired to his chambers.

But a few moments later, Florentine came into his rooms. She had changed out of the pageboy's clothes and was wearing her most beautiful dress.

'My love,' she said and moved across the room to embrace her betrothed, but he turned from her and shouted, 'Oh, unfaithful wretch. A servant told me that you went off with a handsome soldier. Have you only just returned?'

'My Lord,' said Florentine softly. 'It is true that I followed a handsome soldier from here. I followed him because he led me to you.'

'Liar,' he said, still in an angry voice.

'My Lord, I speak the truth. I followed the soldier and he took me to the Saracen. There I sang for him and he was so moved that he released you. And together you and I journeyed home, parting only a few minutes ago.'

'But I journeyed with the pageboy who sang for the Saracen,' exclaimed Alexander.

'It was I,' said Florentine. And as she spoke, she took the band of white cloth from around her girdle and gave it to the astonished Alexander.

'Why did you not reveal yourself to me as you journeyed with me?' he asked.

'To test you. Had I revealed myself to you, you could only have behaved properly in my company. But as I was in disguise, you had every chance to be unfaithful with any maiden you met on your journey. I had to be sure that you still loved me as much as I love you. We have been separated for so long, your heart could have changed.'

'My darling. I loved you when I set out on my journey and every day of our separation my love for you grew tenfold. Now I love you more than life itself.'

'And I love you with equal strength,' replied Florentine.

And from that day, Florentine and Alexander were never parted.

GYULA AND EMELKA

The River Vah flows through southern Slovakia; and three hundred years ago there was a large castle at Lowenstein that stood on a high cliff overlooking the river.

The castle was owned by a rich landowner who had one daughter. She was called Emelka and she was the most beautiful girl in the whole region. She could have married any one of a hundred rich suitors, but she fell in love with a handsome young servant called Gyula.

When her father found out about it he was furious. 'You want to marry Gyula?' he roared. 'Impossible. Why, he's nothing but a servant.'

'I will marry no one else,' cried Emelka, with tears streaming down her pretty face. 'As long as he lives, I shall be his.'

Her angry father paced up and down the vast library, and suddenly came up with a way of getting rid of Gyula.

His brother in the north of the country owed him a large sum of money, so he sat down and wrote to him. 'Brother, the bearer of this letter is a thief and a cheat. Unfortunately, he is popular in the district so I am unable to punish him. Throw him into your deepest dungeon and keep him there for all time. If you do this, your debt is cancelled.' He signed and sealed the letter, and summoned Gyula. When the handsome youth came before him he said, 'Take this letter to my brother and wait for a reply.'

Gyula set off that very day and rode hard and long to reach his master's brother within two days. The brother took the letter from Gyula and read it in astonishment. 'This letter claims that you are a thief and a cheat, yet you look like an honest lad to me. I am commanded to cast you into my deepest dungeon, yet I cannot believe that you are deserving of such a fate.'

Gyula thought for a moment and then explained to the brother that his master wanted to rid of him as he had fallen in love with Emelka.

'Obviously you cannot return to Lowenstein, but I will not imprison you. You must volunteer for the army and go and fight the Turks. I will tell my brother that you drowned while trying to cross the Vah.'

And so Gyula went off to join the army and a messenger was sent to his master saying that he was dead.

Poor Emelka. When she heard the tragic news she was distraught and for week after week, and month after month she stayed in her room weeping until she had no more tears to shed.

The months turned to years, and Emelka's father made plans for her to marry his wealthy neighbour. The preparations were made and Emelka unsmilingly watched as her wedding dress was stitched and the castle was decorated with spring flowers.

On the morning of her wedding, her handmaiden went to awaken Emelka and was horrified to find her mistress dead, an empty phial of poison clasped in her hand.

Emelka's father was heartbroken. For weeks he did nothing but sit in the sun-filled garden calling out his daughter's name.

Meanwhile, Gyula had proved to be a brave soldier. He was quickly promoted to officer rank and after several fierce battles he was made colonel and then general. He was a good officer and much loved by his men. When peace came he had become very rich and he knew that Emelka's father could not refuse to allow him to marry his daughter.

He rode back to Lowenstein, hardly stopping to rest and after several days' journey he arrived late one night at the river Vah. The moon was full, and Gyula could see the vast castle towering above him on the opposite side. He forded the river and rode towards the castle. Suddenly his horse stopped dead and refused to move forward one inch.

Puzzled, Gyula dismounted and prepared to make the rest of his journey on foot. As he walked through the small wood at the bottom of the castle cliff, he stopped as surely as his horse had done. What he saw in front of him terrified him so much that his heart almost stopped beating. For in a moonlit clearing the shadowy figures of ghostly maidens were dancing. They all wore thin wedding dresses and carried posies of flowers. Their hair was decorated with small blossoms. 'The Wilis!' exclaimed Gyula. He had heard of them from his old grandmother. They were the ghosts of girls who had killed themselves rather than marry someone they did not love. And they were doomed to dance until they found their true loves.

A soft breeze sprang up and the maidens stopped dancing. They glanced around and saw Gyula looking at them. One by one they floated past him, murmuring, 'You are not my love'. Until the very last one floated by and stopped in front of him. 'You are my love, my Gyula,' she said.

Gyula looked into her face and saw that it was his beloved Emelka who stood before him. Even in death, she was very beautiful. Her face was white and her lips were the palest pink. Her eyes shone as she whispered Gyula's name over and over again. She laid down her posy and slowly took a chain from around her neck which she gently slipped over Gyula's head.

'Dance with me,' she whispered.

And Gyula danced. She was ice cold to touch and no matter how fast they danced she remained ice cold. Gyula grew more and more tired, but Emelka had so enchanted him that he could not stop.

For dance after dance they moved across the clearing until Gyula could go on no longer. He slumped down on the dewy grass.

They found him there the following morning. He was dead.

His body was carried into the castle and Emelka's father was called for. He immediately recognized Gyula and when he saw the chain around his neck he knew it instantly, for he had given it to his daughter many years before. He sank to his knees, sobbing bitterly. 'Forgive me,' he murmured. 'Please forgive me.' And he ordered his servants to bury Gyula beside Emelka. 'I parted them in this life,' he whispered. 'Please bring them together in the next life.'

And so Gyula and Emelka, who had been denied happiness in this world, were buried side-by-side to be together for ever.

KING SVATOPLUK

It was the feast day of Saint Peter and Saint Paul, and in the cathedral at Velehrad the townspeople were about to celebrate mass. The Archbishop himself was at the altar waiting. The choirboys were singing sweetly, and the heads of most of the congregation were bowed in silent prayer. The crimson robes of the priests shone in the morning sunshine that streamed through the beautiful stained-glass windows. It was a scene of great beauty and of heavenly peace.

The congregation finished their prayers and sat up straight to await the Mass. The Archbishop stood silently in his place and waited. He waited and waited.

Suddenly the peace was broken by the voice of a small child. 'What are we waiting for?' he asked his mother.

'I don't know, child,' his mother replied. 'Hush.'

'But I am getting hungry,' the child persisted. 'Mass should have been over by now.'

The man directly behind tapped the woman on the shoulder and whispered to her. 'King Svatopluk commanded the Archbishop to wait until he arrived, before celebrating the Mass.'

'But the King is out hunting,' said the child. 'I saw him ride out of the castle this morning.'

The child had spoken so loudly that the Archbishop could not help but overhear. He signalled to the choir to begin the Mass and began to read the great words of the beautiful service.

Just as he was about to beckon the worshippers forward to take the wine and the bread there was a mighty commotion as the great wooden doors swung open and the king stormed in. He was dressed in his hunting clothes and his sword was in his hand. 'How dare you start without me, Holy Man!' he shouted at the Archbishop.

'And how dare you enter the house of God with your sword drawn?' retorted the Archbishop, purple with rage. 'Get out of here!'

'You tell me to get out?' roared Svatopluk. 'I am your king.'

'God is my king,' the Archbishop roared back. 'Now leave His house.'

'I leave this house and I curse you and your God,' said Svatopluk.

The townsfolk were horrified to hear such blasphemy.

'And you,' continued the furious king, pointing at the Archbishop, 'you have until dawn to leave my lands.'

The Archbishop stepped forward. 'Mark my words, Svatopluk. Until now you have been a good ruler. Good fortune has smiled upon you. You have been fortunate in battle. Peace now rules the land. But now your fortune has ended.'

Svatopluk stormed from the cathedral and the Archbishop continued with the service.

The very next morning at dawn, the Archbishop left Svatopluk's kingdom and as he crossed the border he noticed the armies of Schlesweig march into Svatopluk's land, clearly ready to battle.

From that day on, for year after year, Svatopluk's land was under constant attack from the armies of Germany in the south and Hungary in the east. The French armies in the west marched against him

as soon as he had repulsed the Hungarians, and when after a long, hard battle the French retreated, Turkish invaders stormed across his south-eastern border.

Svatopluk was so busy planning and plotting with his generals that he forgot all about the Archbishop and his curse; until one day he was walking through the camp and overheard two soldiers talking.

'My family is starving, for there is no food, now that we are constantly at war!' said the first.

'Mine too,' said the second. 'It is all the King's fault. He should never have cursed God.'

Svatopluk went back to his tent and spent the night in deep thought. The next morning before anyone awoke, he rode out of the camp. He rode for three days and three nights until he came to the monastery on the Mount of the Holy Virgin. In the shade of a beautiful elm tree he took his sword from its sheath and plunged it into the ground. He knelt down and kissed it, just where the blade crossed the handle. He made the sign of the cross and vowed never to make war again and to spend the rest of his days serving God and man.

He went inside the monastery and begged to see the Abbot.

When the Abbot saw the king, he knelt down before him, much afraid, for he knew Svatopluk to be a cruel man.

'Father,' said Svatopluk. 'It is I who should kneel before you. Pray rise, I come to seek God.'

And from that day on, Svatopluk spent all of his time in prayer, travelling over the kingdom preaching God's word. Nobody recognized him, for his appearance was greatly changed.

And once, when he stood outside the cathedral where he had cursed God, so long ago, an old woman came up to him and said, 'You have something of the look of the old king about you.'

'What happened to him?' asked Svatopluk.

'He disappeared,' replied the old woman. 'Strange, but from the day he disappeared things began to get better. Maybe he sacrificed himself as a penance. If he did, I bless him for it.'

And Svatopluk was happy.

ILYA MUROMETS

Once upon a time in a small village in Russia, there lived a humble peasant and his wife and their son, who was called Ilya Muromets. Ilya was thirty years old and he was crippled. He could not use his legs to walk and his arms and hands hung uselessly by his side.

Each morning his mother and father would carry him from his bed, wash him and feed him, and sit him by the fire. There he would remain all day until his poor parents returned from their labours in the fields.

One day, while his parents were out, there was a loud knock upon the door. 'Come in,' cried Ilya from his place by the fire. 'The door is on the latch.'

The door opened and three men entered the poor cottage. Ilya could see from their clothes that they were pilgrims, on their way to the holy shrine of St Andrew.

'Rise from your chair, Sir, and bring us some water,' said the first pilgrim, who was older than the other two.

'Alas, good pilgrim, I am unable to rise, for I was born crippled and can neither walk nor use my arms,' replied Ilya.

The old man stepped forward and laid his hands on Ilya's brow. The other two knelt beside him and the three prayed quietly. Suddenly Ilya felt a rush of power flow to his legs. Without thinking he moved his arms to touch his legs. He jumped up and cried, 'I have never been able to move my arms before. I have never been able to stand before. You are indeed holy men that can give me strength. Sit, holy fathers, warm yourselves by the fire and I will bring you wine and not water.'

With that, Ilya rushed down to the cellar and brought them the best wine that his poor father could afford. The three men drank thankfully and then the eldest handed the jug of wine to Ilya. 'Drink the rest of this,' he said, 'and you will have the strength of ten heroes.'

Ilya did as he was bid and as he drank he could feel the strength of ten heroes flow through his limbs. 'Thank you,' he cried joyfully. 'How can I ever repay you?'

'You must serve Mother Russia and protect her from her enemies. For this you will need the strength of one hundred and ten heroes. We have done our best. You must journey forth and seek out the giant Svatogor. Befriend him and he will give you all the strength you require for your task.' With that the three holy men bade Ilya farewell and returned to their pilgrimage.

Ilya rushed out to where his parents were toiling in the fields. When he got there, they were sound asleep, tired out by their exhaustion. Ilya looked at the work they had done. For hour after hour they had toiled, but all that they had managed to do was to clear a small patch of their field. Ilya smiled lovingly at his sleeping parents and set to work. With the strength of ten heroes running through him, it was only a matter of a few minutes before he had cleared the entire field. When he had finished, he awoke his parents, who were amazed to see what had happened. Ilya explained that the Holy Men had given him the strength of ten heroes, but that he needed the strength of one hundred and ten to defend Mother Russia from her invaders. His father then said, 'You must take my old horse, for the giant Svatogor lives many miles from here.'

But Ilya had grown so strong that the old horse could not carry his weight, so the kind parents spent every penny that they had, and bought Ilya a fine young horse. Ilya fed it lovingly every day and soon the horse was strong enough to carry him to meet Svatogor.

Svatogor lived near the Holy Mountain many miles from Ilya's home. For three days and three nights Ilya journeyed until, at last, he came to the mountain. Hanging from a huge fir tree, Ilya spotted a hunting horn. On it was inscribed: 'Let him who seeks Svatogor blow three times.'

Breathing the breath of ten heroes Ilya put the horn to his lips and blew hard. The air was rent with three loud blasts. A few seconds later the very ground began to shudder as though an earthquake was about to rip the world apart. Ilya stood firm and heard a voice from far above call 'Who seeks Svatogor?' Ilya looked up, as far as he could see. There towering above him, astride a vast horse, was Svatogor. He was so tall that his head seemed to touch the sky. When he raised his hand, he almost touched the sun.

'Ilya Muromets,' replied the peasant's son.

'And what do you want of me?' demanded Svatogor.

'The strength of one hundred heroes.'

'Humph,' retorted the giant and with that he bent down and swept poor Ilya, horse and all into his saddle-bag.

Svatogor commanded his horse to move on, but the poor beast stumbled.

'How do you expect me to move, with all that weight in the bag?' asked the horse.

Svatogor took Ilya and his horse out of the bag and set them down

again. 'You must be strong to make my horse stumble,' he said. 'Come, we will ride to my Holy Mountain and be friends.'

And so Ilya and Svatogor rode off to the Holy Mountain. Svatogor was so impressed by Ilya that together they set out to protect Russia from her enemies. But Ilya always remembered that somehow he had to get Svatogor to give him his extra strength so that he could fulfil his destiny.

One day, the two were riding out together when they came upon a high pine tree. In its shade there lay a large coffin bearing a strange inscription. 'Let the one whom this coffin fits lie in it.'

Ilya dismounted and lay in the coffin, but it was far too large for him.

'It's more likely to fit me, Ilya,' said Svatogor. He dismounted and clambered into the coffin. No sooner had he done so, than the lid slammed shut.

'Ilya,' cried Svatogor, 'take my sword, cut through the locks and release me.'

Ilya did as his friend asked, but the sword was too heavy for him even to lift.

'Lean over the coffin,' came the muffled voice of Svatogor from within the coffin, 'and I will breathe more strength into you.'

Again Ilya did as he was bid. Svatogor took a deep breath and blew as hard as he could. Ilya felt the power seep through the lock of the coffin and into his blood. He tried to pick up the sword and was surprised at how light it now felt in his hands. With a mighty blow, he brought the sword down on the coffin. But before it touched the wood, a band of iron appeared just where the blade fell.

'Lean over the coffin and I will breathe more strength into you,' cried Svatogor.

Ilya did so, and again he felt the power surge through him. He brought the sword down and with a mighty clang the iron band smashed through and the lid sprang open. There lay poor Svatogor, dying from his efforts. His face was as white as a blizzard and his breathing was as soft as a zephyr.

'Ilya,' he whispered, 'you now have all my strength. Go and fulfil your destiny. Free our beloved Russia from the invader. But first sit with me until I die and then bury me in the shade of this tree.'

With tears in his eyes, Ilya did as Svatogor asked. When nightfall came, the giant breathed his last breath and died. Ilya toiled all night and dug the giant's grave. As dawn broke and the sun began to bring colour to the landscape, Ilya laid his friend in the earth and prayed for his soul. He rode off with a heavy heart vowing that never would he forget Svatogor. Every battle he fought and every victory he won would be dedicated to the giant's memory.

After several days' journey, Ilya drew close to the town of Chernigov where he intended to rest for a few days. As he rode over the summit of the hill that shaded Chernigov, Ilya saw that the city was under siege. Around the city walls were the tents of the Tartar armies. Three standards flew from each of the tents and Ilya immediately knew that the army was led by three Tartar tsarevitches and that each Tsarevitch had forty thousand men at his command. The poor townsfolk of Chernigov stood no chance against such an army. The only sound that Ilya could hear was the wailing of the townsfolk. This saddened him. But soon his sadness turned to anger. And as his anger rose, so too did the wind. 'Ilya,' it seemed to be saying, 'remember that you have the strength of Svatogor as well as the strength of ten heroes.'

With a great roar, Ilya drew Svatogor's mighty sword and spurred his horse into a gallop. Faster and faster they rode down the hillside and into the Tartar camp. With the strength of one hundred and ten heroes flowing through him, Ilya was invincible. Wave after wave of attacking Tartars tried to dismount him and each one met the same bloody reply. The three tsarevitches soon realized that nothing they could throw against him would defeat Ilya Muromets and those who still lived withdrew back over the hill into their own lands. Word soon spread amongst Russia's enemies that the country was no longer weak and defenceless, but was protected by a mighty warrior called Ilya Muromets.

The townspeople of Chernigov begged Ilya to stay with them and rule over them, but Ilya could not. 'Are there not still foreign armies in the north around Kiev? I must do for the citizens of Kiev what I did for you.'

The townsfolk protested. Did Ilya not know that to go to Kiev meant crossing the mighty Blacklands which were damned by the wicked Nightingale, whose whistle made the earth tremble, blackened the sky and scorched the land. 'He whistles his terrible whistle if anyone tries to cross the Blacklands,' warned the townsfolk.

But Ilya was determined.

'At least let us give you something to protect you,' said the mayor and handed Ilya a golden crossbow.

In the morning, Ilya set off with the good wishes of Chernigov's people ringing in his ears.

As he came near to the Blacklands, Ilya's heart sank. The land was bleak and flat. The sun was covered by huge black clouds. The only thing growing was a clump of oak trees right in the middle of the dreadful heath. Summoning every ounce of courage, Ilya rode forwards and neared the oak trees.

'Who dares ride across my Blacklands?' demanded a voice from far above Ilya. He looked up and saw an enormous bird circling above him. It was nothing like the nightingales that Ilya knew. It was as big as an eagle and as cruel as a vulture.

'Ilya Muromets,' shouted the brave hero.

The bird landed on top of an oak tree and opened its beak, about to release its terrible whistle. As it lifted its head back, Ilya drew an arrow from his quiver and fired it from his golden bow. The arrow was accurately fired, for before the bird could make any sound the arrow pierced its throat and it slumped to the ground. Ilya dismounted and picked up the dying bird. 'You are indeed as mighty as I have heard,' croaked the bird. 'I curse you and yet I hail you as the mightiest warrior in all of Russia.' With these words, the bird let out its dreadful whistle for the last time and died. Ilya tied a rope around its neck and strapped it to his saddle. He rode on across the Blacklands. But they were no longer black. The sun was bathing them in a golden glow. Flowers were springing to life. Trees were budding and birds were singing.

Before long Ilya arrived at Kiev. He made his way to the royal palace and begged for an audience with the Prince. When he explained what it was he wanted, his wish was granted.

As he entered the throne room, the dead bird in his hands, the whole court rose and cheered.

'Sire,' Ilya said as he knelt before the throne, 'I bring you the enchanted ruler of the Blacklands. Dead.'

The Prince was incredulous. But on examining the bird, he saw that what Ilya had said was true. 'You may have anything that you want,' he said in deep gratitude.

'Sire, to rid the north of the invaders is all I want. Give me command of your armies and together we will ride out to meet the enemy in battle.'

The Prince happily agreed and a few days later the two men rode through the city gates of Kiev at the head of the most splendid army ever assembled by a Prince of Kiev. When word had spread of Ilya's gift to the Prince, every man and boy in the city had rushed to join up, and every woman and girl had stitched them the most splendid uniforms.

The battle was long and bloody. At one point the Prince began to fear that even with Ilya against them the invaders were invincible.

166

His men were being well beaten on the right and left flanks, and in the centre they were only holding their own. Suddenly at noon, when the sun should have been at its highest, the clouds gathered and blackened the sky. A strong wind began to blow from behind the Kiev army, forcing their soldiers forwards and the invaders' armies backwards. The wind blew stronger and stronger forcing the invaders further and further back, until they were overtaken by the Kiev soldiers, who, seeing the Tartars running before them, were given fresh spirit. By nightfall the last Tartar was either dead or had been driven out of Russia for ever.

Of Ilya Muromets there was no sign.

Some say that he rode off when he saw that the battle had been won and continued to fight tyranny and injustice whenever he found it. But one soldier knew differently. When the tide of the battle had turned and the Kiev armies were winning, he had looked around him to see what was happening behind him. He hardly believed what he saw. For just as the wind was blowing its strongest, a gap appeared in the heavy clouds and a hand swept down to earth and gathered Ilya Muromets upwards as easily as if he had been a feather.

And there was a wonderful expression of pure joy on Ilya's face as the clouds closed behind him.

ISIS AND OSIRIS

Egypt was once ruled over by the god Osiris. He was a wise and much-loved ruler. He taught his subjects how to plough their fields, how to build houses, to make pots and to fashion pots on wheels. He taught them to sing songs, to read and to count. The people loved him greatly.

Their happiness was complete when Osiris took a wife. She was the lovely Isis and she was so good-natured and kind that she was soon as popular as her husband with the people of Egypt. A son was born to the happy pair, which made their joy absolute. They called him Horus.

There was only one thing that marred Osiris' happiness. His brother Typhon was an ill-tempered youth, who was as quarrelsome as he could possibly be. He never had a kind word for anyone and if he had the slightest chance to do an evil deed, he would grasp it eagerly.

Typhon loathed his brother. He was jealous of his popularity with the people. He envied him his beautiful wife and lovely son. He believed that he would make a much better ruler than his brother.

'If I were king,' he would say to himself, 'I would make the people work much harder to make me richer. I would force the men into my army and make war to extend my empire. My brother has no idea how to use his power.'

Now, as well as being ruthless and ambitious, Typhon was not the sort of man to sit around and do nothing to realize his dreams. So he made a secret pact with the queen of neighbouring Ethiopia and with several discontented Egyptian princes. In exchange for their support, he would give them huge amounts of money when he grabbed the throne.

One day, when Isis and Osiris were swimming in the warm sea, Typhon crept out from behind a tree and carefully measured the mark that Osiris' body had made as he lay in the sand. With stealth he tiptoed away and went to his jeweller.

'Make me a chest to these measurements, exactly. Decorate it with the most precious jewels in your possession and bring it to my palace as soon as it is ready.'

For many a week the jeweller toiled at his work and eventually it was finished. When Typhon saw it he was greatly pleased and rewarded the craftsman well.

That evening Typhon invited Isis and Osiris to a great banquet. He also asked his princely allies. The feasting went on well into the night and when at last everyone had eaten their fill, Typhon clapped his hands. The great doors of his room swung open and his servants carried in the jewelled chest. There were gasps of astonishment from all in the room. Isis and Osiris were genuine in their appreciation of the magnificent chest. Typhon's allies were laying a carefully re-hearsed trap.

Typhon announced that whoever the chest fitted the best, should have it. Immediately all the allies rushed to try to lie in the chest, but, of course, it fitted no one. Typhon turned to his brother and said, 'Osiris, why don't you try?'

Osiris stepped forward and lay in the chest. It fitted him perfectly, but before he could stand up again, Typhon's allies rushed forward and slammed the lid down. They locked it tightly and carried it from the room.

Poor Isis watched in horror as she saw the men take the chest to the highest tower in the palace and cast it into the river below. She ran from the room and made her way down to the river banks. There she saw the chest float down to the sea. For day after day she followed it in a fragile papyrus boat. Each time she almost caught up with it, a gust of wind would blow it further ahead.

Eventually, the chest was blown ashore in the kingdom of Byblos. It came to land in the shade of a magnificent tamarind tree and no sooner had it reached the shade, than the tree's branches stooped down and wound themselves around the chest. Isis screamed as the bejewelled chest disappeared into the very trunk of the tree.

She ran to the spot and collapsed, weeping dreadfully.

For three days and three nights she lay there until, on the fourth morning, the King of Byblos passed. As soon as he saw the tree which had grown to superb maturity he commanded that it be cut down and taken to his palace there to be used as a pillar. He took pity on the weeping woman at the base of the tree and ordered that she come to the palace. The weeping Isis mournfully followed the small procession into the city.

Isis was sent to the servants' quarters where she taught the slaves the feminine wiles that she had learned when she had ruled Egypt. She made them skilful in the art of decorating their faces in the Egyptian way, and helped them oil their hair with scented oils.

Word of her ways soon spread to the ears of the Queen and she commanded that Isis be brought before her. Isis charmed the Queen with her beauty and wisdom and soon she was made nurse to her child.

As time passed, the baby began to remind Isis of her own child in far-off Egypt and she came to love it as strongly as if it were her own. She was no longer a rich queen, so there was only one gift left to her with which she could endow the child. As a goddess, she was immortal and she decided to make her charge immortal, too.

One night as the Queen slept Isis began to bathe the child's body in the flames of immortality. Each night thereafter as the Queen slept, Isis made another part of his body immortal. And as the flames of immortality bathed the child, Isis would change herself into a beautiful dove and circle the pillar which contained the sleeping body of Osiris.

One night when Isis was flying round the pillar and the Queen's chamber was enveloped in the warm glow of the flames of immortality, there was a dreadful storm which awoke the Queen.

When she saw her child's body bathed in fire, she screamed.

Isis flew down to the foot of her bed and transformed herself back to human shape.

The poor Queen was terrified. 'Please do not be alarmed,' said Isis,

stepping forward, and she explained who she was and how she came to be there. 'Your child is so like mine that I wanted to give him my gift of immortality. That is why he is bathed in flames.'

'But, the bird . . . you were a bird . . .'

'My husband, Osiris, is locked in a jewelled chest, imprisoned in that tamarind pillar. I fly round him so that he knows I am near.'

'My poor Isis,' said the Queen. 'Had I but known who you were we could have released Osiris. But now my husband loves the tamarind pillar so much. And when he learns of our son's immortality, he will be jealous and banish him from the land.'

'In that case,' said Isis, 'we must plan . . .'

For the next few days Isis continued to play the part of handmaiden to the Queen. One night when she was serving the Queen and the King, she nodded silently to the Queen.

'My love,' said the Queen. 'Would that we were immortal, then we could live as happily as we are now, forever.'

'Immortality is only for the gods,' said the King.

'Excuse me, Majesty,' said Isis. 'But in my land it is said that the mighty tamarind tree has the gift of immortality.'

'The tamarind tree?' exclaimed the King.

'Yes, Sire. It is said that he who is not afraid to stand in the burning wood of the tamarind tree will be granted eternal life.'

Isis was so convincing that the King believed her. But he was very afraid.

'Would I become immortal if I did so?' he begged Isis.

'Sire, it is said that the child who is heir should be one to gain immortality. For the parents are pleased to know that their heir will ensure that their names last as long as his immortality.'

'Bring my son,' the King commanded.

'But husband,' the Queen said in great alarm. 'What if what has been said is untrue.'

'If it is untrue and our child dies, then fear not, for we will have another. But if it is true and our son becomes immortal, then our names will live as long as his immortality.'

The child was brought before the King, who commanded that the tamarind pillar be cut down and burned.

His orders were obeyed and soon the huge pillar was burning fiercely with the child in the middle of the flames. The courtiers were amazed when the child appeared to be quite unconcerned and slept peacefully as the flames grew higher and higher.

'It is true,' cried the King, hugging his wife. 'Our dear son is becoming immortal.'

172

Suddenly all the courtiers gasped as with a mighty crash a be-jewelled chest fell from the flames. The crash was so colossal that the lock smashed open. Isis rushed forward and embraced her beloved husband. Before anyone could move she turned herself back into a dove and Osiris into a mighty eagle.

Together the two flew back to Egypt, but when they arrived they were grieved at what they saw. They had left behind a happy land, and now it was a sorrowful sight. The people who had once gone smilingly about their business now were in chains.

Isis and Osiris flew on until they reached their palace. Osiris knew enough about his brother to realize that although he would never dare kill their son, he would never let him be free, so they flew to the topmost room in the topmost tower, and sure enough, there was their beloved son, who had now grown tall and strong.

The couple flew into the chamber and immediately transformed themselves back to the human form. 'My son,' said Isis and ran forward to embrace him. The boy was startled, but he knew instantly that the woman was his mother.

'We must get away from here,' said the boy. 'There are many escaped slaves in Babylon who will march against Typhon to free Egypt once more. All they await is a leader.'

Isis and Osiris regained their bird shapes and changed Horus into a steely hawk. The three flew off to Babylon where they recruited a large army.

They trained hard for many months and, eventually, Osiris decided that they were ready to march against Egypt. The march was long and hard, but the soldiers were pleased to be returning home and they marched in high spirits. When they crossed the border they met with little resistance, for the attack was completely unexpected. And as they freed more and more slaves, their numbers swelled tenfold.

After several days' marching and several skirmishes, the slave army found itself facing the combined might of the forces of Typhon, the Abyssinian Queen and the Egyptian princes.

The battle was long and hard. It lasted for several days and the balance swung backwards and forwards. First the slaves took ascendancy and then they were driven back by the forces of Typhon; then the slaves would find fresh heart and push forward again. And so the battle continued, until eventually the knowledge that if they were beaten they were doomed to a life of continual slavery, gave the slaves the final amount of heart needed to win and they managed to beat off the last attack of Typhon's forces.

Isis and Osiris demanded that Typhon and his princes be brought before them.

'Brother,' said Osiris, 'show repentance and I will forgive you.'

'Never,' cried Typhon and spat on the ground before him.

'In that case . . .'

And Osiris waved his hands in the air, and instantly Typhon and all his princes were transformed into tamarind trees, which they remain to this very day.

ISHTAR IN HELL

In Egypt, Ishtar was the goddess of love and faithfulness. She also brought happiness to those who worshipped her, and she liked nothing more than looking down on earth and watching the people enjoy themselves. If anything threatened to destroy the joy that she created, she would do her utmost to put it to rights. She would calm the seas if a storm went on for too long. If gales threatened to bring danger, she would blow in the opposite direction and cause the gales to lessen.

Ishtar had a sister called Ereshkigal and one day, she said to her lover, Tammuz, 'I am going to go and visit my sister.'

Tammuz was horrified, for Ereshkigal was the goddess of Hell. Whoever saw her was cast into Hell and never seen again.

'You cannot,' he cried. 'I will never see you again if you do, and I love you too much to bear that.'

But Ishtar was insistent. 'She is my sister, she will not harm me. When we were children, we laughed and loved together. She will remember that and not let me come to harm.'

And so, despite Tammuz's constant pleadings, Ishtar set off on her journey.

Tammuz was sad, for he did not believe that he would ever see his beloved again.

After a long and tiring journey, Ishtar arrived at the gates of her sister's palace, in Hell. It was a gloomy, forbidding place and Ishtar was afraid. But she remembered the love that she had felt for her sister and refused to believe that any harm would come to her, so she knocked loudly at the heavy wooden door.

After what seemed like hours of waiting she heard the sound of shuffling footsteps at the other side of the door. 'Who is there?' a creaky voice demanded.

'The goddess Ishtar comes to visit her sister Ereshkigal.'

'Go away,' the voice replied. 'The goddess of Hell only sees those who come to visit her for eternity.'

'Go and tell my sister that Ishtar is here. She will see me.'

The footsteps slowly shuffled away.

'Ishtar!' said the surprised Ereshkigal. 'Why has she come? I must see her, for I remember the love that we had for each other. Bring her to me.'

'But mistress,' said the little hunch-backed man who had talked to

Ishtar from the other side of the door, 'if she comes in, I must do to her what I do to all men and women who enter your palace.'

'I know,' said the goddess, 'but I must see her. Bring her to me.'

And so, the little man returned to the outside door.

'You may enter,' he said to Ishtar when he had opened the door, 'but first you must give me your shawl.'

Ishtar did as he asked and entered the palace of Hell.

He led her through a long passage with a door at the end of it. As they passed through the door, he suddenly wrenched the golden ear-rings from her ears.

'Why did you do that?' the angry Ishtar demanded.

'It is the law of Hell. No one can see Ereshkigal unless they are naked of all precious things.' And the two proceeded deeper into the castle.

They came to another door and as they passed through it, the little man ripped the golden necklace from around Ishtar's neck. Again she angrily asked him why he had done it and again she was told that it was the law of Hell. At the third door, Ishtar was robbed of her beautiful rings and at the fourth of her golden belt. At the fifth her bracelets were ripped from her wrists and at the sixth the golden chains from around her ankles. As they went through the seventh door there was not a single precious thing around Ishtar's body and in the chamber beyond, there stood Ereshkigal waiting for her sister. The two women embraced and wept, Ishtar because she was so happy at seeing her sister, Ereshkigal because she, too, was happy to see her beloved sister, but also because she knew what she must do.

After they had stopped crying and had begun to laugh, as they remembered the happiness of their childhood days, Ereshkigal said to her sister, 'Have you left anything precious behind you? Did my slave remove all your precious things?'

Ishtar was surprised at the question, but nodded. 'Yes,' she said. 'I have nothing precious left.'

'Then,' cried Ereshkigal, 'you must stay here for eternity. For it is the law that only those who stand in my presence with something precious may return.' With that, she swept out of the room leaving the horrified Ishtar alone. The little hunchback entered the room chuckling to himself. 'Come, Ishtar. A chamber has been prepared for you. I hope you find it comfortable, for it is yours for all time.'

He grabbed her by the wrists and pulled her roughly into a luxurious chamber. He threw her onto the silken bed and then left her alone, locking the door behind him with the key of timelessness.

Ishtar wept. And as she wept, rainclouds gathered in the skies

above the land and the rain began to fall. She wept for days and days and it rained on Earth for days and days. And then she became very angry and banged on the door with all her might. She banged for day after day, and the thunderbolts clashed for day after day in the skies above the Earth.

From his place above the Earth, Tammuz could see what was happening. He had tried to warn Ishtar and she had ignored him. But his love for her was as strong as ever and he had no choice but to set out for Hell to try to rescue her.

He travelled for day after day, until he stood before the gates of the Palace of Hell. He knocked at the heavy door and after a long wait a voice from the other side said, 'Who stands before the gates of the Palace of Hell?'

'Tammuz,' he replied. 'Let me in.'

'Why are you so eager to enter Hell? Most men spend their lives trying to avoid it.'

'I come to see my beloved Ishtar. Let me in.'

The hunchback opened the door and with a wicked smile on his face, bade him enter. He led him along the long passage and as they passed through the door at the end of it, he ripped the golden crown from Tammuz's head.

'Why did you do that?' Tammuz demanded angrily.

'It is the law of Hell,' explained the hunchback. 'No one can see Ereshkigal unless they are naked of all precious things.'

At the second door he plucked the golden lyre from off Tammuz's shoulder, and at the third the rings from his fingers. At the fourth, the red ruby on his tunic was taken from him and at the fifth his beautiful golden belt. The sixth door cost Tammuz his quiver of golden arrows and the seventh his golden bow.

'Who stands before Ereshkigal?' she demanded as Tammuz was taken into the chamber behind the seventh door.

'Tammuz,' he declared. 'I come for my love.'

'And who is your love?'

'Ishtar, your sister.'

'Ishtar is here and here she must stay. She stood before me with nothing precious and only those who stand in my presence with something precious may return.'

'But you trick them. Your hideous servant robs everyone of all precious things.'

'As he has done to you,' said Ereshkigal. 'You have nothing precious, so you must stay here, locked in your chamber by the key of timelessness.'

178

At that the hunchback grabbed Tammuz by the wrists and began to pull him from the presence of the goddess of Hell.

'Wait,' cried Tammuz. 'I still have the most precious thing in the world!'

'Nonsense,' shouted the hunchback. 'I took your golden crown and your golden lyre. Your rings and your fine rubies are all gone, along with your belt and your arrows and your bow. You have nothing precious.'

'I still have my love for Ishtar. That is the most precious thing I possess and nothing you can do can steal that from me.'

'Let him go,' Ereshkigal's voice was soft and thoughtful. 'And bring Ishtar to me.'

The hunchback did as his mistress commanded and a few minutes later Ishtar was shown into the room. When she saw Tammuz she smiled and ran towards him, and in the sky, the sun shone for the first time since Ishtar had been locked in by the key of timelessness.

'My love, my precious love,' she wept as she embraced Tammuz.

'Your *precious* love,' said Ereshkigal. 'Then when you stood before me you were bearing something precious.'

'Of course,' said Ishtar. 'My love for Tammuz is much more precious than the things I lost on my way to your presence.'

'Oh, dear sister,' smiled Ereshkigal. 'Why did you not say that? Did I not tell you that those who stood in my presence with something precious might return? Here you both stand with your love for each other, your most precious possession. You may return. Do not think badly of me for what I did. I had to, for it is the law and it has to be applied to all, regardless of who they are. Now go. Be happy. Be together always.'

And so, Ishtar and Tammuz made their way out of the Palace of Hell to their own palace where they still live happily to this day.

THE VOYAGES
OF SINBAD THE SAILOR

There was once a rich merchant who had a son called Sinbad. When the merchant died, he left Sinbad a vast amount of money and precious jewels. Sinbad was lazy and spent all his day with undesirable friends, squandering his wealth. Within a few years he had spent most of his inheritance.

One day he happened to pick up an old book and his eyes fell upon these words:

'Three things are more important than any other: the day of death is more important than the day of birth, the living dog is more important than the dead lion, and poverty is less important than the grave.'

He thought about these words for some time and realized how silly he had been. So he sold what was left of his possessions and decided to invest the money he raised in a journey overseas to buy precious things which he could resell at a profit when he returned. He would spend what he had raised on hiring a ship and crew and with anything left over, he would buy goods to sell overseas to pay for his purchases.

So that is what he did. He went to the bazaar and spent some money on goods for trading. Then he hired a few porters and ship and crew, and then they set sail. They crossed the Persian Gulf and sailed into the Sea of Levant.

One day, the ship approached a beautiful island and the captain cast anchor. The merchants were enchanted by the loveliness of the place and were eager to set their feet upon land. So they went directly ashore. There some lit cooking fires, others washed in the island's clear streams and still others, Sinbad amongst them, walked about enjoying the sight of the trees and greenery.

They had spent many hours in these pleasant pursuits when all at once the ship's lookout called to them from the gunwale,

'Run for your lives. Return to the ship. That is not a real island, but a great sea monster stranded in the sea on whom the sand has settled and trees have sprung up so that he looks like an island. When you started your fires it felt the heat and moved. In a moment it will sink with you into the sea and you will all be drowned. Run! Run!'

All who left, left their gear and goods and swam in terror back to the ship. But Sinbad had walked too far to get away in time. Suddenly the island shuddered and sank into the depths of the sea; the waters surged over Sinbad and the waves crashed down upon him. He had nearly drowned when a wooden tub in which the crew had been bathing floated his way. He jumped into it and began to paddle with his arms towards the ship. The captain, however, was in such a fright that he set sail immediately with those who had reached the ship, heeding not the cries of the drowning.

Darkness closed in around Sinbad and he lay in the tub, certain that death was at hand. But after drifting for an entire night and a day, the tides brought him to the harbour of a lofty island. He caught hold of one of the branches and managed to clamber up onto the beach. Alas, he could walk no farther, for his legs were cramped and numb, and his feet swollen. So he crawled on his knees until he came upon a grove of fruit-laden trees amidst springs of sweet water. Sinbad ate and drank and his body and spirit began to revive.

After several days, Sinbad set out to explore the island. As he walked along the shore he caught sight of a noble mare tethered on the beach. He went up to her and she let out a great cry. Sinbad trembled in fear and turned to leave.

Before he had gone very far, a man came out of a cave, followed him and asked, 'Who are you?'

'Sinbad,' the surprised merchant replied.

'Where have you come from?' asked the man.

'I am a stranger who was left to drown in the sea, but good fortune led me to this island.'

When the man heard Sinbad's tale, he took his hand and led him to the entrance to the cave. They entered, descended a flight of steps and he found himself in a huge underground chamber as spacious as a ballroom.

Sinbad looked around and said, 'Now that I have told you of my accident, pray tell me who you are, why you live under the earth and why that mare is tethered on the beach?'

And so the man began his story:

'I am one of many who are stationed in different parts of the island. We are grooms of King Mirjan who guard and protect all of his horses. The mare you saw was one of a magical breed that eats not hay, but is nourished by the light of the moon.

'Every month when the moon is at its fullest, we bring the mares to the beach and then hide ourselves in these caves. In the morning when the moon has worked its spell, we return with the mares to our master. And now I shall take you, too, to the king.'

The rest of the grooms soon arrived, each leading a mare and the grooms set out, journeying to the capital of King Mirjan. The groom introduced the king to Sinbad, wherupon Mirjan gave him a cordial welcome and asked to hear his tale. So Sinbad related all that had happened. When he had finished the king said, 'Your rescue is indeed miraculous. You must be a blessed man destined for great things.' And the king promptly made Sinbad his harbour master, showered him with gifts and all manner of costly presents.

Sinbad lived in this way for a long while. And whenever he went to the port, he questioned the merchants and travellers for news of his home, Baghdad, for he was weary of living among strangers and

hoped to find some way to return home. But he met no one who knew of his beloved city, so he despaired.

One day a large ship came sailing into the harbour. When it had docked, the crew began to unload the cargo while Sinbad stood by and recorded the contents. 'Is there anything left in your ship?' Sinbad asked when the crew seemed to have finished.

'There remains in the hold only assorted bales of merchandise whose owner was drowned near one of the islands on our course. We are going to sell the goods and deliver the proceeds to his people in Baghdad.' When Sinbad asked for the drowned merchant's name, the captain replied, 'Sinbad the Sailor'.

On hearing this, Sinbad let out a great cry.

'O captain, I am that Sinbad who travelled with you. I was saved by a wooden tub that carried me to this island where the servants of King Mirjan found me and brought me here. These bales are mine and I pray you to release them to me.'

But the captain did not believe Sinbad.

'O captain,' Sinbad exclaimed, 'listen to my words. I will tell you more about my voyage than you have told me, then you will believe me. '

So Sinbad began to relate to the captain the whole history of the journey, up to the tragedy of the island. The captain then realized the truth of Sinbad's story and rejoiced at his deliverance saying, 'We were sure that you had drowned. Praise be to the power that gave you new life.'

The captain gave the bales to Sinbad, who opened them up and made a parcel of the finest and costliest of the contents as a present to King Mirjan.

Having done so and honoured with even costlier presents from King Mirjan, Sinbad returned to Baghdad with the crew of the ship.

With all the presents that the King had given him, Sinbad was rich and settled down again in Baghdad.

Sinbad was leading a most pleasurable life until one day he took it into his head to travel around the world. So he brought a large supply of merchandise, went down to the harbour and booked passage on a brand new ship. At last, fate brought him to an island, fair and green filled with fruit-bearing trees, fragrant flowers and singing birds. Sinbad landed and walked about, enjoying the shade of the trees and the song of the birds. So sweet was the wind and so fragrant were the flowers that he soon fell into a deep sleep. When he awoke he was horrified to find that the ship had left without him.

Giving himself up for lost he lamented, 'Last time I was saved by fate, but fate cannot be so kind twice. I am alone and there is no hope for me.'

He was so upset that he could not sit in one place for long. He climbed a tall tree and, looking in all directions, saw nothing but sky and sea and trees and birds and sand. But after a while his eager glance fell upon some great thing in the middle of the island. So he climbed down from the tree and walked to it. Behold, it was a huge white dome rising high into the air.

Sinbad circled around it but could find no door. As he stood wondering how to enter the dome, the skies darkened. Sinbad thought that a cloud had hidden the sun, but when he looked up he saw an enormous bird of such gigantic breadth that it veiled the sun.

Then Sinbad recalled a story he had heard long ago from some travellers. It told of a certain island where lived a huge bird called the roc, which fed its young on elephants. As Sinbad marvelled at the strange ways of nature, the roc alighted on the dome, covered it with its wings, and stretched its legs out on the ground. In this strange posture the roc fell asleep. When Sinbad saw this he arose, unwound his turban and twisted it into a rope with which he tied himself to the roc's legs.

'Perhaps,' he thought, 'this bird will carry me to inhabited lands. That will be better than living on this deserted island.'

In the morning the roc rose of its egg, for that is what the dome was, and spreading its wings with a great cry, soared into the air dragging Sinbad along, but never noticing him. When the roc finally alighted on the top of a high hill, Sinbad, quaking in his fear, wasted no time in untieing himself and running off. Presently he saw the roc catch something in its huge claws and rise aloft with it. Looking as closely as he dared Sinbad realized it was a serpent as gigantic as had ever roamed the earth; yet it seemed puny compared to the roc.

Looking further around, Sinbad found that he was on a hill overlooking a deep valley, which was surrounded by mountains so high that their summits disappeared into the clouds. At the sight of the wild and impassable country Sinbad moaned, 'Woe is me: I was better off on the island. There I had fruit to eat and water to drink, but here there are neither trees nor fruits nor streams and I will surely starve.'

Then Sinbad took courage and went down into the valley. Imagine how amazed he was to find that the soil was made of diamonds and it swarmed with snakes and vipers as big as palm trees. Sinbad ran for his life. Again he lamented at his misfortune.

As Sinbad walked along the valley, a roc flew overhead and dropped a slaughtered beast at his feet. Looking at the beast he had an idea. He took his knife from his belt and cut the meat into large, sticky pieces. When he had done this he threw the chunks into the valley. Suddenly the air was filled with huge eagles who swooped down into the diamond-filled valley and picked up the meat. Because the meat was so sticky, the precious stones stuck to it. Sinbad ran

after them and shooed them away, picking up the diamonds as he did so.

When he had gathered all the diamonds, he unwound his turban and lay all the meat on it. He tied it around himself and lay on his back and waited. A few minutes later, one of the huge eagles flew overhead and seeing the juicy meat, swooped down. He picked the meat up in his might talons, the turban and Sinbad with it. They flew for many miles, until Sinbad saw that they were passing over a huge, blue lake. He let out a loud cry and the startled bird dropped him, diamonds and all.

Sinbad landed in the lake with a large plop. Fortunately he was a good swimmer and swam as fast as he could for the shore. He walked along the sandy beach until he came to a small village. He asked one of the men there, how he could get to the nearest port. The man scratched his head and said, 'The nearest port is many miles from here, much too far to walk. We only have one horse in the village, so we could not sell it to you, no matter how much you offered.'

Sinbad showed the man his diamonds. 'Sir,' he said, 'if your horse is strong enough to carry two, I will give you ten diamonds for a lift. You and I can both ride on its back, and with the money you get for the diamonds you can buy ten hundred horses.'

So the man agreed to do this and the two set off. It was a long and tiring journey, but eventually they reached the port. There Sinbad sold some of the diamonds and bought beautiful silks and golden ornaments with the money he received. He hired a boat to take him back to Baghdad, and when he arrived he sold all his goods for a huge profit and settled down in the town again, living a most pleasurable life.

But as time passed he once again grew weary of his idle life of ease and comfort. So once more he laid in a considerable supply of merchandise to trade, and set sail in a fine ship with a company of merchants. For weeks they travelled on calm seas, stopping at many ports and gaining great profits through their trade. But one day, when they were far out at sea a mighty storm arose. The waves lashed the ship and the gales drove them they knew not where. The next morning when the storm had calmed, the captain climbed up to the gunwale and scanned the ocean in all directions. Suddenly he let out a great cry and tore his garments in despair.

'O my fellow travellers,' he cried, 'the wind has driven us far off course and we have run aground at the Mountain of the Hairy Apes. No man has ever left this place alive. We are doomed.'

Hardly had he finished speaking when thousands of apes were upon them, surrounding the ship on all sides, swarming about like locusts. They were the most fearsome creatures, only two feet tall, but covered with black hair, evil-smelling, black-faced and yellow-eyed. They gnawed at the ship's ropes and cables, tearing them in two, so that the sails fell into the sea and the powerless ship was stranded on the mountainous coast. Then the apes chased all the men off the ship, stole the cargo and disappeared.

Sinbad and his companions were left on the mountain island where they fortunately found fruit and water. They ate and drank and then decided to explore the island.

They had walked for a mile or two when they came across what looked like an uninhabited house. As they came close to it they could see that it was a tall castle and the gate was open. They went in and found themselves in a large courtyard which was completely empty. They lay down and fell asleep, hoping that the castle's owner would return before nightfall.

All at once the earth trembled under them and the air rumbled with a terrible noise. The owner had returned and he was a gigantic creature shaped like a man but as tall as tree, with eyes like fiery coals and teeth like elephant's tusks. His mouth was like a well, his lips hung loose onto his chest and his nails were as long and sharp as lion's claws.

The merchants almost fainted with terror at the sight of him. Then the giant seized Sinbad, who was but a tiny plaything in his hands, and began to run his mighty hands all over him, prodding him here and there. But Sinbad was too thin for the giant's huge appetite, so he put him down and picked up another. Finding him too thin as well, the giant tried another and another until he came to the captain of the ship, who was a fat, broad-shouldered man. The giant found him tempting enough to eat and promptly did so. That done he lay down and fell asleep. In the morning he got up and left the castle.

The next night the giant returned and again the earth trembled, and again he went through all the men until he found one tasty enough for his supper.

When the giant departed the next morning the terrified men decided that they could not sit by and watch the giant eat them all.

'Let us try to slay him,' they said. 'We will build a raft of firewood and planks and keep it ready at the shore.' As soon as the giant came home, he grabbed one of the men and ate him for his dinner. He lay down and fell asleep shortly afterwards.

When the men were quite sure that the giant was sound asleep, they took two iron spits and heated the ends in a fire, until they were as red-hot as the coals themselves. They crept up to the sleeping giant and thrust the glowing spits into his eyes.

His scream rent the air and he jumped up fumbling for the men. But he was quite blind and he could not prevent the men rushing to the raft.

But even when they had passed beyond the giant's reach, they could find no respite from danger, for the sea was stormy and the waves swollen. One by one the men died until there were only three men and Sinbad left. Finally the winds cast them upon an island where they found fruit to eat and water to drink. Exhausted by their hazardous voyage, they lay down on the beach and went to sleep.

They had barely closed their eyes when they were aroused by a hissing sound and saw that a monstrous dragon with a huge belly was spread in a circle around them. Suddenly it reared its head, seized one of Sinbad's companions, and swallowed him whole. Then the beast left and Sinbad said, 'Woe to us. Each kind of death that threatens us is more terrible than the last. We rejoiced at our deliverance from the sea and apes and the giant, but we are now at the mercy of something even more evil.'

The frightened men climbed into a high tree and went to sleep there. Sinbad rested on the top branch. When night fell, the dragon returned. He looked to right and left and finally discovered the men in the tree. He stood up on his hind legs and swallowed Sinbad's companions. Again, the dragon left satisfied with his dinner. Then Sinbad climbed down and resolved to find some way to save his life. So he took pieces of wood, broad and long, and made a cage with them. He crept into the cage and when the dragon returned he saw Sinbad sitting in the cage. He immediately tried to eat him, but he could not get his jaws round the cage.

All through the night, the dragon circled around Sinbad's cage, hissing in anger. But when the dawn came and the sun began to shine, the dragon left in fury and disappointment.

Sinbad ran to the beach where he spied a ship on the horizon. He broke a branch off a tree, unwound his turban from his head and tied it to the branch. He began to wave it like a flag and at last, one of the sailors spotted him and the ship turned to shore. They cast anchor and took the grateful Sinbad aboard, and carried him back to Baghdad.

One day, several months later, Sinbad was visited at home by a company of merchants who talked to him about foreign travel and

trade, until the old wanderlust came back to Sinbad, and he yearned
to enjoy the sight of foreign lands once more. So Sinbad resolved to
join them on their voyage and they purchased a great store of precious goods, more than ever before. They set out and sailed from
island to island.

After several months of travelling and trading they sailed into
a furious storm which tore the sails to tatters. Then the ship founder-
ed, casting all on board into the sea.

Sinbad swam for half a day, certain that his fate was sealed, when
one of the planks of the ship floated up to him and he climbed on it,
along with some of the other merchants.

They took turns paddling and soon the current drove them to an
island. Sinbad and his companions threw themselves onto the beach,
ate some of the fruit that they found there and then each man fell
into a troubled sleep. The next morning they began to explore the
island. Coming across a house, they were about to knock at the door
when a host of half-naked savages ran out, surrounded them and
forced them inside where the king awaited. The king extended

a most cordial welcome and invited them to dinner. Gratefully they sat down and were immediately served such food as they had never tasted in their lives.

Sinbad, however, was not hungry and he refused all the food that was offered to him. He was soon glad that he had done so, for as the men tasted the food they lost all their senses and began to devour it like madmen possessed of an evil spirit. Then the savages gave them coconut oil to drink, whereupon their eyes turned around in their heads and they continued to eat even more ravenously than before.

Seeing all this, Sinbad grew anxious for his safety. He watched carefully and it was not long before he realized that he was amidst a certain tribe of savages of whom he had once heard a traveller tell. Every man who came to the savages' country was given food and oil which made their stomachs expand and at the same time to lose their reason and turn into idiots. In this way, the unfortunate victims never stopped eating. Every day they were led out to pasture like cattle and grew fatter and fatter. When they were judged fat enough, the savages slaughtered them and sent them off to market.

So Sinbad understood the evil folk that he had fallen among and watched sadly as his friends ate and drank. The savages paid no attention to Sinbad, for as the days passed he grew thinner.

One day he slipped away and walked to a distant beach. There he saw the old man who was the herdsman, charged with guarding his friends. As soon as the herdsman saw Sinbad, so gaunt and bony, he realized that this was not one of the madmen and wanted to help him escape.

'If you take the road to the right,' the herdsman said, 'it will lead you away from the house of the savages.'

Sinbad followed the kind old man's advice and did not cease travelling for seven days and seven nights. He stopped only to eat and drink, for the path was strewn with roots and herbs and water was plentiful. On the eighth day he caught sight of a group of men gathering peppercorns.

'I am a poor stranger,' he said to them. 'May I have a peppercorn?'

One of the men threw him a handful and Sinbad told them the story of the hardships and dangers that he had suffered.

The men marvelled at Sinbad's tale and brought him to their king, to whom he repeated his tale. The king instantly liked Sinbad and invited him to stay in his sumptuous palace.

One day the king invited Sinbad out to ride with the hunt. Now Sinbad had noticed that neither the king nor his citizens had saddles on their beautiful steeds.

'Why, O Lord, do you not have saddles? Riding is much easier with them.'

'What is a saddle?' the king asked, for he had never heard of such a thing before.

Sinbad offered to make one for him, so that he could ride in greater comfort. In a few days, Sinbad had fashioned a magnificent saddle of polished leather with silk fringes and presented it to the king. The king tried it and was delighted. The next week his Vizier asked Sinbad to make a saddle for him as well. In a short time, everyone wanted a saddle, so Sinbad went into business and became a prosperous saddle maker.

Then one day the king said, 'Sinbad, I have such affection for you that I cannot permit you ever to leave. I must therefore insist that you marry one of our women so that you will remain here for the rest of your days.'

So Sinbad married a beautiful and rich lady of noble ancestry and lived with her in peace and contentment.

One sad day, however, Sinbad's wife took ill and died within a week. The mournful Sinbad was about to make arrangements for a funeral in accordance with the customs of his own country when a messenger arrived from the king.

'My lord offers you deep condolences and asks that the funeral be conducted according to the customs of our land,' the messenger said.

Sinbad agreed, for he wished only to honour his wife.

Now it happened that the customs of the country were very strange. When a woman died she was buried in a deep cave and her husband, still alive, was buried with her so that she might have companionship in the afterlife.

On the day of the funeral, the whole town arrived in front of Sinbad's house and they walked in procession to the burial cave — a vast underground cavern that ran beneath a mountain. The body of Sinbad's wife was lowered down. Then the townsfolk lowered him down on a rope ladder.

Sinbad found himself in a cave filled with rotting bodies and skeletons, for it had served as a burial site since time immemorial. It was a horrible, foul-smelling place and Sinbad again lamented that the greed that had made him leave Baghdad had ended in such a way. There was no escape from the cave of death.

The day after the funeral, Sinbad noticed a mountain goat at the far end of the cave. Seeing that the beast was fat and healthy, Sinbad realized that there must be another opening in the cave, one unknown to the townspeople. So he followed the beast and after

a while saw a shaft of light. Indeed, it was another opening. Sinbad joyfully climbed out and found himself high over the sea on a steep cliff which only an animal so agile as the goat could climb. Although he felt sure that he was to die there, he was thankful that he would not die in the cavern of death.

When Sinbad was near to death, a ship passed by and spotted him. The ship cast anchor and with the help of strong ropes, the sailors scaled the cliff and rescued Sinbad.

When he arrived back in Baghdad, Sinbad promised his friends and relations that he would never leave them again. This time he kept that promise.

ALADDIN

In far-off China there once lived a magician who was as ugly as he was wicked. His magic was tremendously powerful, but he was not satisfied with it. He wanted to be the most powerful and the richest magician in the whole of the world, for he knew that there were others who could equal him.

One day as he was walking in the market place his eyes fell upon a ring that was brighter than any ring that he possessed. It glittered in the bright sunshine and threw off dazzling patterns of red and blue on the canopy of the jewel-seller's stall. The magician had to have it and after long bargaining with the jewel-seller, a price was agreed which satisfied both men.

The magician rushed home with his new treasure and as soon as he was inside, he hurriedly pulled off all the rings that he was wearing and slipped the new one on. He moved his hand hither and thither, and marvelled at the glorious colours that the ring cast off. With greed and lust in his eyes, the magician watched the beautiful patterns until he could bear it no longer and he lovingly stroked the ring. Suddenly, the room darkened and was filled with smoke. The magician was terrified and began to shake with fear. He shook even more when a voice boomed out, 'Who calls the Genie of the Ring?'

'The what?' asked the magician, his voice trembling as much as his knees.

'Who calls the Genie of the Ring?' the voice repeated.

'I did, I suppose,' said the magician.

'And what do you want, oh Master?' the Genie of the Ring asked.

'What can you give me?' asked the magician.

'Money, jewellery, precious metals, rich cloth, enough to satisfy most men.'

'I am not most men,' said the magician. 'I want power. I want to be the richest and most powerful man in the world.'

'For that you need the Genie of the Lamp, not the Genie of the Ring.'

'Where can I find this Genie of the Lamp?'

'Come, I will show you,' said the Genie and with a rush of wind and a blaze of sparks the two were suddenly transported to an oasis far from anywhere. In the centre of the oasis there was a trapdoor.

'There you will find the Genie of the Lamp. Under the trapdoor,' said the Genie of the Ring.

The magician rushed forward and pulled at the trapdoor. But it refused to move, even by as much as an inch.

'Foolish man,' scoffed the Genie of the Ring. 'I offered you enough to satisfy most men and you wanted more. Only one person in the whole world can open the door.'

'Who?' demanded the magician. 'Who can open the trapdoor?'

'Aladdin. Aladdin, the washerwoman's son. Anyone else who enters the garden will die instantly,' laughed the Genie and with a rush of wind and a blaze of sparks he was gone.

The magician rubbed his eyes in disbelief and suddenly found himself back in his own home.

He immediately summoned all his servants and commanded them to find out where Aladdin, the washerwoman's son, lived. One by one his servants went out and searched, and one by one they returned with no information. The magician angrily sent them out again and eventually one of the servants came back with the news that Aladdin lived in the poorest district of the town, some distance from the magician's palace.

The very next morning the magician set out to see Aladdin, and even his own servants did not recognize him. His long, dirty finger-nails had been cleaned and cut. His straggly hair and greasy beard had been washed and trimmed and he was dressed in fresh, newly-laundered clothes. He quickly made his way to where Aladdin lived and when he saw the boy he rushed up to him and put his arms around him.

'Aladdin. My dear nephew. We have never met, but I am your poor father's brother. I have been travelling for many years, visiting holy places.'

'My father's brother?' said Aladdin. 'No one has ever mentioned that my father had a brother.'

'No matter, child. It is the truth. Take me to your mother. My poor brother's wife.'

The boy did as he was told and the two went into the steamy laundry where Aladdin and his mother lived.

'Sister-in-law,' cried the magician as soon as he saw Aladdin's mother.

'Sister-in-law? My poor husband had no brother,' said the woman.

'He did. Indeed he did. But we quarrelled many years ago and I have been on pilgrimage ever since.'

The woman did not believe him at first, but when the magician took ten gold coins and gave them to her, saying 'Take this. Buy some clothes for the child,' she was happy to believe him.

For several days the magician stayed with Aladdin and his mother, insisting on paying for everything.

One day, about a week after his arrival the magician asked the woman if he could take Aladdin on a journey for a few days. By this time the widow was convinced that the magician was her brother-in-law and gave her consent.

The man and boy travelled together for several days until they came to an oasis. 'Aladdin,' said the magician. 'Raise the trapdoor, child, and bring me the lamp that you will find down there.'

Aladdin did as he was told and lifted the trapdoor. There was a flight of stairs and the magician then told Aladdin to go down them and bring him the lamp. Aladdin went down the steps and found himself in the most beautiful garden that he could ever have imagined. The trees were laden with precious jewels that dazzled Aladdin's eyes with their magnificent colours — there were pearls, diamonds, rubies and many, many more. At the end of a golden path, Aladdin could see the lamp. He made his way towards it and tried to lift it, but it would not budge. 'Uncle,' the boy cried. 'I cannot lift it on my own. Come and help me.' But the magician was afraid and called back, 'Try harder, nephew, for I cannot come into the enchanted garden.'

The boy tried and tried, but it was no good. He kept calling for his uncle and still his uncle refused to come down. After many hours the poor child was exhausted and made his way back to the steps. But the magician was furious. 'Ungrateful wretch!' he screamed. 'You shall stay there for ever. If I cannot have the lamp, then no one will.' And with that he slammed the trapdoor down, leaving Aladdin in the enchanted garden.

Poor Aladdin. He ran back through the garden looking for a way out, but there was none. Eventually he made his way back to where the lamp was and unthinkingly tried to lift it. He was amazed when he did so quite easily. He ran back to the trapdoor and shouted, 'Uncle, I have it. I have it.' But the magician was miles away and no one heard Aladdin's cries. Aladdin sat down and wept. As he did so his hands rubbed the lamp, and suddenly there was an enormous puff of smoke and with a blaze of sparks, the most enormous Genie appeared before Aladdin.

'You called me, Master. What is your command?'

'M ... M ... M ... Master! C ... C ... Command,' stuttered Aladdin.

'Yes, Master! I am the Genie of the Lamp. Anything you wish shall be granted.'

'Then take me home,' cried the astonished boy and in an instant

Aladdin was outside his own home. 'Mother,' he cried and rushed inside to tell her everything that had happened to him.

'We need never be poor again,' he said and rubbed the lamp. When the Genie appeared Aladdin asked him to bring gold and silver and fine clothes; and in an instant the Genie did as Aladdin had commanded. For many days, whenever Aladdin or his mother

wanted anything they summoned the Genie, who did as he was asked.

One day, Aladdin was in the market when soldiers of the Sultan's army appeared and began to push the crowds roughly to one side. 'Stand back,' they cried. 'The Sultan's daughter is coming and she must not be seen. Turn around.' Everyone did as they were commanded and the Princess passed through the market place. Now Aladdin had obeyed the soldiers, but found himself looking into a large mirror. As the Princess passed by, Aladdin saw her reflection in the glass and instantly fell in love with her. He ran home as fast as he could and burst into the house. 'Mother,' he gasped. 'I have seen the Sultan's daughter.'

His mother was horrified. 'But it is instant death for anyone who casts eyes on the Princess. It is the law.'

'I saw her in a looking glass,' said Aladdin. 'Mother. I must marry her!'

'Marry her!' exclaimed his mother. 'Aladdin, child, we are poor people. You cannot marry the Princess.'

'But the lamp,' said Aladdin. 'With the Genie we can become as rich as the Sultan.'

And so, despite his mother's doubts, Aladdin summoned the Genie. He commanded him to build a vast palace and to fill it with jewels and precious things.

Before the mother and son could blink, they found themselves in a sumptuous room furnished with gold and silver. Their clothes were made of the finest silks and jewels sparkled from their fingers.

The next morning the Sultan awoke as usual and went to his window to look out over his capital. He blinked once, then twice, then three times. For where there had been a vast park, the night before, there now stood the most beautiful palace that the Sultan had ever seen.

The astonished Sultan immediately summoned his Vizier and demanded an explanation. The Vizier hurried from the palace and into Aladdin's splendid new home.

When Aladdin saw the Vizier approach, he went to meet him. 'Tell your master that the palace and all the precious things are for the Princess if he will give me permission to marry her.'

The Vizier ran back to the Sultan and told him what Aladdin wanted. The Sultan ordered that his daughter be brought to him, dressed in her most beautiful clothes. 'Go and bring this Aladdin to me,' he called to the harassed Vizier.

As soon as the Princess saw Aladdin she fell as deeply in love with him as he had with her.

'How did you come to build such a magnificent palace overnight? How is it that you are obviously so rich, yet I have never heard of you?' demanded the bewildered Sultan.

'Sire, my fortune I made in a far-off land. By trade,' said Aladdin, who did not want anyone else to know of the Genie of the Lamp. 'I had one million servants toil silently the night to build the palace.'

'And why do you want to marry my daughter?'

'Because, sire, I had heard of her beauty, and now that I see her for myself I see that I was told wrongly, for no words can describe such beauty. Sire, allow me to marry her. I will make her happy. She will want for nothing.'

The Sultan thought for a few seconds. He loved his daughter very much and did not really want to lose her. But he loved riches, too.

198

'Very well, I consent,' he said, 'but only on condition that you take her to the palace across from mine, and that you both live there for ever.'

Aladdin was overjoyed and promised to bring the Princess back.

The wedding was the grandest that had ever been seen, and the couple were as happy as happy could be to live in their splendid palace. Everyone who saw them was astonished at how completely happy they were together and expected them to live there for ever and ever. And that is exactly what the lovers planned to do; but they had made these plans without considering the wicked magician.

Thousands of miles away, the magician was wondering what had happened to Aladdin. One day, about three weeks after Aladdin and the Princess had been married, he went into a great book-lined room and from the back of a secret drawer he took out his crystal ball. Murmuring some strange incantations, he rubbed his hands over the ball. Imagine his horror when he saw Aladdin and the Princess in their splendid palace. His voice got louder and louder and soon he was screaming a strange spell at the top of his voice. He turned three times and vanished into thin air.

He reappeared at nightfall outside Aladdin's palace. He walked around the walls and saw that it was heavily guarded. He wanted the lamp more than ever and as the night passed, he made his plans to get revenge.

The next morning, he watched as Aladdin set out on a fine horse, obviously going hunting. He then made his way to the market where he bought several beautiful new lamps.

Soon he was back outside Aladdin's palace, shouting, 'New lamps for old! New lamps for old!' From deep inside the palace, the Princess heard the strange call, and suddenly remembered the old lamp that her husband kept in a cupboard. 'How well pleased he will be to have a fine new lamp,' she thought to herself and ran to fetch it.

'Lampseller,' she called from a window. 'Wait. Here is an old lamp for a new one.'

The magician's greedy hands grabbed the lamp and his eyes lit up with joy. He had the lamp. 'Thank you, Lady,' he called up to the Princess. 'Here is your new lamp,' and with that he was off.

He rounded a corner out of sight of anyone and rubbed the lamp. Instantly the Genie appeared. 'What do you require, oh Master?'

'Take Aladdin's palace and the Princess to my home in Africa.'

No sooner had he spoken than there was a loud gust of wind. The palace was being hammered by a violent dust storm, and when the dust cleared, the palace had vanished.

When the Sultan awoke from his afternoon nap, he went to his window as he now always did to admire his son-in-law's magnificent palace. Imagine his horror when all that he saw was the park that had been there before. He immediately summoned his Vizier and demanded that Aladdin be brought before him. It took a few hours to find the young man, but eventually he was brought before the furious Sultan.

'What have you done with my daughter? Where is the palace?' the Sultan demanded.

Aladdin could only shake his head in astonishment as he had no idea what had happened.

'Take him away,' roared the Sultan. 'Throw him into the deepest dungeon and let him remain there until my daughter is returned to me.'

Poor Aladdin was dragged away and cast into the deepest, darkest dungeon in the palace.

Meanwhile, thousands of miles away in the depths of darkest Africa the poor Princess was weeping and begging the magician to take her back.

'Keep the palace, but let me return,' she begged.

'Never,' replied the magician. 'Now you are here, here you will stay. Not as a princess, but as my wife. Prepare yourself, my dear, for tomorrow we will be wed. Tonight we will feast.' With that, the magician departed and left the poor girl to her thoughts. She thought long and deep, and after many hours she came up with a plan.

That evening, she dressed herself in her most beautiful robes, rubbed the most expensive perfumes on her soft skin and waited for the magician. She ordered her servants to bring her the most succulent meats and the sweetest fruits. To drink, she ordered the most potent of all the wines in the cellar. When the magician appeared later, she greeted him with a deep curtsey.

'At last you have come, my master,' she said.

'Ah,' sighed the magician. 'I can see that you have thought over my proposal and are going to be sensible.'

'Come, drink with me,' the Princess said softly.

She poured two glasses of wine and watched as the magician drank deeply. She quickly filled his glass and beckoned him to the table. All through the meal she laughed and smiled and kept the magician's glass full, while she hardly drank at all.

'You are without doubt the most powerful man in the world. That weakling Aladdin is nothing compared to you,' she said after they

had eaten. 'Where does your power come from?' Before he could answer, she filled his glass yet again. 'Let us drink a toast to your power,' she said and watched with great satisfaction as the magician emptied his glass.

'My power,' the magician said, 'comes from this old lamp.' As he spoke, he took the lamp from under his cloak. 'I only need to rub it gently...' He never finished his sentence. The Princess had filled him so full of wine, that he slipped to the floor, completely drunk.

The Princess picked up the lamp and rubbed it gently. Immediately the Genie appeared. 'What do you command, oh Mistress?'

'Take this man and set him in a place from which he can never escape.'

The Genie stooped down and picked up the sleeping magician as easily as if he had been a piece of fluff. He disappeared for the flick of an eye, and was back. 'What else, oh Mistress, do you command?'

'Take me and my palace back to where we belong,' said the Princess.

There was a sudden rush of wind and in an instant the palace was back in its proper place.

The next morning, the Sultan awoke from his troubled sleep and went to the window to look sadly at the park where the palace had once stood. He blinked once, and then twice, and then three times.

'Vizier!' he shouted. 'Come quickly. Look!'

Within a few minutes, Aladdin had been released from his deep dungeon and was reunited with his beloved wife.

'You are indeed a powerful magician, Aladdin, who can make palaces appear and disappear. But do not do it again. Next time I will not be so merciful!'

Aladdin was quick to agree, and he and his Princess lived happily together for many, many years.

And the lamp? It was locked away in the deepest dungeon in Aladdin's palace, and it is probably still there to this day.

RAMA AND SITA

In distant India the lands around the city of Ayodhya on the banks of the river Saragu were once ruled by the wise King, Dasaratha. He had three wives. The first was called Kausalya and they had a splendid son, Rama, who was heir to Dasaratha's throne. His second wife, Kaikeya, was the mother of his son, Bharata, and his third wife, Sumitra, bore him fine twins, Lakshmana and Satrughna.

The king, his three queens and their four sons were all very happy. Only Kaikeya was occasionally jealous that Rama would one day rule over the kingdom rather than her own beloved Bharata.

Rama grew up as tall and handsome as his father, and one day Dasaratha announced, 'Rama, you have now grown to manhood. It is time that you took a wife and had children of your own. I have chosen for your bride the lovely Sita.'

Rama had never met Sita, but it was the custom at that time for fathers to choose their sons' brides. It was also the custom that the sons never saw their brides until the wedding day.

The marriage was duly announced, and preparations for the great occasion were soon underway. On the day before the ceremony, Rama looked out of his window and saw the bridal procession enter the city gates. There were mighty elephants and beautiful horses. Graceful cheetahs strained at their leashes, adding excitement to the magnificent procession. In the centre, a huge white elephant decorated with gold carried a curtained box on its back, and Rama knew that in it sat his future bride.

That night he was unable to sleep. He was worried in case Sita's beauty proved to be an exaggeration, and by morning he had convinced himself that his bride would be old and fat and probably toothless, too.

Imagine his delight when Sita was revealed to be as beautiful as had been rumoured. She was tall and graceful and her dark eyes shone with happiness when she looked at her handsome husband for the first time. At once she fell in love with Rama, and he too fell in love with her.

The marriage ceremony was long and impressive. The music was enchanting and afterwards all the courtiers were invited by Dasaratha to a splendid banquet. There was much jollity and laughter and clapping as the sumptuous feast was carried in. Suddenly, when the merriment was at its height, Dasaratha slumped forward, his hand on his chest. The guests were silent as the court physician quickly examined the king and then whispered to the three queens. 'He is dead,' the physician said in a sad voice, and the guests watched, horrified, as the king's body was carried from the room.

A little later, Kaikeya left the palace and went into the hills beyond. She made her way to a small clearing and gathered some curious-looking herbs. She quickly returned to the palace and made an infusion of them. When it was prepared she went to the chamber where the king's body was lying and said to the other two widows and all their children who were there,

'Stand aside. Let me draw near.'

They all did as they were told, and the woman raised her husband's head gently off the pillow. She parted his white lips and poured a little of the liquid into his dead mouth. She then laid his head back on the pillow and rubbed more of the herb infusion all over his body.

A few seconds later, Kausalya screamed, 'He's breathing! He's breathing! Kaikeya has brought him back to life.' And sure enough, Dasaratha's chest was moving up and down, drawing air into his lungs. A moment later, his eyelids flickered open and soon he stirred, as if awakening from a deep slumber. The astonished onlookers knelt before him as he held out his hand to Kaikeya. 'You have brought me back to this life. You may have any two wishes and if it is in my power to grant them, I shall do so.'

Kaikeya did not hesitate. 'Declare my son Bharata your heir instead of Rama, and banish Rama from here for fourteen years.'

'But mother,' cried Bharata. 'I do not wish to be king. Rama is the rightful heir.'

'Quiet,' commanded Dasaratha. 'I gave my word. Bharata, you are now my heir. Rama, I command you to leave here and live in the jungle as a penitent.'

'I will obey,' said Bharata. 'But when the fourteen years are up and Rama is free to return, I will hand over the reins of power to him.'

'I must go where my husband goes,' declared Sita. 'If he leaves for fourteen years, then I, too, will go.'

'You cannot,' said Rama. 'The jungle is a dangerous place. It is no place for you.'

'I WILL go,' repeated Sita.

'And I too,' said Lakshmana.

And so, the very next morning, Rama, his newly-wedded wife and his half-brother prepared to leave the palace.

Rama's mother stepped forward. 'I have but one gift for you,' she said handing a sword to Rama. 'It is an enchanted sword. Wherever it is aimed it will fall.' And she kissed her son and her stepson tenderly.

Lakshmana's mother stepped forward. 'I too have a gift,' she said, and gave him a bow and a quiver of arrows. 'This quiver will never run empty. The arrows will always find their targets.'

Then Satrughna, Lakshmana's twin brother, stepped forward. 'Take this,' he said and thrust an alabaster pot into Sita's hand. 'It is the infusion that brought the king back to life.'

And so bearing only the sword, the quiver and bow, and the pot, the three made their way out of the palace. Dasaratha watched from his chamber, his heart heavy with sadness, for he knew that he would not live another fourteen years to see them return.

The three travelled long and far and eventually came to Mountain Chitrakutu where the Holy Hermits lived. Valkimi, the leader of the hermits, came forward to greet them. 'Prince Rama,' he declared, 'I had heard that you and your brother were to come here. And this lovely creature must be Sita. I wish you all happiness.'

Rama and Sita thanked him.

'You must build yourselves a hermitage before the rains start. You will be helped.' And he bowed and left the three of them to search for a suitable spot.

The news soon spread to the other hermits that Rama and his bride and half-brother had arrived and all of them helped to build a fine hermitage.

Hermits live a simple life and are quiet and gentle people. After a short time, the three found that the tranquillity of the Holy Mountain was as beautiful and peaceful as the jungle around it and they began to be very happy. Their happiness grew deeper every day and for year after year they lived in great contentment. Sita became more and more beautiful as the years passed, and Rama's love for her grew with each setting of the sun.

In the jungle all around the Holy Mountain, there lived demons. They did not bother the hermits because they knew they were able to resist any of the temptations they could offer, but those unwise enough to travel in the jungle at night were often scared by the shining eyes and eerie laughter of the demons as they roamed the jungle.

One day, as Rama and Sita knelt quietly in prayer at the altar outside their hermitage an ugly old woman passed. She was Shurpanakha, sister of the master demon. She fell in love with Rama as soon as she looked at him. She was used to getting anything that she wanted and when she called out to Rama, 'Come, oh beautiful warrior. Come and be my husband,' she was astonished when he replied, 'Woman, I am married already.'

Just then Lakshmana came out of the hermitage. He had grown more handsome than Rama and Shurpanakha fell in love with him, too.

'Come both of you. We will live in my brother's palace in the jungle. I will make you both rich and we will be happy, the three of us,' she said.

'And leave our beloved Sita,' laughed Rama. 'Go, old hag. Leave us alone.'

No one had ever called Shurpanakha an old hag before and she became furious.

She ran towards Sita and grabbed her around the neck. Her scrawny hands tightened around the poor girl's throat squeezing the life out of her.

Rama pulled his enchanted sword from its sheath, where it had lain untouched for years, and brought it down on Shurpanakha's nose. The old hag screamed terribly as her hands flew up to stop the ghastly flow of blood gushing from the hole where her nose had been.

'I will have my revenge for this,' she shouted as she ran off into the jungle.

When her brother saw the ghastly mess that Rama had made of Shurpanakha's face, his fury matched Shurpanakha's. He immediately sent fourteen thousand evil demons to kill Rama and his wife and half-brother.

The battle was long and horrible; fourteen thousand against two. But Lakshmana's magic quiver never ran out of arrows and each arrow fired killed every demon in its path.

Shurpanakha watched in astonishment as wave after wave of demons were slaughtered by the magic arrows. She looked in terror as she saw an arrow fly straight towards her brother and bring him down, along with one thousand demons. Terrified and angry, she ran from the hermitage and fled through the jungle to the palace of Ravana, king of all demons. When she told him her story, Ravana wanted to send even more demons after Rama, but his son, Manan, said, 'Wait, father. If we send ten million demons after Rama, it will be no use. He and his brother are clearly invincible. But Sita is not. We must lure her away from Rama and Lakshmana. They will surely die of grief.'

And so Ravana and Manan made their way to the hermitage and waited for their chance. It came a few days later. Rama went out hunting, leaving Lakshmana to guard Sita.

Disguising his voice as that of Valkimi, the leader of the hermits, Manan, called out, 'Help! Somebody help me!' Lakshmana rushed out of the hermitage into the undergrowth to search for Valkimi. Further and further away from the hermitage, Manan lured him, and as he was still searching, Ravana ran into the house and grabbed the terrified Sita from her chair. Although she struggled fiercely, the demon was far too strong for her and he dragged her into the jungle.

When Rama came home, he listened, horrified, to his brother's tale. The two men sadly went to Valkimi's hermitage and told them their story.

'I cannot help you,' said Valkimi. 'Only Sugriva and his councillor Hanuman would know where Sita has been taken. You must go to them at Mount Rshyamuku and ask for their help.'

So Rama and Lakshmana went and collected the sword, the bow and arrow and the alabaster pot and made their way to Mount Rshyamuku.

Sugriva and Hanuman listened to the two brothers. Hanuman

stroked his long beard and said, 'Go into the clearing and light a fire of sandalwood. As the smoke rises, a bird will appear. Ask it where Sita has been taken and it will help.'

Rama did as Hanuman had said. He collected sandalwood and made a big fire. As the smoke whirled into the air, a magnificent bird flew down and asked, 'What do you want of me, oh Rama?'

'How do you know who I am?' asked Rama.

'I know everything,' answered the bird.

'Where is Sita, my wife?' begged Rama.

'She is being held by Ravana at his palace on the island of Lanka.'

'How can I get her out? Please tell me!' pleaded Rama.

'You alone cannot,' said the bird. 'You need the aid of Louhi, leader of the monkeys.'

'Monkey! How can monkeys help me?'

'Monkeys are as intelligent as humans. I can fly to Lanka, but you cannot fly with me. Louhi can lead you to the shores across from Lanka.'

'How can I find Louhi?' asked Rama.

'Wait here,' said the bird and flew off.

An hour passed. Two. Rama was about to make his way back to Lakshmana when there was the sound of footsteps approaching the clearing. Rama watched in astonishment as an enormous monkey approached him and said,

'I am Louhi. I have come to lead you to Lanka. Go and collect your brother and be back here at dawn.'

'But monkeys cannot talk. I must be dreaming,' said Rama.

'Rama! The gods are pleased with the devotions you have offered them since your exile. With them, anything is possible. They give us the gift of communication to help you. Now go.'

At dawn the next morning, Rama and Lakshmana returned to the clearing where Louhi was waiting for them. He beckoned them to follow and the two brothers went into the jungle behind the monkey. For three days and nights they went deeper and deeper into the thick undergrowth, until they came to a lake that was so large that the other side was not visible from the shore. In the middle of the lake, Rama and Lakshmana could just make out an island. 'There,' said Louhi, 'is where Sita is being held.'

'But how are we to rescue her? If we sail out, we will be spotted and destroyed,' said Rama. 'We must somehow get them to leave the island and bring Sita to the shore.'

Louhi beckoned to some birds. 'Fly over to the island and tell the Princess Sita that help is at hand,' he ordered and the birds flew off.

Meanwhile Sita was miserable and frightened. She was being held prisoner in the most beautiful palace she had ever seen. Every room was more sumptuously furnished than the next. The furniture was all made of pure gold and studded with precious jewels. The carpets were of finest silk and rich fabrics hung on every wall. The gardens were a glorious sight. There were the greenest of green lawns and flower-beds containing orchids and roses and gardenias, as well as sweet-smelling herbs that filled the air with a wonderful aroma. Fountains played everywhere sending sparkling streams into the blue, blue sky above. Yet all that Sita wanted was to be reunited with her beloved Rama. Every day, Ravana asked her to be his wife and every day she refused.

'I would,' she said, 'rather die.'

Sita was walking in the gardens when a bird landed in the pathway in front of her. She was astonished when she heard it speak.

'Princess,' the bird said, 'Rama and his brother are on the shore waiting to rescue you. You need be patient for only a few more hours. Be not afraid of anything that happens and do what Ravana tells you to do.'

Before the astounded Sita could say anything, the bird flew off . . .

It alighted on the shore where Louhi and the others were waiting. 'She is safe but sorrowing,' said the bird. 'I told her that help was at hand.'

'Good,' said Louhi. 'Now go into the jungle and tell all the monkeys to come here tomorrow morning.'

The next morning every monkey in the jungle obeyed Louhi and by the time the sun was high in the sky, there were more than one million monkeys on the shores of the lake.

'Now,' said Louhi to the bird, 'return to the jungle and tell every stinging insect to come here.' The bird immediately flew off.

'Go and cut down branches and fashion clubs from them,' said Louhi to the monkeys and they set about doing that.

Just when the sun was at its highest, the sky grew darker and darker. Every stinging insect had followed the bird. There were millions of them.

'Attack the island,' commanded Louhi.

Within minutes there was panic on the island. The demons raced hither and thither trying to escape the vicious stings of the insects, but it was useless.

'Leave this island,' thundered Ravana. 'You,' he shouted at Sita, 'come with me.' He grabbed poor Sita, pulling her to the shore and onto a boat. They were almost the last to leave. In front of them,

210

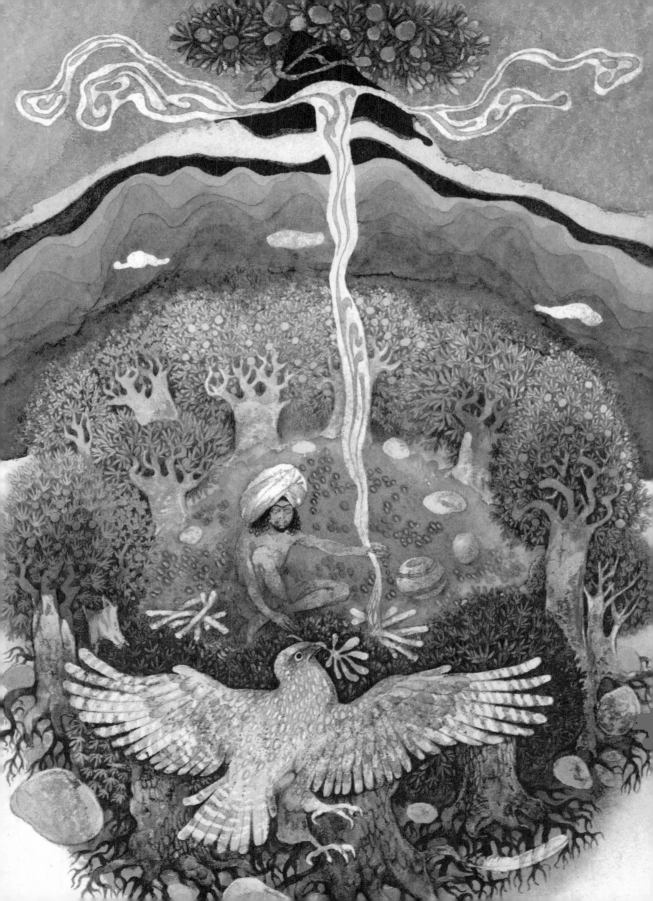

hundreds of thousands of demons were rowing as hard as they could to reach the shore and escape the insects.

Louhi and all the other monkeys were hiding in the undergrowth around the lake. Louhi waited until he saw that Ravana and Sita had landed and then he shouted, 'Attack!'

The demons watched horrified as wave after wave of monkeys rushed out of the undergrowth bearing clubs. The battle lasted until night fell without either side gaining victory. When it was dark, the monkeys retreated to the undergrowth and the demons sought refuge in their boats. Ravana had not let go of Sita, so she had no chance of escape. She had seen her beloved Rama in the midst of the fighting, his enchanted sword killing demon after demon. Lakshmana had fired arrow upon arrow, and each one had killed every demon in its path, but there were still many more demons on the banks of the lake than there had been at the hermitage a few days before.

As soon as it was light the next day the battle began again. Despite the courage of the monkeys and the enchanted weapons of Rama and Lakshmana the demons began to gain ascendancy. The monkeys began to retreat, and Sita watched in horror as she saw twelve demons come upon Rama from behind. Rama's sword was flashing to right and left, but by the time he realized what had happened it was too late. The demons felled him to the ground and in an instant Rama was dead.

Sita screamed and lurched back horrified as Ravana, seeing what had happened, turned to her and said, 'Now Sita. Rama is dead. Marry me.'

'I would rather die first,' replied Sita, tears of sorrow streaming down her face.

Night fell and it was obvious that the monkeys were being beaten. They had seen the brave Rama fall to the ground and they had lost their fighting spirit.

Lakshmana carried his dead brother from the battlefield into a clearing in the undergrowth. With his eyes misty from tears, he began to dig a grave for Rama. The soil was soft and it was not long before he had completed his sad task.

He lifted his brother gently and laid him in the grave. He knelt down beside it and said softly, 'Oh Rama. If only things had been different, you would be ruling in our father's kingdom. But now, you are dead. If only our father had not died at your wedding . . .'

Suddenly Lakshmana remembered that although their father had died he had been brought back to life by their step-mother's magic infusion. He then recalled that their step-brother had given them what was left before they set off on their long exile. He knew where it was, so he ran as fast as he could to the battlefield.

The monkeys were sitting around dejectedly. Lakshmana could see Louhi talking excitedly to a group of them, and he ran over to where they were. 'They want to go back to the jungle now that Rama is dead. They see no way that the battle can now be won,' said Louhi . . .

'If Rama came back, would that put new spirit in them?' asked Lakshmana.

'Of course, but that is not possible,' said Louhi.

But Lakshmana smiled. 'Remember what you said to my brother. The gods can do anything. Gather as many of your troops who are left and meet here at dawn tomorrow.' With that, Lakshmana ran to collect the alabaster pot. It was exactly where he remembered it should be. He picked it up and ran back to his brother's grave.

Rama lay in the shallow grave, the moon shining on his dead face. His eyes were closed and his lips were blue.

His heart beating quickly, Lakshmana cradled Rama's head in his arms and he poured some of the infusion into his mouth. The rest he spread over Rama's body and rubbed it into his skin.

Nothing happened. Rama remained as dead as he had been. Lakshmana waited and waited for what seemed like forever. He knelt down and wept, and as he cried one of his tears fell into Rama's open mouth. Lakshmana looked down at his brother for one last time before he would cover him with earth. His heart nearly stopped beating as he suddenly saw Rama's eyelids flicker, and he wept even more as Rama stirred as if awakening from a deep sleep.

'Brother,' he cried as Rama stood up, 'you are alive!'

'Yes,' whispered Rama softly. 'And only you could have brought me back.'

Then he stepped out of the grave and the two half-brothers embraced. Together they walked arm-in-arm back to the camp. The monkeys stared in amazement as Rama appeared.

As the sun rose the demons reappeared to finish off the battle.

They had expected to face an already-defeated army that would take only a few minutes to beat into submission.

Instead, they were met by almost as many monkeys as before, for word had spread back to the jungle and every monkey who had not come at first, now appeared — determined to win.

With their new fighting spirit and with surprise on the demons' side, the new battle was short. Within one hour the demons were in retreat.

Ravana watched, horrified, from his boat in the lake, Sita at his side. When he saw that all was lost, he commanded his oarsmen to row him to the other side of the lake. Rama saw what was happening, grabbed Lakshmana's quiver and arrows and quickly ran to the shore. His aim was steady and the arrow was true. Ravana fell, dead, into the water and Rama swam towards the boat.

With their leader slain, the remaining demons fled in all directions. Rama clambered onto the boat and embraced Sita — his beloved wife.

The reunited husband and wife rowed back to the shore where Lakshmana was waiting for them. Louhi stood slightly aside while the three rejoiced at being together again. After a few minutes he shyly approached them.

'I must now return,' he said. 'The monkeys have gone back. Remember that with the gods all things are possible.' And with that Louhi lumbered off into the undergrowth.

Rama, Sita and Lakshmana looked towards the island for the last time and started off on their journey back to the hermitage.

When they arrived Valkimi and the other hermits on the Holy Mountain were overjoyed. 'Rama. Sita. Lakshmana. You have returned. The gods have been good, let us give them thanks.'

The four made their way to Valkimi's temple and gave thanks to the gods for the safe return. When they had finished their devotions Valkimi said, 'It is now fourteen years since you came here. You may now return to Ayodhya.'

The following morning Rama, his brother and his wife set off to return to Ayodhya. They arrived a few days later and went straight to the palace. As they approached, a guard saw them and ran to tell Bharata that Rama, the true king, was on his way.

Bharata ran out to welcome them. 'Brothers,' he shouted. 'Sita. You have all returned. I am thankful, for we heard of the events at Lanka.'

'I suppose,' said Lakshmana, 'that you are now so used to ruling that you have no intentions of giving up your throne.'

'On the contrary,' laughed Bharata. 'I could not be happier. My mother acted as she did because she was jealous. I never wanted to rule. The throne is Rama's by right. Our father died many years ago and our mothers followed him to the grave shortly after. Brothers. Sister-in-law, I rejoice at your return. I have never called myself king; only Regent, ruling in your absence. Come, let us be friends.'

And the three brothers and Sita went into the palace where Lakshmana's brother, Satrughna, was waiting for them.

There were great celebrations throughout the country when Rama took his rightful place as ruler of Ayodhya with Sita as his queen. He appointed Lakshmana as ruler of the northern province, Bharata as ruler of the southern province and Satrughna as ruler of the eastern province. He gave the western province to the hermits of Mount Chitrakutu as a way of thanking the gods for Sita's safe return from the demons.

And unlike his father, he did not take more than one wife. He was happy with Sita and he knew that their children would never have to go through the tortures that they had endured, because of another wife's jealousy.

ORION

If you look up into the sky on a clear, dark night, you may be able to see a group of stars called Pegasus. There are hundreds of stars in Pegasus, and one of them is called Pelai.

Pelai lived in a magnificent palace with his lovely wife and their beautiful daughter. One day the daughter looked down to the Earth and saw a young hunter called Orion. Orion was as tall and handsome as any of the gods in the sky and the girl fell in love with him immediately.

Orion was out hunting one day shortly after the girl had first seen him, and as he turned into a clearing in the forest, he came upon the most beautiful girl he had ever seen. It was the daughter of Pelai, who, as soon as light had come to the sky, had slipped out of her night palace and come down to earth. Orion fell in love with her as deeply as she had fallen in love with him. The happy couple spent the day hunting and laughing and walking hand-in-hand through the forest, as lovers do. When night approached, the girl said, 'I must leave now. I must return to my father's palace in the night sky. We can never meet again. For I am allowed but one trip to your world. If I try to come back, my heavenly light will be put out forever.'

Orion was heartbroken. 'Then I must come to you,' he whispered.

'Your love will have to be the strongest of all if you are to ascend to the sky and live with me,' the girl said gently, and disappeared.

Poor Orion. His love was the strongest of all. But how could he find a way to the heavens?

Day after day, Orion would climb to the highest cliffs, scale the tallest trees, and even, in utter despair, reach out as far as he could. But it was of little use. The night sky was as far away as ever. Orion sat down and wept. As he shed his tears, an old woman walked by. 'My son,' she said as she passed, 'why do you cry? You are young. You are handsome. What has made you so sad?'

'Oh woman,' wailed Orion. 'Love has made me weep so,' and he explained his plight to the old woman.

She listened silently and when he had finished she said, 'There is only one way for you to ascend to the heavens. You must gather your most precious possession and offer it to the night gods tomorrow when the moon is high. If they are pleased with your offering, they will take you to live amongst them.'

Orion was overjoyed and rushed home to find his most treasured possession. As a hunter, his bow and arrow were of great value to him, so he gathered them up. He was about to leave his humble hut and return to the clearing when he remembered the belt that his parents had given him when he had reached manhood. It was studded with precious stones and his parents had sacrificed much to afford it.

With his bow and arrow and his belt he ran back to the clearing and waited until the sun was at its highest. There was a thin veil of cloud covering the stars, but exactly when the moon should be at its highest, the sky cleared and Orion could see the shining stars.

Suddenly, a soft voice whispered in the breeze, 'Orion, what is your most precious possession that you can offer?'

'My bow and arrow, by which I make my living,' said Orion.

The breeze wrenched the bow and arrow from his hands and Orion watched it disappear upwards and upwards.

A few seconds later the breeze whispered, 'It is indeed a precious gift, but we want your *most* precious possession.'

So Orion took the belt from around his waist and held it up to the stars. Again the breeze wrenched it from his hands and Orion watched as it disappeared heavenward.

'It is indeed a precious gift, but there is something else that you have that is even more precious,' whispered the breeze.

'I have nothing else of value,' cried Orion.

'There is one thing so precious that if you offer it to the gods they will grant you your wish.'

'Nothing. There is nothing more,' sobbed Orion.

'Then I leave,' breathed the wind.

'No. Wait!' cried Orion. 'My most treasured possession, I cannot give away, for it is not mine to give. It was entrusted to me and in return I gave a similar gift.'

'What is it?' demanded the breeze.

'It is the love that my sweetheart gave to me. That is my most treasured possession.'

As soon as he had said the words, the breeze became stronger and wrapped itself around Orion pulling him upwards and upwards and upwards, until at last he was in the sky looking down at the world.

'My love,' a voice behind him whispered. Orion turned round and there was his beloved. 'You had to know that my love was your most treasured possession before you could come here. I am so happy that you knew it.'

The happy couple embraced and have been together in the sky ever since.

THE LITTLE PRINCE
OF THE SUN

The islands of Tonga lie in the South Seas, and many hundreds of years ago they were ruled by a very powerful king. He had one daughter who was said to be the most beautiful girl in the world, and he was very proud of her. But the king was so jealous of her beauty that he refused to let anyone, other than her handmaiden, see her.

The handmaiden felt sorry for her beautiful mistress and one day she said to her, 'It is so sad that you are always shut up within the palace walls. Why, you cannot even swim.'

'I have heard of swimming, but although I know I would like it, my father would never allow me to go to the seashore,' said the princess.

'It is your birthday tomorrow,' said the maid. 'Why do you not ask your father if you can go out as a special treat.'

So, the princess went to the king and asked if, just this once, she could leave the palace and go swimming.

The king thought for a minute and said, 'I hate to see you sad, so I will arrange something as a surprise.'

The next morning, the king escorted his daughter down to the seashore. All his subjects had been commanded to stay indoors so that they could not see her. During the night, the king had had a shaded causeway built out to the nearest island.

'There, my daughter,' he said. 'You may walk out to the island and there you may spend the day swimming, out of sight of any of my people.'

So the princess went out to the island and happily splashed about in the warm, deep green water. After an hour or two she lay down on the sand to rest. While she lay there, the god of the Sun passed over the island and shone down on the princess. As his rays warmed her she smiled up at him and her smile was so beautiful that he immediately fell in love with her.

The next day the princess asked her father if she could return to the island and she looked so beautiful, kissed by the sun, that her father willingly gave his permission.

And so, every day from then on the princess swam in the warm seas around the island and would then lay down and allow the sun to kiss her, for she grew to love the sun as much as he loved her. The two lovers were blissfully happy and eventually the princess gave

birth to a handsome baby boy whom she called 'Little Prince of the Sun'.

As the child grew, he became the most handsome boy in the islands. He could run faster than anyone else, throw the javelin further and swim long after the others had tired. He was also very proud and would boast to his friends, 'The king is my grandfather, and my mother is the most beautiful woman in the world. I am the best among you all.' And because he was so strong and proud, the others always agreed with him.

One day he went too far. He picked a quarrel with the smallest boy in the village and forced him to the ground. As he sat astride him, the little prince forced him to say, 'You are the best in all the islands, because your grandfather is king, and your mother is a beautiful princess.'

One of the other boys watching suddenly shouted, 'Your grandfather may be king and your mother a beautiful princess, but who is your father? At least we all have fathers and you do not.'

And all the other boys began to taunt him, calling, 'Who's got no father? Who's got no father?'

The little prince was enraged and began to chase the others away, but their taunts rang in his ears. 'Who's got no father? Who's got no father?' And he began to cry. Huge salt tears rolled down his cheeks as he ran back to his house. 'Mother,' he called and threw himself into her arms. 'The boys in the village said I do not have a father. Tell me, who is my father?' And he cried so hard that his whole body became racked with pain.

The princess felt so sorry for her son that she said to him, 'My child, do not cry. Your father is a great king. No one in the whole world has a father as powerful as yours.'

'But who is he?' demanded the child.

'Other children have ordinary mortals as their fathers. But you, my son, are the child of the god of the Sun. He is your father!'

The boy stopped crying immediately. 'If my grandfather is king, and you, my mother, are his daughter, and my father is the sun, then I am much too grand to live on this island. How can I talk to the other boys if the sun is my father?'

The princess was horrified at these words, but before she could ask anything the boy continued, 'I must leave here and go and visit my father.' He stood up and kissed his mother tenderly. 'I will come back when I have spoken to him.'

And with these words he left the house despite his mother's pleadings. She ran towards the door to call after him, but the boy had disappeared into the forest and she never saw him again.

The Little Prince of the Sun crossed the forest and went to the cove where his boat was anchored. He hoisted the sail and when the tide was high enough he pushed his boat into the water. The wind blew him towards the east and at mid-day the sun was right overhead. The Little Prince cried out to him, 'Father! Father! Stop, it is me, your son.' But the sun did not hear him and continued his journey to the west. The Little Prince tried to follow him, but the wind blew him in the wrong direction. He watched sadly as his father raced across the skies and slipped out of sight over the western horizon.

That night the Little Prince was all alone in the dark, dark ocean. When it was at its darkest, the Little Prince remembered that the sun rose in the east, so he raised his sail and sailed to the point where his father would rise from the sea in the morning.

When the first rays of light spread over the ocean the next morning, the Little Prince called out, 'Father! Wait for me.'

'Who calls me?' asked the sun.

'Me. Your son,' said the Little Prince. 'You must know me. I am the son of the Princess of the Islands of Tonga and of you, god of the Sun.'

'You are my son?' asked the sun.

'Yes, I am. Oh please stop and talk to me.'

'My son, I cannot. What would the people say if I did not shine in the sky? I must go or I shall be late.'

'Please stay. Hide behind a cloud and come down and talk to me,' pleaded the Little Prince. 'If you are behind a cloud, the people will not know that you have come down to talk to me.'

The sun admired the boy's intelligence and wit, so he called on a cloud and under its cover he slid down to the surface of the water. There the father and son talked. 'Tell me of your life on the islands,' said the sun.

So the boy told his father of his mother and of his grandfather; about his friends and how he was the best swimmer and the fastest runner in all the islands. And the sun told the Little Prince many of the secrets of the sky. Eventually the sun told the child that he must continue his journey across the sky or else men and women would begin to get alarmed. 'Stay here till night comes and my sister, the moon, appears. When she leaves the water to begin her journey across the sky, call to her and tell her that you are her nephew, my son. She will offer you a choice of two gifts.'

'And which one should I take?' asked the boy.

'One is called Melaia and the other Monuia. Ask her for Melaia and you will have eternal happiness. If you disobey and take Monuia, then great misfortune will come your way. Goodbye, my son.'

And the sun went back behind the cloud and began to race across the sky. The people looked up and said, 'Look. The sun is late and is now rushing across the sky much faster than usual.'

The Little Prince took down his sail and stayed where he was until nightfall. When the night came he raised his sail and skimmed across the ocean to where the moon would rise. The moon saw the boat and the handsome young boy sailing in it.

'Boy,' she called out. 'Why do you sail like the wind across the seas to look into my face?'

The Little Prince stopped his boat right in front of the moon and said, 'I am the child of your brother, the sun, and the princess of the Islands of Tonga. My name is the Little Prince of the Sun and you, Moon, are my aunt.'

The moon was astonished and said, 'How wonderful to have a human nephew. But move your boat, for I must begin my journey. Look, the stars are already in the sky.'

'If I do, Aunt, you must give me the gift that my father said you would offer me.'

'I have two gifts in my possession,' laughed the moon knowingly, 'which one did the sun tell you to ask for?'

Now the Little Prince was a devious child. When he was told to do one thing he always did the other. Always! So he said to the moon 'My father told me to ask for Monuia. So may I have it, please?'

The moon was horrified. 'He said Monuia! Are you sure that he did not say Melaia?'

'No, Aunt. He said that you were to keep Melaia and that you were to give me Monuia.'

'I cannot give him Monuia,' said the moon to herself. 'Surely my brother would not want to harm his son.'

So she took Melaia from her purse and handed it to the boy. 'Here,' she said, 'here it is. But you must not open it until you are safe on your own island.'

Unbeknown to both the moon and the boy, the sun had been watching all this from the opposite horizon. He had delayed his setting until the moon had talked to her nephew. When he saw what had happened, he was furious, and with the last ray of light he stretched out across the sky unseen by either his son or the moon. He removed Melaia from the boat and put Monuia in its place. He returned Melaia to his sister's pocket.

222

As the boy sailed away, the moon began to rise in the sky and to hurry across it to make up for lost time.

The people below looked up and said, 'How strange. The moon was late and now she is running through the stars.'

The boy sailed on and across the ocean until he was in sight of his own island. 'I cannot wait to open my present until I am home, surely it will not matter if I open it before.'

So he picked up Monuia from where it lay and took it out of its covering. His eyes lit up with joy when he saw the most beautiful oyster shining in the dying light of the moon.

'Such an oyster must contain a magnificent pearl,' and he took his knife and opened the oyster. Inside there was such a pearl as no man had ever seen before. The Little Prince was about to take it from the shell when, as if by command, a storm began to blow. The little boat was tossed around on the waves, but the boy was oblivious to the danger. He could not keep his eyes away from the pearl. Suddenly from out of the stormy seas every type of fish began to rise to the surface and to swim towards the little boat. There were dolphins, sharks, tuna fish, eels, and even whales. But still the Little Prince was unaware of anything but the pearl.

The storm continued and more and more fish were swimming towards the boat. Just before they came close to the boat, they submerged and swam under it. As if by magic they all surfaced at once, tossing the boat high out of the water.

Poor child. He was tossed out of the boat and he landed deep in the ocean. He stood no chance of saving himself. He was dead before he knew what was happening. As he splashed through the surface, the oyster snapped tightly shut and nipped the top of his little finger off.

The Little Prince's body was never found. It lies deep down in the South Seas. The oyster, however, was washed ashore on his island a few days later. Inside it there was the most magnificent black pearl shaped like the top of a finger. No other pearl like it has ever been found before or after.

You see, Monuia was the goddess of the tide, which the moon controls and which can bring danger to those who disregard her.

HAMISH
AND THE GOLDEN FISH

Long, long ago in the misty valley of northern Scotland, there lived a boy called Hamish. He had two brothers, and the three boys lived in a small whitewashed cottage with their widowed mother.

The widow worked hard to make ends meet. Hamish did his best to help her, but his two brothers were as lazy as lazy could be. When Hamish went fishing to catch something for the family to eat, his two brothers would still be in their beds. As Hamish stood patiently helping his mother to wind wool and to spin, his two brothers would be roaming the hills or carousing in the village.

The widow loved her children equally, but she hoped that when she died the two brothers would see sense and work as hard as Hamish.

The sad day came when the widow died and with a heavy heart Hamish dug her simple grave. When night came he carved a cross and the next day the three brothers mourned deeply at their mother's graveside.

But the following morning, they lay in their beds and shouted to Hamish, 'Where is our breakfast?' and Hamish set to and cooked breakfast. 'Hamish, the hens need feeding,' they called from beds, and Hamish went to feed the hens. 'Don't forget to milk the cow,' they yelled, and Hamish did as he was told.

This went on day after day. One day, about a month after the widow had died, the brothers cried, 'Hamish, there is no salt fish left. Go and gather your line and catch some fish to salt.' And Hamish did as he was told.

He set off, up the mountain to where the bubbling stream widened to a deep pool. Hamish had often had good luck there and this particular morning was no different. Within an hour, he had caught enough fish to keep the three of them for one month. He was ready to go home when he decided to cast his line one last time. Imagine his surprise when he pulled the line up and there, on his hook, was a golden fish! Not only was it golden, but it was wearing a golden crown on its head. Hamish was rooted to the spot.

'What do you think you're up to?' the fish suddenly said.

'What!' Hamish cried out in amazement. 'Who spoke?'

'Who do you think spoke? Me, of course. There's no one else here, is there?' the fish said angrily.

'But fish don't speak,' said Hamish.

'Of course we speak,' the fish mocked. 'How else do you think we communicate with each other. But I am the only one that can speak your language.'

'You must be a very important fish,' said Hamish, 'if you can speak to humans.'

'Well, I was important. In fact I was king of the pool. But not now,' said the fish sadly. 'Now that you have caught me, I expect that I'll end up smoked and brown like a kipper. Unless you throw me back.'

Now the fish was very big, and looked very tasty, but Hamish was quite sorry for it. After all, he was obviously a very important fish.

'I'll tell you what,' said the fish. 'If you throw me back, I'll grant you three wishes. I am a magic fish.'

'Very well,' said Hamish. 'I wish that my brothers would work as hard as I do. I wish that the hens would lay ten times more eggs than they do, and that the cow would give ten times more milk.'

'Very well,' said the fish. 'Now throw me back.' And Hamish did.

By the time Hamish got home, his brothers were in bed, for it was very late. The next morning Hamish got up early as usual but did not begin to prepare breakfast. After all, his brothers should now be as hardworking as he. But half an hour later his brothers shouted from their beds,

'Hamish, where is our breakfast? Come on lazy. We're hungry. And then you can collect the eggs and milk the cow.'

'Perhaps the magic will start tomorrow,' thought Hamish as he cooked his brothers' breakfast. He went out to collect the eggs and was sorry to see that there were no more than usual. And the cow gave her normal amount of milk.

'Oh well,' thought Hamish, 'it must start tomorrow.'

But the next morning, his brothers stayed in bed and the hens laid as usual, and there was no extra milk. And Hamish worked as hard as ever before.

One day a month later, his brothers called, 'Hamish, there is no more fish left. Collect your line and go fishing.' And Hamish did as he was told.

He set off up the mountain to the pool and cast his line. There were many fish and Hamish caught almost more than he could carry. He decided to cast his line just once more before going home, and sure enough, he caught the same golden fish with the golden crown.

'Put me back, and I'll make you rich,' said the fish.

'You told me last time that you would grant me three wishes if I put you back,' said Hamish.

'Silly,' said the fish. 'Whoever heard of a fish that could grant wishes.' Hamish grabbed his mallet and quickly killed the cruel fish. He took it home and prepared to cook it. His brothers were out in the village. When Hamish cut the fish open, imagine his surprise when a purse of gold fell from the fish's stomach. 'Someone must have dropped it in the pool, and the fish must have swallowed it.'

With all the gold in the purse, Hamish knew that he was rich, so before his brothers returned, he packed his bags and left. They never saw him again, and when they came home, all they found was a half-cut fish lying on the kitchen table.

CONFUCIUS

More than fifteen hundred years ago, in China, one of the five ruling spirits, the Lord of the Night, looked down on his people and was saddened by what he saw. Everyone had forgotten the old ways: wars were being fought for no other reason than territorial gains; neighbour cheated neighbour, and son cheated father. Bribery was common and corruption was rife.

He decided to send among the people a man of such perfect goodness that all would come to love and respect him and follow his example of peace and understanding. He would stop wars and restore happiness to family life.

He searched the country for a good woman who would bear this child, and after many months he found her in the town of Lou, in the province of Shan-Tung. He watched her for many days and when he was satisfied that she was the perfect mother to bring up the child, he appeared to her in dream one night and said to her, 'Woman, you are going to have a child who will become a king without a crown.'

Sure enough, nine months later, the woman gave birth to a son which she called K'ong-tseu. When he was born, there was a piece of red thread around his left foot. Today, fifteen hundred years later, we still know about this child, for he became Confucius, the great Chinese prophet.

He was a very odd-looking little boy and as he grew to manhood he became even odder. He was exceedingly tall and his face, unlike the yellow colour of other Chinese, was very dark — almost black. His mouth was enormous, stretching almost from ear to ear, and his lower lip never quite met his top one, so that his perfectly white teeth could always be seen. His voice was deep and beautiful to listen to. He seemed almost to hypnotise all who listened to him.

He had a disciple called Yan-Hui. One day Confucius and Yan-Hui climbed a mountain known as Tai-schan which was sacred to the people of the province of Shan-Tung. Confucius pointed his finger towards the south and said to Yan-Hui, 'Do you see that river over there?'

'Yes,' replied his companion.

'Follow its course with your eye.'

Yan-Hui did as he was told.

'What do you see?' asked Confucius.

'The river flows past the gate of the town of Wu.'

'Is there anything in front of the door?'

'I can see something white but I cannot make out what it is. It is like a piece of paper billowing in the wind,' said Yan-Hui.

'It is not a piece of paper, it is a white horse,' replied Confucius.

'Come now, Confucius,' said Yan-Hui. 'Even you could not make out what it is at this distance. It is many miles to Wu.'

'We will go and see,' said Confucius, and the two men climbed down the hill and set off along the dusty track to Wu. As they went Yan-Hui told everyone who passed that his friend claimed to have been able to see a white horse outside the gates of Wu from the top of Tai-shan. The people were incredulous and many of them followed ready to mock the odd-looking man when he realized his mistake.

By the time they got to Wu, there were many hundreds of people following Confucius and Yan-Hui. There, in front of the gates was the most magnificent white charger anyone had seen. Its coat glistened and shone in the sun. Its mane and its tail were the colour of newly-minted gold, and its body and legs were perfectly shaped. The people were stunned and excited at the same time.

'How could anyone have seen this from so far away?' they said to one another.

'Who is this man?' they asked.

Soon there was a loud babble of conversation among the people that grew louder and louder as each second passed.

It stopped suddenly when Confucius held up his hand and fixed the crowd with his dazzling eye.

He began to preach to them and his voice was so beautiful and his message was so simple and honest that the people listened for hour after hour.

Eventually word of Confucius spread right across the province and into every corner of the country. People flocked to hear Confucius's message and many who heard it were so impressed that they put their bad ways behind them and began to live good lives.

One day, many years later the Prince of Wu was out hunting with some of his friends. He fell some way behind them and was galloping to catch up when a small deer appeared in his path. He reined in his horse quickly, for the deer showed no signs of moving. The Prince dismounted and went to 'shoo' the deer off. To his surprise, he noticed that the deer had a piece of red thread wound around his left foot. The deer looked up at the Prince and moved away in such a way as if he was deliberately trying to draw the Prince's attention to the red thread.

When the hunt was over, the Prince returned to Wu and told Confucius about the strange happening.

Huge tears welled up in Confucius's eyes. 'It is a sign from my father, the Lord of the Night, that I must prepare myself for death. I have not done well enough. I have changed some people, but not enough to please my father.'

The Prince was saddened and said, 'But Confucius, no one could convert the whole world. Everyone has changed who has heard you speak, and although there are still wars, and dishonour amongst families, the world is a much better place now than it was before you began your mission.'

'No matter,' cried Confucius, 'it is not enough. I must follow my father's wishes.'

That very night Confucius died and his body was placed in a tomb, outside the city walls. The people mourned him greatly and he became known as Confucius the Omniscient. Within a few years the whole of China began to follow his doctrine and his religion became the official religion of the land.

Many hundreds of years passed, kings died and new kings took their place. The land came to be ruled by the Emperor Tsin-Shi-Huang. He was cruel and mean. He ruled his subjects with an iron hand and whatever he said had to be obeyed on pain of certain death.

Everything that he did was contrary to the ways of Confucius.

One day he rode into the city of Wu and asked his minister, 'Is this the place where that old fool Confucius has his tomb?'

'Yes master,' replied the minister. 'His tomb is outside the city walls, about a mile from here.'

'Take me to it,' commanded the King.

The King and his retinue rode out to the tomb. When they reached it Tsin-Shi-Huang ordered that it be opened. The people were thunderstruck.

'But Sir,' they protested. 'That would be sacrilege.'

'To disobey me is sacrilege,' shouted the King, purple with rage. 'Open it.'

Reluctantly, his orders were obeyed, and the stone that guarded the entrance of the tomb was rolled back. The King entered the cavern, astonished to find that the air inside it was not at all musty, but quite fresh.

As his eyes grew accustomed to the darkness, he was astonished to see that there was a couch that looked new and on the ground underneath it there was a pair of beautiful red silk slippers.

230

The King sat down on the couch and kicked his own shoes off. He slipped his feet into the silk slippers and was delighted to find that they were unusually comfortable. He looked around the tomb. It looked more like the office of a working man, than the tomb of a dead one. He noticed a desk in one corner and went over to it. On the leather top there was a pot of ink and a quill pen. Alongside was a sheet of paper with fresh writing on it. The puzzled King picked up the paper and was horrified when he saw what was written on it.

'Tsin-Shi-Huang, you live the life of a degenerate,
You enter my tomb and rest on my couch.
You wear my slippers. You are not fit to do so.
You will die at Schakiu.'
The frightened King ran from the tomb and ordered that it be closed at once. He mounted his horse and rode away as quickly as he could.

From that time on the King refused to go anywhere near Schakiu. No matter what the occasion was he would not go.

One day, about a year later, he was out riding. His horse stumbled over a rock and Tsin-Shi-Huang was knocked off the horse's back. His head hit the rock and he was rendered unconscious. For many days he lay in a deep coma. Nothing would bring him round. Eventually the court physician said that only one man had the power to revive the King — the wise Doctor of Schakiu.

The almost lifeless body was put into a carriage and taken to that town. There, the Doctor made an infusion of many herbs and held the steaming bowl under the unconscious King's nose. Within a few minutes the King's eyes opened and a few minutes later he was sitting up on his bed.

'Where am I?' he asked his physician.

'Sir. We had to bring you to Schakiu, for only the Doctor here knew how to revive you.'

At that the King burst out laughing. 'Why,' he roared, tears of laughter running down his cheeks, 'that old fool Confucius prophesied that I would die here. But I have been given life here. Ha.'

No sooner had he spoken, than his eyes opened wide. They almost popped out of his head. His face went red, then blue, then purple. It was as if invisible hands were squeezing the life out of him, for he could not breathe. A few seconds later, he slumped back dead. The horrified courtiers rushed up to him, but it was too late. The prophecy of Confucius had come true.

Tsin-Shi-Huang had died at Schakiu.

THE STRANGER
WITH THE CURLY BEARD

Many hundreds of years ago in China, the area that is now Peking was covered by a mighty lake. It was as deep as the Pacific Ocean and when the winds blew huge waves would crash onto the shores. In the lake there lived the Dragon King and his ugly old wife.

As the population grew, the people needed more land to build houses on and to create fields to grow crops to feed themselves. A wonderful plan was drawn up, canals were dug all around the lake and the waters were drained away leaving a magnificent plain where the city of Peking was build.

The Dragon King and his wife were furious at being driven from their home. They swam up the canals and into the river and made their home in a much smaller lake hundreds of miles from their old home. There, night after night they plotted to have their revenge and vowed to destroy the city of Peking and the people who lived in it.

They waited for year after year until the time was ready.

Their chance came when they heard that all the men in Peking were out of the city building a huge wall to keep China's enemies out of their land. They swam down the rivers and along the canals until they were standing on a small hill overlooking the city. The Dragon King weaved a spell and turned himself and his wife into a ragged, poor old man and woman. He snapped his fingers and a large hand-cart appeared. On it were two magic vats, that could never be filled, no matter how much water was put in them.

When night came, they went round every well in the city and pumped the waters into their unquenchable vats. Just as dawn was breaking, they had emptied the last one, and they slipped out of the city before anyone was awake.

When the women rose from their beds and went to the wells to draw water for the day, they were horrified to find there was no water in any of the wells. Not even a drop.

They sent a messenger to tell their husbands, who were busy at their building. General Liou Po-Ho was thunderstruck when he heard the news, for he alone realized what had happened. He knew that there was only one solution.

Only one man could save the city, so he called all the men together and said to them,

'Men of Peking, you have heard what has befallen our city. One of you and only one of you can save Peking. Which one is it?'

At that, all the men rushed forward shouting and begging to help. The General heard each one and shook his head, until a strange little man said, 'General. It is me. I know how to save our city.'

Everyone laughed, for the man was very small and strange-looking. The strangest thing about him was that his beard, unlike everyone else's, which were straggly and straight, was a mass of thick curls.

'How do you know it is you?' asked the General kindly.

'Sir,' said the stranger with the curly beard. 'Only one person is powerful enough to have emptied all our wells.'

'The Dragon King,' said the General. 'And if you know that then you must know how to foil him, for you must be . . .'

'His half-brother,' said the stranger.

The General said to his assembled men, 'Many years ago when I was a boy I was standing by the canal banks when the great sluice were opened for the first time to empty the lake. I saw the Dragon King and his wife swim by, vowing to have their revenge, and chuckling that the only man who could stop them would be his half-brother, who had long since left the land to travel abroad. This man with the curly beard is that half-brother. Only he knows how to save our city.'

'Sir,' said the stranger with the curly beard. 'I need the services of your bravest soldier and your fastest horse. The soldier will need the sharpest lance he can have.'

Immediately all the men rushed forward to volunteer. The old man looked them all up and down and eventually pointed to one and said, 'You are Kao-Liang. You are the bravest soldier. You will save our city.'

'What must I do?' asked Kao-Liang.

'Follow the marks of the wheels of the water cart and you will come upon the Dragon King and his wife. They will be changed into a sad and helpless couple toiling to pull their water cart and you may feel sorry for them. Do not. Gallop at full speed towards them and pierce the vats with your lance. All the water will run along the tracks back to the wells.'

'That sounds the simplest of things,' said Kao-Liang.

'The difficult part is still to come. Although the water will run back to the wells, for you to escape you will need every ounce of your courage. Once you have pierced the vats you must turn and gallop away. You must not look back until your horse has taken one hundred paces. No matter what you see you must not look back.'

234

Kao-Liang agreed and one hour later rode out on the fastest horse, carrying the sharpest lance.

He soon picked up the tracks of the cart and rode off in their direction. Soon in the dust of the road he saw an old couple bent double, pulling the water cart. They were so frail and shrunken that, just as the stranger with the curly beard had said, he felt sorry for them. But mindful of his words he put the kindness out of his mind and galloped at the cart, his lance at the ready. As fast as lightning he galloped, and with a mighty crash he pierced the vats with his lance. They burst open with mighty explosions, just as Kao-Liang turned his horse and galloped away.

The sky went black and the sound of horrible laughter filled the air. Kao-Liang rode as fast as he could and behind him he could hear the sounds of hundreds of horses chasing after him. He felt as if a whole army was at his heels and he wanted to look back to see. But his courage did not fail him and he rode on and on. The ground trembled under the thudding of the horses' hooves. Sweat fell from his brow and his heart beat faster and faster. He felt his horse slow down as though something was pulling his tail, but still he did not look back. And all the time he was counting . . . eighty-nine, ninety, ninety-one, ninety-two . . .

When he got to one hundred he looked round.

But he had made a mistake. In his excitement he had miscounted and taken one pace too few. He had only gone ninety-nine paces and not one hundred.

As he looked round he saw a huge wall of water rush towards him. He spurred his horse on, but the water foamed and roared after him. Poor Kao-Liang. Within ten steps the water had overtaken him and he was lost forever under its frothing surface.

Immediately, the water calmed down and flowed gently along the cart tracks and back into the wells of the city of Peking. The citizens were happy but their happiness was tinged with sadness, for Kao-Liang had been the most popular young man in the city. Soon their sadness turned to anger.

'Why had Kao-Liang died? Why could the stranger with the curly beard not have ridden out after his half-brother, the Dragon King?' they asked themselves. An angry mob gathered and marched to the palace of General Liou Po-Ho, demanding the blood of the stranger with the curly beard.

The General looked furious as he appeared on his balcony to calm the mob down. 'How dare you,' he thundered at them. 'Instead of demanding his blood, you should be grateful to the man with the

curly beard. He alone knew how to save our city from certain death. He knew that Kao-Liang may have to sacrifice his life, but Kao-Liang was aware of the risk he was taking, and went gladly to save us. I am ashamed of you and if Kao-Liang is looking down on you from the Palace of the Eternal Heavens then I hope that he is ashamed of you too. Return to your homes. Remember, things become more appreciated if sacrifice has been made for them. We used to take our water for granted, but now that Kao-Liang has given his life that we may have water, we know how precious it is. We must always remember the lesson taught to us by the stranger with the curly beard.'

QUETZALCOATL

Long, long ago in the continent of South America, a large part of the land was ruled by the Serpent of the Snow. The Serpent of the Snow was a fierce warrior who, whenever his domain was threatened by invading armies, would lead his men into battle and inspire his soldiers with his brave leadership and incredible courage. His men loved him so much that they followed his example and the army became invincible.

He was also a wise ruler and all the people in the land loved him dearly.

One day the armies of neighbouring Golhoucan marched against him and invaded the northern part of his kingdom.

The Serpent of the Snow rallied his soldiers and marched off to meet the invaders. They were led by the wicked Chilalman, who was as mean as the Serpent of the Snow was generous, and as cowardly as he was brave. Chilalman did not lead his armies, but directed them from behind. If the tide of battle turned against him, Chilalman was the first to turn and flee.

The Serpent of the Snow knew this, so he was very surprised when he saw that Chilalman was sitting on a fine white horse at the head of his armies.

When Chilalman saw the Serpent of the Snow ride toward him, he called out, 'This time, Serpent, you have met your match, my power is greater than yours.' And saying this he drew an arrow from his quiver, fixed it into his bow and aimed straight at the Serpent's heart.

But the Serpent of the Snow managed to swerve to avoid the arrow.

Chilalman was furious, for the arrows had been given to him by the witch Uitznuac, who had promised him that whoever the arrow was aimed at would fall dead. Chilalman drew another arrow and fired it, but the Serpent was too quick for it. Again and again Chilalman fired at the Serpent, but each time the same thing happened.

Eventually the quiver was empty and the Serpent led his armies into the middle of Chilalman's. The battle did not last long, for Chilalman's men were as cowardly as he was, and seeing the fear in their master's face, they lost any heart they had had before they saw the way in which the Serpent had ducked Chilalman's arrows.

When the battle was over, the Serpent of the Snow rode back to where the arrows had found their mark. He picked them all up and ordered them to be burned.

When the flames of the fire were at their highest, they suddenly parted and from them flew the most beautiful bird that the Serpent or his men had ever seen. Its breast was the brightest green and its wings were the most dazzling red; its eyes were deep blue and its beak and talons were as bright as purest gold.

The Serpent of the Snow was so moved by the bird's beauty that he knelt down before it. Seeing this, his soldiers did the same, and the bird flew low over them and came to land at the Serpent of the Snow's feet.

'Thank you, for you have released me from the curse of the witch Uitznuac. She captured me and imprisoned me in the arrows. Only one as great as you, Serpent of the Snow, could have escaped from my path, and only one as true as you could have released me from Uitznuac's curse. Rule well and wisely in your land, and if you ever need my help you will find me at the Palace of the White Gold in the mountains of Guatemala.'

With that the bird flew off and from that day the people of the Serpent's kingdom worshipped him as a god. They named him Quetzalcoatl.

Whenever they needed his assistance, which was not very often, they went to his palace and he gave what they asked. And if Quetzalcoatl heard of anyone in need, he would bring relief. If he saw, as he flew about the countryside, anyone in pain, he would bring consolation. If he saw hunger, he would bring food and wine. The people came to love him as dearly as they loved the Serpent of the Snow, and they built temples to him and dedicated themselves to him.

The Serpent had twin sons, and he passed a law that when he died, the kingdom was to be divided between the two. One of them was to rule the land north of the Great River all the way up to the mountains of Guatemala and the other was to rule south, down to the mountains of Mexico.

The sad day came when the Serpent died and his kingdom was divided as he had wished.

The son who ruled in the south was called Cintoetl and he was as brave and wise as his father. He ruled his part of the kingdom wisely and well and the people loved him.

The son who ruled in the north was called Tollan. He was weak and foolish. He loved being flattered and spent all of his time hunting, or seeking pleasure. He handed over the government of his land to whoever flattered him most. These flatterers were greedy and selfish men. They cared nothing for the people. All that mattered to them was to gather riches for themselves, and power for their families. They raised taxes and made the people work for them for little reward.

As Quetzalcoatl flew around the countryside he was sad at what he saw, and he did his best to bring some relief to the poor peasants, but their misery was such that there was little that he could do.

One day when Tollan was out hunting, he saw Quetzalcoatl sitting sadly in the branches of a tree. He was envious of the love that his people had for the beautiful bird, so he quietly dismounted from his horse and crept towards the tree. When he was close to the bird he drew his bow and taking careful aim, he fired an arrow at him. The arrow pierced Quetzalcoatl's wing making it impossible for him to fly away. Tollan took a large bag from his belt and unceremoniously dumped the bird in it.

With a greedy smile on his face, he rode back to his palace and proudly showed his courtiers his prize. At first they were horrified, but soon they gathered round and mocked Quetzalcoatl.

'Where is your power now?' asked one.

'There is nothing you can do to help the people,' mocked another.

Tollan ordered that a cage be built for the bird, so that when his courtiers came to see him, they would always be reminded that it was he, Tollan, who had captured the bird.

'Just think,' said Tollan. 'If I can capture Quetzalcoatl as easily as I did, I must be much mightier than he. The people should worship me as their god, and not this silly bird.'

And so all the temples that had been built in Quetzalcoatl's honour were pulled down and new ones built. The people were ordered that on no account was Quetzalcoatl to be worshipped, and that Tollan, the most powerful king on the face of the earth, was to be their new god.

Everyone were horrified at this, but such was the power that Tollan and his favourites held over them that they had no option but to obey.

When Cintoetl in the south heard of his brother's doings he was furious. He immediately sent messengers to his brother to demand that Quetzalcoatl be released and that the temples to him now be rebuilt.

'Tell my brother,' sneered Tollan, when he had heard what the messengers wanted, 'that Quetzalcoatl is now mine. I am more powerful than him and that if Cintoetl wishes to rebuild Quetzalcoatl's temples he will have to beat my armies first.'

240

When this message was repeated to Cintoetl he sent his brother an ultimatum.

'Unless my ambassador reports to me within one week that the temples that have been built in your honour have been raised to the ground and those dedicated to Quetzalcoatl have been rebuilt, my armies shall march against you in battle.'

Tollan read the message and laughed out loud. He went up to the cage where Quetzalcoatl now spent all his days and plucked a feather from his tail. He ordered his court painter to paint his face on the feather.

When this was done, he said, 'Take this to my brother. He whose face is shown on the feather is mightier than the bird from whence it was plucked.'

At these words all the courtiers applauded and mocked the poor bird once again.

Cintoetl's ambassador rode from Tollan's palace and journeyed all through the night to deliver the sacrilegious feather to his master.

As soon as he saw it, Cintoetl ordered that his armies get ready for war. A week later all was ready and Cintoetl rode out at the head of a mighty column of warriors. On the tunic of each soldier there was an image of Quetzalcoatl on their hearts.

When they approached the border, Cintoetl stopped and turned to speak to his men.

'I would do anything rather than fight my own brother and his armies. We fight, not for gain, or reward, but for what we believe in. Had it not been for Quetzalcoatl's help in the past, many of our people would have died or starved. Whenever he saw anyone in need, he helped, and now that he is in distress we must fight to the last man to release him from his misery.'

The army crossed the border into Tollan's kingdom. A few miles further on they crossed a small range of foothills and there, in the valley below, they could see Tollan and his army waiting to meet them.

All of Tollan's soldiers bore an image of him on their tunics. Tollan himself was sitting astride a magnificent black charger. On his wrist he held Quetzalcoatl. The bird was hooded and chained to Tollan's wrist like a falcon waiting to be released and flown.

'Brother,' cried Cintoetl. 'I give you one last chance. Release Quetzalcoatl and return to your palace. Tear down your temples and build new ones in honour of the mighty bird.'

'I am more powerful than Quetzalcoatl,' shouted Tollan. 'It is right that my people worship me as a god.'

No sooner had the words been spoken than an arrow whizzed past Cintoetl's ear and thudded into the tree behind him. The feathers in the arrow were the bright green ones from Quetzalcoatl's breast. Cintoetl drew his sword and spurred his horse into action. His men did the same and soon his army was galloping across the plain to meet Tollan's soldiers.

The battle was long and bloody. By dusk there were many dead on both sides, the grass of the plain was coloured red with the blood of hundreds of soldiers and horses.

As dusk gave way to darkness, the battle continued and it was fought all through the night. Tollan ordered that his archers dip their arrows in burning tar and fire them into Cintoetl's armies. The flaming arrows burned many soldiers horribly, and as a second volley lit up the night sky, Cintoetl's men took flight and ran from the battlefield.

As they rode after them in pursuit, one of Tollan's men stumbled over a body. As he rolled over, he recognized that it was Cintoetl. His face and arms were burned black, and he was bleeding from a wound in his side. He ran across to Tollan and told him what he had found. Tollan galloped to where the soldier pointed and saw his brother lying there.

'He is dead,' he thought to himself and took the hood from off Quetzalcoatl's head so that the bird could see for himself that his would-be saviour lay dead in the field of battle.

As he did so, there was a low groan from beneath him, and Tollan realized that Cintoetl still lived. He ordered that a stretcher be brought to him and that his brother be taken to his palace.

When Cintoetl regained consciousness a few hours later he was horrified to find himself in a cage, at the right-hand side of Tollan's throne. On the other side he could see Quetzalcoatl sitting dejectedly on his perch. Between them Tollan sat on his throne.

'So brother, you have come back to consciousness,' sneered Tollan. 'Welcome to our palace. You see now that I am mightier than you and the bird that you worship. Fool, to question my power.'

All the courtiers took up this cry and soon the chamber echoed with the word 'Fool'.

Cintoetl was horribly burned. His face was black and the flesh on his arms was red and raw. As the courtiers filed past his cage, taunting him with the cry 'Fool,' one girl said to Tollan, 'Sire, this man is your brother and he is in pain. Show him how merciful you are and let me tend his wounds.'

'We are merciful,' said Tollan. 'Do what you will with him. But he may not leave his cage. Nurse him, so he is well when I have him executed.'

The girl, who was called Cochtocan, went to her chamber and collected some soothing oils and towels. She returned to the throne room and Tollan unlocked the cage. She rubbed the oils into Cinto-etl's wounds and dried them with the cool towels.

Every day she came to him to care for him.

At first she could hardly bear to look at him because he was so deformed by the flames that had burned him, but as her oils began

to do their work, the blackness left his face and the flesh on his arms became less red and less raw. Soon he was as he had been before. His handsome face and dark eyes attracted the girl, and his gentle manner was in marked contrast to that of his brother, Tollan.

One day, Cintoetl asked Cochtocan why she had treated him so kindly, after all, their people were enemies.

'Because you are a human being. I would do the same for anyone, no matter who or what he was.' And as she spoke, she smiled, and her smile was so lovely and caring that Cintoetl felt himself warm towards her.

Each evening as he lay in his cage, the taunts of Tollan's courtiers and the plaintive cries of Quetzalcoatl ringing in his ears, he began to think of Cochtocan and to look forward to her visits.

The day came when his wounds were completely healed, but still the girl continued to come to him. When he asked her why, she told him that Tollan had commanded that as soon as he was healed, he was to be put to death, for Tollan was afraid of his brother.

'I tell him that you are still not well,' said Cochtocan, 'and he believes me.'

'For how long will he carry on believing you?'

'Not for much longer. For you are well, and I cannot go telling him lies.'

'Then you must help me escape,' said Cintoetl.

'I cannot. Tollan would kill me if he found out.'

'But you could come with me,' said Cintoetl.

'Why should I want to do that?' asked Cochtocan, her eyes lowered.

'Because . . . because . . . I love you and would like to make you my wife.'

The girl began to cry. 'Oh Cintoetl, I have loved you since the moment when first I saw you lying, horribly burned in the cage. But Tollan keeps the keys on a chain around his waist. He never lets them out of his sight. He lets me in here, and lets me out.'

'Then here is what you must do,' said Cintoetl, and explained his plan to Cochtocan.

The next evening all the courtiers were gathered in the throne room. Cochtocan approached Tollan's throne and knelt before him. 'Sir,' she said, 'Cintoetl is now completely well and is ready for what you have in mind for him, but first as I nursed him back to health, I crave one favour.'

'Whatever you ask,' said Tollan.

'I wish to carry Quetzalcoatl on my wrist to watch the execution.'

Tollan laughed out loud. 'Why, you are a girl after my own heart. Of course you may.'

The following morning all the court stood in the yard outside the throne room. Tollan and Cochtocan came out and nodded to everyone. They all bowed back. Quetzalcoatl was chained to Cochtocan's wrist. Tollan clapped his hands, and immediately Cintoetl was brought out into the sunshine.

'Brother,' said Tollan as he stopped in front of him, 'I kept you alive and brought you back to health so that all could see you die at my command and know how powerful I am.'

With that, Cintoetl was dragged to a pole in the yard in front of a line of archers.

'Each of these archers is an expert and never misses his target,' said Tollan. 'But only one has the order to kill you. You must shout out a number and that archer will fire, but only the right number will kill you. The others will just miss you.'

'And if I refuse,' cried Cintoetl.

'Then Quetzalcoatl will die . . . very, very slowly . . .'

'Then do your work.'

Cintoetl was blindfolded and made to stand against a high wall.

The crowd hushed as they saw him take a deep breath. For a moment all was silent, then Cintoetl cried out 'Seven'.

An arrow whizzed through the air and thudded into the wall behind Cintoetl.

The crowd gasped. They hushed again as they saw Cintoetl ready himself to call out another number, but before he could do so, Cochtocan slipped the chain from around Quetzalcoatl's talons and the bird was free. It made straight for Tollan and before anyone knew what was happening, the bird had gouged his eyes from his face. Tollan screamed as the blood gushed from the space where his eyes had been . . . He was a foul sight.

In the commotion no one was paying any attention to Cintoetl and Cochtocan. She ran towards him and slipped the blindfold from his eyes. They ran to the gate where two horses were waiting.

Soon they were out of sight of the palace, with Quetzalcoatl flying above them. None followed, for Cochtocan had loosened all the shoes from all the horses apart from the two that they were riding.

Soon they were back in Cintoetl's land and the people rejoiced when they saw their king back amongst them.

Within a few days an army was ready to march against Tollan and this time there was hardly any fight. With Tollan unable to command his troops the war was over in an hour.

Cochtocan and Cintoetl were married and lived happily ever after. Quetzalcoatl was restored to his Palace of the White Gold and peace reigned in the land for ever more.

THE MAGIC TREE

One day at the end of the last century, a small white boy was walking across a plain in the middle of Africa. His parents had recently arrived in the continent to try to farm the barren land. The boy was very tired so he sat down in the shade of the only tree that he could see for hundreds of yards around. As he sat in the shade a soft breeze began to blow and stirred the twigs of the old tree.

'So someone has come again. I have no more magic. Go away.'

The boy was frightened. 'Who said that?' he cried in terror.

'I did,' said the breeze in the tree.

'But I . . . I . . . don't understand.'

'You want nothing from me?' asked the breeze in the tree.

'Only the shade of your branches,' said the boy. 'Why do you ask?'

'Child. I have been here for many hundreds of years. I was planted by the god of the Creation to serve the tribes that once lived here.

'When I grew to maturity there were many peoples living all around. They were poor but hardworking. They tilled the soil and planted their crops and they were happy. There were four main tribes and two or three minor ones and they all worked together in harmony. One day the elders came to me and said, "Give us some relief from our poverty. We work in the hot sun from morning until night and we barely scrape a living."

'So I gave them the gift of a wonderful animal. It could survive on only a little grazing and it could breed quickly. The people were very happy, and with the animal they became rich and prosperous. It gave them much milk. Their carcasses were full of fine meat. Clothes could be made from their skins, and their bones could be used to make beautiful ornaments.

'The tribes became so rich that they stopped tilling the land and brought in servants from far away to do the work for them.

'At first, they treated the servants well, but as they became richer, they became greedier and began to be cruel and harsh.

'One night the servants' witch doctor came to me. He had painted his body in bright colours and he wore horns on his head. There were ornaments around his neck and over his shoulders.

'"Oh tree," he said to me. "We have heard that you have magic power. When we came here at first we did not mind working for our masters. They treated us with kindness and consideration. But now they are cruel and treat us badly. They whip us and starve us, no matter how hard we work for them. Give us our freedom".

'I did as they asked. I told the witch doctor that at the next full moon I would make the breeze blow through my branches and call all the villagers to me. I would keep them there until the slaves had made good their escape.

'And when the full moon came, I called the tribes to me. I used my magic to root all the tribesmen to the spot while their servants escaped. I held them there for two days to give them time to get far away, and when I knew they would be safe, I released their masters from my magic.

'But the servants were not only content with their freedom. They took all the herds and left nothing for their old masters.

'I did not think that the tribes would know that it was I who was responsible for the freedom of their servants, but they soon realized what had happened.

'They came back later and said, "Tree. We realize that you gave our servants their freedom and we know, too, why you did so. We treated them so badly. But now we have nothing. Help us."

'And so I gave them a seed that would grow into a rich grass that would feed them and any animals that they had. And they planted it and they grew rich again. But they had learned their lesson. They cultivated their own fields and cared for their own animals. And they were happy.

'But then the white man came. And he was envious of the lush fields and fat livestock. So he took them for himself and made slaves of the tribes. They returned to me and asked yet again for help. I gave them a germ that would cause fever in the white man. "But you must not touch anyone who catches the fever, otherwise you too will die," I said.

'They took the germ and soon many of the white men caught the fever. At first there was no danger to themselves. But one stupid girl had fallen in love with her white master and as he lay in his fever she kissed him, and so she became ill. And then her family. Soon the fever had touched all the people, black and white, and it spread to the animals.

'Within weeks everyone was either dead or had left the area and I was left alone with my magic. So I called to the god of the Creation. "My magic has brought nothing but pain and tyranny and suffering. Take it from me."

'And the god of the Creation replied, "I'll do as you ask, but I leave you one gift."

' "What is it?" I asked him.

'"I will not tell you. But from now on you will have one gift to bestow on anyone who comes to you."

'To this day I do not know what it was. But no one comes here any longer, so it does not matter.'

By this time the little white boy was feeling refreshed, so he stood up and left the shade of the tree.

He told no one what he thought had happened.

His parents decided to build their house quite close to the tree. At first it was a simple structure, but they worked hard and they prospered. Soon they could afford to extend it. They built terraces and verandahs and the house became the most important in the area.

One day some builders came and erected a fine seat around the trunk of the tree.

The following day the boy and his mother and sister came to sit on it and enjoy the shade that the tree's branches afforded.

'How wonderful it is to sit in the cool shade on such a hot day as this,' said the boy's mother. 'We are so lucky to have this tree so close to the house.'

'It's almost like a gift from the gods,' laughed the daughter.

And the little boy looked up into the tree's branches and smiled.

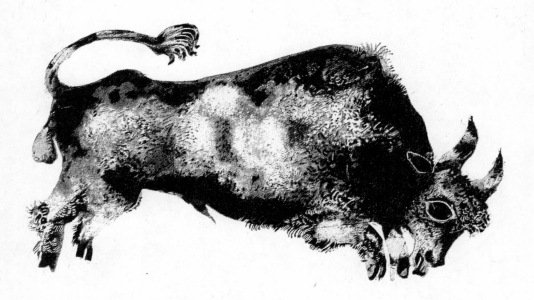

NAMA AND THE ELEPHANT

There was once a very beautiful girl called Nama who lived with her parents, her brothers and sisters in the village in the south of Africa. Apart from her beauty, she was also set apart from the other girls in the village by the fact that her mother was the youngest of seven children, and so was Nama. As the seventh child of a seventh child, Nama had been given the gift of magic powers by the gods which her people worshipped.

One day, when Nama had gone to draw water from the well, an elephant happened to pass. He looked at the lovely black girl leaning over the well and immediately fell in love with her.

When she made to return to the village, he followed her and noticed which house she entered. He went into the jungle, picked some beautiful flowers and returned to Nama's house. He stood outside and trumpeted as loud as he could. Nama and her parents and her brothers and sisters rushed out of the house to see what all the noise was about and were naturally surprised to see an elephant standing there, holding a rose in his trunk.

'What do you want?' asked Nama's father.

'I want to marry your daughter,' said the elephant.

The family all began to laugh. 'Imagine,' they said to each other. 'An elephant wants to marry our Nama,' and the more they said it the more they laughed.

'I don't see what's so funny,' said the elephant. 'I am willing to pay quite a lot for her.'

'Willing to pay for her,' said the father and the whole family stopped laughing immediately; after all, business was business, and daughters did have to get married eventually . . . 'How much?'

The elephant said a certain amount and Nama's father replied, 'That's not quite enough. After all, our Nama is the most beautiful girl in the neighbourhood, but it is enough to start bargaining. Come into the house out of the sunshine. Wife, bring us something cool to drink.'

And so the elephant and the father entered the house to discuss the matter further, while Nama's brothers and sisters ran off to tell everyone that Nama was going to marry an elephant. Soon the whole village had heard the news, and when Nama's father and the elephant had reached a bargain and left the house, the villagers were all waiting to hear how much the elephant had paid. When they did hear, they were aghast. It was more money than most of the villagers had ever imagined. The elephant must love Nama a great deal to pay so much. Nama was not even consulted. She was only a woman, and they did not count for much in those days.

No one took any notice of her tears and her wailings. Once the bargain had been made, she was helped up on to the elephant's back and sent on her way to her new home.

As they passed through village after village, everyone came out of their houses to wave, for word had spread quickly of the elephant who had paid a king's ransom for his human bride. Their curiosity was for the elephant, and no one took any notice of poor Nama, weeping on the elephant's back.

Eventually, they came to where the elephant lived. In a large clearing in the jungle there was an enormous palace, and as they stopped outside it the elephant trumpeted as loudly as he could. A few seconds later, an old female elephant came out of the palace.

'Mother,' said the elephant, 'I have brought home a bride.'

'Where?' asked the old elephant, expecting to see a fine young elephant beside her son.

'On my back. Isn't she beautiful?' said the proud elephant.

'Indeed,' said the mother. 'For a human being she is very beautiful, but she is not an elephant's wife. She cannot be.'

'She is my wife. I paid a king's ransom for her.'

The old elephant was very sad. Like all mothers she wanted her son to marry and have youngsters, but this would not be possible with a human bride. But she knew how strong and obstinate her son was, and for his sake she did her best to pretend to be happy. She helped Nama off her son's back and showed her to a splendid room.

News spread round the elephants in the jungle, and soon all the elephants came to call and to look at the elephant's human bride. The old female elephants smiled sympathetically at their friend, for they knew how sad she must be, and the young males were all envious of their friend for having married such a lovely human girl. The young females were not at all friendly, after all; one of them should, by rights, have married the fine young elephant, not this young upstart human.

And poor Nama was miserable.

For weeks she stayed in the palace and would not leave it. One day she could stand no more and said to her husband, 'Please let me go. You are very kind, but I do not love you. How could I? After all you are an elephant and I am a human.'

252

The elephant became angry and said, 'I am an elephant but I love you and you are human. Why cannot you love me?'

'I cannot,' cried Nama and ran from the room.

Every day from then on she asked the elephant for her freedom and the elephant always refused. 'I paid your father a king's ransom for you, why should I give you up! I cannot get it back. So you must stay.'

Many months passed, and Nama remained as beautiful as she always had been, but her sadness had become almost unbearable. Even the elephant was touched by her melancholy.

One day he said to her, 'I will let you go if your father will repay me the money I paid for you.'

So Nama wrote to her father and asked him to do as the elephant had asked, but her father wrote back and told her that he had lost all the money that he had received, as well as everything he had had before. He was as poor as poor could be, and it was impossible for him to repay the money. Nama must stay where she was and be happy.

Nama showed her husband and his mother the letter. The elephant was very happy, but his mother was very upset, for she could see how unhappy Nama was.

'Shortly after you came here, you told me that you were the seventh child of a seventh child and had magic powers,' she said to Nama one day. 'Is there nothing you could do to repay the money?'

'Nothing,' said Nama. 'It is not the kind of magic that can conjure up money. At its most powerful, all it can do is change the form of growing things. There is nothing . . .' She stopped suddenly, for she had had an idea.

That night while everyone slept, Nama went into the forest to where she knew a certain flower would be in bloom. She plucked four handfuls of the fullest blooms and returned to the palace where she mixed them with some special herbs and boiled everything together until the dawn came.

The next night she went to another clearing where another flower grew and she gathered four handfuls of the fullest blooms. She returned to the palace and boiled them together with some more herbs.

The next night she mixed the two lots together and boiled and boiled them until the liquid had become a thick smooth cream.

As her husband slept she rubbed the cream into the dull tusks that grew out of his face.

The next morning she said to her husband, 'May I return to my people?'

254

'How can you, Nama?' said the elephant. 'Your father has no money to buy you back. You must stay here and try to be happy.'

'But I have now repaid the dowry,' said Nama. 'Look at yourself in a glass,' said Nama.

The elephant sent a servant to bring a glass, and when he looked in it he was astonished to see that his dull tusks now gleamed as white as the purest snow.

'What have you done?' he asked Nama.

'I have repaid the dowry,' replied Nama. 'The tusks that used to be made of matted hair are now fashioned in the finest ivory and are worth more than my father paid you.'

The elephant was as good as his word and allowed Nama to return to her village where her family rejoiced to see her. Nothing but ill-luck had befallen them since she had left, but soon after her return their fortunes changed and they became rich again.

Back in the jungle, the old female elephant did her best to console her son. She knew how much he had loved Nama and how broken-hearted he was. But time is a great healer, and it was not long before the elephant had fallen in love again, this time with a beautiful young female elephant. Everyone was very happy and when their first child was born, it too had fine ivory tusks like his father.

And that is why all elephants have ivory tusks. Because an elephant fell in love with a girl called Nama, a long, long time ago.